BIRDS IN THE SKY

BY

ASHLEY ANTOINETTE

BIRDS IN THE SKY Copyright @ Ashley Antoinette

All rights reserved. No part of this book may be reproduced in any form or by any means without prior consent of the Publisher, except brief quotes used in reviews.

ISBN: 978-1-7355171-1-7

Trade Paperback Printing January 2021
Printed in the United States of America

This is a work of fiction. Any references or similarities to actual events, real people, living, or dead, or to real locales are intended to give the novel a sense of realism. Any similarity in other names, characters, places, and incidents, is entirely coincidental.

Distributed by Ashley Antoinette Inc.
Submit Wholesale Orders to:
owl.aac@gmail.com

DEDICATION

The reflection of your soul shines through the imprint I leave on the world. I will finish all you started. My dear grandmother, my ancestor, my example of power wrapped in femininity. Rest my love. I will hold up your name, Annette Snell. I miss and love you.

LETTER TO THE FANS

Ash Army! My army! My motivators! My reasons! Hey y'all!!! Here we are! In a different place, a new place, a brand-new world. I thought it was time to take a break from Ethic land and introduce you to some new folks. They're shy though. They are a completely different vibe and they don't like a lot of people. They're funny acting so this one isn't for everyone. It's exclusive and you have chosen to dive into their souls and become acquainted. I hope you enjoy them and much as I did. They are slowly but surely making room for themselves inside my heart. Can't wait to discuss! Happy reading!

-xoxo-

Ashley Antoinette

THE VIBE LIST

My All, Mariah Carey
Grateful, Mahalia
Comfortable, H.E.R.
I Been, Ari Lennox
Mindblown, Tink
More Than Enough, Alina Baraz
Stand Still, Sabrina Claudio
Karma, Summer Walker
Cats Got My Tongue, Trey Songz
Put U On, Dani Leigh
At Your Best, Aaliyah
Dying 4 Your Love, Snoh Aalegra
Love Again, Daniel Ceasar x Brandy
Come Together, Chris Brown x H.E.R.
The Weekend, SZA
Need U Bad, Jazmine Sullivan
Unravel Me, Sabrina Claudio
This Way, Kahlid x H.E.R.
Thinkin Bout You, Frank Ocean
Hit Different, SZA
Against Me, H.E.R.
You Do, DVSN
Pack Lite, Queen Naija
Wasted, Summer Walker

Bad, Wale
Like This, Mitch x Ann Marie
Too Deep, DVSN
Above and Beyond, Jhene Aiko
Losing, H.E.R.
Homies, Savannah Re'
10 Seconds, Jazmine Sullivan
Best Sex Ever, Vedo
Last Time, Giveon
Thunder and Lightning, Jhene Aiko
Permission, Ro James
Finders Keepers, Shateria
Let it Go, Summer Walker
When You Touch Me, Brandy
Love All Over Me, Monica

CHAPTER 1

*I am thinking of youuuuuuu
In my sleepless solitude tonight
If it's wronggg to love youuuuu
Then my heart just won't let me be right
Cause I've drowned in you
And I won't pull through
Without you by my sideeeeeee
I give my allllllllll*

Demi looked up from the smoky table in the middle of the bar. Past the people on the dance floor, past the beautiful, half-dressed, woman in front of him who was desperately sending "fuck me" vibes, through the haze of the club, until finally his eyes landed on the stage. He didn't frequent spots like this. A hole in the wall spot on Flint's Northside but money lured him there. He wondered what had lured her to a place so seedy. It was beneath her. A voice like that, a face like that, one that he couldn't seem to tear his gaze away from belonged in a stadium. What the fuck was she doing in a crevice like this? Fate intersected their paths in the underbelly of the ghetto, a place where most wouldn't feel safe. Hell, he didn't feel safe, but she appeared so comfortable that Demi felt himself letting out a bit of discomfort in the form of a deep sigh. Demi heard the conversation going on around him. He was present in body only. His mind was on the girl with the burgundy lips on stage. She sang with her eyes closed and it made him want to close his too, to meet her wherever she was disappearing to in the dark. He would put every dollar he had on it that wherever she went, behind those closed lids, was peaceful. The way her forehead relaxed, and her neck leaned to the right as she robbed the joint of their view of those dark eyes told him so. She was exceptionally beautiful, but somehow ordinarily so. The floor-length dress she wore matched her golden skin tone and he was offended by the way it surfed the waves of her petite frame. She was thin, but graceful, like the ballerina he used to shake up in his snow globe as a kid. Her blonde locs were shoulder-length and swept to one side. If she wasn't royal, it would be a shame because Demi just wanted to bend a knee to her. This honey-hued beauty was a queen.

I give my alllllllll to haveeeee,
just one more night with youuuuu.

Small woman, giant voice. She gave him chills.
"Demi, are you listening to me?"
Suddenly, the girl across from him was like the commercial that came on right when the show was getting good. Nails to a chalkboard, his temple flexed but his gaze didn't reveal his temperament. Poker face. Poker champ. It was important to never wear his heart on his sleeve in his line of work. An

undetectable threat. No announcements, just action. Demi was a mystery wrapped in Gucci denim and a five-hundred-dollar t-shirt. He blended in well, too well, because he was a product of the ghetto too; not this one, but once you've seen one, you've seen them all.

"I missed that. You speaking good to me?" he asked, tearing his gaze from the stage and refocusing on the table.

"I want to do more than speak good to you," she said, biting her lip.

Demi licked Hershey-colored lips, the kind of lips that smoked blunts daily and ate pussy to perfection, before giving up a faint smile. White-ass teeth between chocolate lips and wafer-colored skin. S'more-colored. The man looked edible and the woman was offering to swallow him whole.

"Is that right?" he asked.

She only smiled. Pretending. Feigning innocence because there was nothing shy about the foot she was caressing his dick with under the table. He reached beneath the table and tapped her foot discreetly. Feet on the floor was the silent direction.

"Why don't you and your girl let us finish chopping up this bi'ness and I'ma get with you before I break out," he said. He motioned for the waitress who attentively came to his side.

"You can put whatever they order on my tab," he instructed. He pulled a Gucci money clip out his pocket and peeled off two hundred-dollar bills.

"I'll keep 'em real busy for you," the waitress replied, leaning down, and touching his shoulder. It was a small price to pay to move the women away from his table.

Disinterested. He was disinterested and tired of being polite. That other side was begging to be set free and nobody wanted to see that side. Plenty of good nights had gone bad for much less than irritation. Demi grabbed her hand and moved it from his shoulder.

"I got a thing about people touching me, gorgeous, it's not personal," he said.

"Noted," she said, smiling. Women always smiled around Demi and he didn't know why because he rarely did. "Lots of looking, but no touching. Damn near impossible when a man like you walks up in here."

"You know how to earn your tips, miss lady," he said.

Again with the smiling before she walked away.

I'd risk my lifeeee to feellllll
Your body next to mine

There it was again. That voice. It was the vulnerability in her tone that hollowed him. Like the song hurt to even sing.

"About this business. Now, tell me why you needed me to come collect money your young hitters supposed to be collecting?" he asked.

"Club owner gave my people a hard time. Said he wasn't paying shit. His exact words were 'tell Demi to suck my dick. I don't pay niggas I don't know,'" the man said.

iiiii-eyeeeee-eeee give my alllll to loveeeee tonightttt

What the fuck, man? He thought, eyes pulling to the sound before cutting them away.

He wasn't a man who lost focus easily. He forced himself to face his mans instead. Kirk sat stone-faced.

"Exact words, huh?" Demi asked.

"You know niggas hate to feel like they not running shit. My young gunner would have laid him down but you said you wanted to keep the club clean," Kirk said. "Too much money being made to dirty it up, and I don't really do the diplomatic approach, so I thought I'd let the boss handle it."

Demi had been moving weight through this club for two years with no issues. It wasn't until the new owner stepped in did things begin to go awry. There was always an issue. The money was always late or short, and this time it hadn't been accounted for at all. He didn't get his hands dirty often but he didn't do blatant disrespect.

"I'll straighten it out. Your people won't have no more problems with collecting from now on," Demi said. "Take the nigga tongue out his mouth or something. Teach him a lesson."

Demi lifted a bawled fist and Kirk tapped it with his own, knowing better than to expect a handshake. It wasn't something Demi did. The touching rule went for everybody.

"You a nutty-ass mu'fucka, my nigga," Kirk said, snickering and eliciting a smirk from Demi.

Kirk took both the women off Demi's hands and Demi moved to the bar. The crowd was slowly growing scarce as patrons downed their last drinks. Demi's eyes scanned the room.

The song ended and the lights came on, pulling groans from those who weren't ready to go home.

The songstress spoke in the microphone.

"Y'all know the rules. You ain't got to go home but you got to..."

"Get the hell out of here," the crowd joined. Her voice surprised him. It was sultry. Warm. Like homemade biscuits on a Sunday morning. It didn't match her at all. There was so much gravity in her tone for such a small woman. She was too thin to pull from such depths to produce that sound.

She probably say a nigga name real proper, he thought.

The club emptied and the band began to pack up, as waitresses cleaned around him.

"You know we're closing," the waitress who had served him said.

"What's her name?" he asked, nodding toward the stage. He was unfocused, a rarity for him, and he knew this was not what had brought him here. He knew he was deviating from the plan, letting distraction pull him away from making this clean and swift. Yet, he had to know. A name said so much about a person. He wanted her name to speak to him. If it was Keisha or Tanisha or something he had heard before, he would be able to fill in the lines. He would be able to assume some things; whether his assumptions be right or wrong, he would get the curiosity out of his head.

"Who? Charlie?" she asked.

He scoffed at the discovery of her name. Now that fit her fine, and just like that, he couldn't assume shit. A pretty girl with a boy's name. His intrigue grew.

"She always look that mean?" he asked.

The waitress glanced to the stage. "Pretty much."

"You tell her to sing that song again and I'll give her ten bands," he said.

"You'll give her what now?" the waitress asked.

He snickered at that, running his tongue on the inside of his jaw as he found amusement in her reaction. "I'll make it worth your while too."

"Consider it done," she said. The waitress walked up to Charlie and Demi took a seat, knocking a fist against the bar subtly as the waitress whispered in Charlie's ear. Her head snapped up, looking in his direction in astonishment.

Are you for sale, Ms. Charlie? He thought. She would be crazy to turn down the offer, but silently, he hoped she would. It was just like Demi to set unrealistic expectations on someone he didn't even know.

"Hey, you, Mr. ATM by the bar! Can you come here for a minute?" she asked.

Demi swiped a hand down his goatee. It was lined so sharp it could have cut him. He hadn't expected her to confront him, only to sing.

He approached her, scratching behind his ear in a spot that didn't itch. He was nervous about her reaction and nervousness was a new friend; they weren't well acquainted.

"So, who are you?" she asked when they stood face to face. She smelled edible, like she had bathed in vanilla extract. Up close, she was blinding. It wasn't just her locs that were golden. Her skin, it was 24 karat. It was him who closed his eyes this time, before blinking away to look at the waitress. She was a bit dimmer. He could stare at her straight on just fine.

"I'm just a man that wanna hear a song," he said.

"My set is over," she said. "Come back next Saturday and get it for free like everybody else." She turned away from him and bent down to begin wrapping up the microphone.

"I'm paying for your time now. Seven days is a long time. I might not make it," he answered.

She stood and turned to him, a bit taken aback.

"Ten thousand dollars?" she asked, her tone disbelieving.

He nodded.

"You do know you could probably get Mariah to sing you the damn song for ten bands, right?"

He felt the smile but didn't show it. Tongue on the inside of his cheek. He glanced off to the waitress.

"She always this difficult?" he asked.

"Don't answer that, Shayla!" Charlie said, with a warning finger. Shayla. Yup. He had some assumptions about a Shayla; but a Charlie? The pretty queen with the defensive demeanor, he was stuck on her. He was drawing blanks. "Bringing weird niggas over here for me to sing." Charlie sighed. "I wouldn't even feel right taking that amount of money. Thank you for the compliment, but no."

Word? He thought. He was pleased. Extremely fucking pleased. *The good shit ain't never for sale. You just got to admire it from afar and wish you could have it.*

"I respect it." The average woman would have sung while taking her panties off for that amount.

"You really gon' make us beg for that ten thousand dollars, Charlie?" her guitarist asked.

"Tim!" she shouted, mouth falling open as the band gave

her a hard time.

"I got a thousand for the three of y'all too if I can get that song," Demi said smoothly. He was applying pressure in the form of Benjamin Franklins.

The band pulled out their instruments and Charlie huffed as she folded her arms across her chest. "Noooo!" she whined.

"Girl, just sing!" Shayla, the waitress said. "Fine-ass man asking you to do what you do every weekend for these cheap-ass niggas in here." Shayla bent down and picked up the tip bowl, shaking the loose change at the bottom.

Demi took a seat and removed a heavy wad of money from his pocket. He placed it in the center of the table. Charlie grabbed the microphone, rolling her eyes. Oh, but when she opened her mouth...

I am thinking of youuuuuuu
In my sleepless solitude tonight
If it's wronggg to love youuuuu
Then my heart just won't let me be right

Demi leaned forward and put his elbows to knees as he lowered his head, rubbing the top of it as his eyes closed with her. He met her there... in the dark.

When he looked up, her fists were bawled at her sides as if she were fighting for this song as she belted the words.

I GIVE MY ALLLLLLLLLL

"Tsss," he pushed a breath of disbelief off his lips as his body went cold. Goosebumps. This girl gave him goosebumps.

She moved her hand like she was directing her own orchestra, and then she snapped pretty fingers and shook her head. She had no business singing in this club. She was a star.

She blushed when she finished the song, and he bit his lip and nodded as she came down off the stage.

"You disappear up there," he said.

"I just love music. Ever since I was a little girl. I'd listen to my mom play these songs and she'd sing, she'd cry. She'd wake me out of my bed at three o'clock in the morning and I would know it was time for me to sing to her and her friends because I could smell the liquor on her breath. She would be so proud when I sang for her. I just kind of never stopped singing since then."

He didn't know what had possessed her to share so much, in fact, he was sure she wasn't really sharing it with him but reminiscing to herself. He just happened to be there to hear it.

"You want to tell me what kind of man spends ten thousand dollars on one song?" she asked. "Who are you? I've never seen you in here."

"Just somebody passing through town. I ain't from around here," he answered.

"Mr. Not From Around Here, do you have a name?" she asked.

"Demi," he answered.

"Charlie," she formally introduced, holding out her hand. Demi looked at it and his skin crawled a bit at the thought of touching her hand, but he shook it anyway, fighting past alarms ringing in his mind. The anti-social gangster felt his gut clench at the parallel of their existence. Rough versus soft.

"I can't take the money but thank you for thinking my voice is worth it. An industry full of music execs thought otherwise, but it's nice to know somebody likes it," she said, smiling.

He nodded, as she bent to grab her bag and her guitar case.

"You play too?" he asked.

"A starving artist must do it all to make a living," she replied. She handed it off to him. "Carry this for me?"

She was assertive, like she had known him for a while, and he was used to taking her marching orders. Like a longtime boyfriend who knew to get his ass off the couch to get the groceries out the car when his old lady got home. He took it from her grasp and smirked at her natural authority. She was sweet, but not all sweet. She had a subtle aggression that he found intriguing because she was so little that he was sure she had never intimidated anyone. Still, her demand was heeded as he found himself walking beside her as they headed out of the club.

"Goodnight, y'all!" she called, turning to give a slight wave.

The band grumbled their goodbyes as he followed her out into the crisp night air. Sixty-one degrees on a summer day was chilling and Charlie shrank as the wind sunk her collar bone as she recoiled.

"My Uber's almost here," she said.

"You make it a habit of hopping in cars with strangers at 2 am?" he asked.

She shrugged.

He turned and walked across the parking lot.

"Hey, where are you going?" she asked, frowning as she quickened her steps to give chase.

He walked to the passenger side of a silver Cadillac and pulled open the door. Charlie stopped walking as she stood in front of the car.

"Uber for the night," he said.

She stalled for a bit and then took out her phone and held it up to his face, snapping a picture.

"In case you kidnap me," she said, deathly serious. She snapped the license plate next and then sent the pictures to her sister.

"You done?" he asked, slightly annoyed. He was too fucking fine to frown the way that he was. Rough. Rugged. Thuggish. There was nothing good about this man and Charlie knew it, yet she was still going to get in the car.

She walked up to him and past him as he held open the door, pausing slightly to look him in the eyes.

"Uber drivers don't have tattoo tear drops on their faces," she said. "Am I safe with you?"

She was so close that he smelled the leftover hint of wine on her breath. She had sipped it periodically throughout her set. Sometimes, holding it in her hand while swaying and singing. She hadn't put on a performance at all. She had set a vibe inside the club. He thought about what she had asked him. Was she safe? The life he led. The circumstances that had lured him to the club that night. He couldn't say she was safe at all with him. He was danger personified, walking in designer clothes and dripping in expensive cologne.

"I think I can handle getting you home," he said.

She slid into his passenger seat as her phone rang. She giggled, covering her mouth as she answered her FaceTime.

"Who is that fine-ass man?"

Charlie laughed as her sister, Stassi, demanded answers through the screen and Demi slid into the driver's seat.

"A crazy man who likes to spend money on frivolous things," Charlie said, smiling.

"Must be nice," her sister answered.

"I'll call you when I make it home," Charlie replied.

"Damn, can I at least hear his voice? I know he has a voice that makes you melt because everything else, girl!"

Charlie turned the phone to Demi.

"Say hi to my sister, Stassi," Charlie said.

Demi gripped the woodgrain steering wheel with one hand as he put the car in drive, and he rested one elbow on the center console.

"How you doing?" he said, only half glancing at the screen, as he tried to focus on the road.

"Hey, handsome, please get my sister home safe and knock the cobwebs off that..."

"Aye, aye! That's enough, bye, Stassi" Charlie interrupted, hanging up abruptly.

"I didn't catch that last part. I like to follow instructions. Let's run that FaceTime back right quick," he said, as he drove.

"You wish!" she said, laughing, and blushing so hard that her cheekbones reddened.

He pointed to the navigation. "Put your address in."

She did as she was told and then settled into the luxury car as a quiet settled over the car.

Charlie turned in her seat, pressing her back against the door and looking at him curiously. Demi's eyes went to the foot in his leather seat and had to turn his eyes back to the road to avoid asking her to remove it.

Demi frowned. She was intruding with her eyes.

"You mad rude with the staring," he said.

Demi giggled. He was annoyed.

"I'm just wondering what this is. This moment, you know? A man walks in a bar and sees a girl. What happens after that?"

"What you want to happen after that?" he asked.

Charlie shrugged. "I'm only here for happily ever after. I've had enough horror stories to last a lifetime," she said, turning back toward the front. She rolled her eyes back to him as she pressed her head against the headrest. "No pressure or nothing."

He bit his lip. "All pressure, baby," he answered. "I ain't afraid to apply a little pressure."

He played in the hair on his chin as he leaned against his door and drove. Charlie reached for the radio and Demi could practically see her damn fingerprints on his screen.

He let her choose the vibe, however, as she hooked her phone up to his Bluetooth without asking.

He wasn't sure why she amused him. Most weren't this assertive in his presence, but Charlie moved like she was the boss. Like, he was pushing her whip and she didn't need to ask for shit inside these four doors. The sound of her voice as she leaned back and closed her eyes invaded their space. She barely let the words leave her lips, in fact, she wasn't saying anything at all. Just letting the music fill her mouth, humming softly, every other lyric as she enjoyed the song.

You say you've got a girl
Why you want me?
How you want me if you got a girl?

Demi watched the music move through her body, despite the fact that she didn't move an inch. Only her finger tapped softly against her thigh. Oh, how he wanted to be that finger, keeping the tempo, to his heart. Why the fuck was his heart beating at her command? He swallowed the lump in his throat, clearing his discomfort as the bridge hit. Her voice was soft as it floated into the air. She wasn't trying, but no effort from Charlie was like an award-winning performance from anybody else. Her voice made goosebumps sprout on his forearms.

I'll just keep him satisfied through the weekend
You're like 9 to 5, I'm the weekendddd
Make him lose his mind for the weekenddd

The lyrics played in his mind long after they ended and as he pulled up to her townhome, he used the button on his steering wheel to lower the volume.

"Thank you for the ride," she said. "Much better than the Uber."

"Not a problem," he replied.

She got out and was halfway to her building when she turned back for the car.

He rolled down the passenger window.

"Hey, do you have somewhere to be?" she asked.

He looked at the clock. Did he? He knew he should probably answer differently but instead, he said, "You get in Ubers in the middle of the night, invite niggas you don't know in your house. You living a real thug life."

Her laughter was warming. It heated his entire middle and Demi glanced down, wondering if she could see the fire she caused. Women were a motherfucka. They were some powerful, voodoo, intuition-having, dick-hardening, motherfuckas. Her essence was created to arouse his nature and everything about Demi was triggered by her, most of all, his intrigue. And Demi wasn't a man who took interest easily.

"I know you. You're Demi. I'm Charlie," she said sarcastically. "Nigga, you coming in or not?"

"I'ma opt-out. You be good, though," he said.

"I'm a little better at being bad," she challenged. "But if you pussy just say that." She shrugged, looking away from him, as a smirk spread her mauve-colored lips. She had licked her lipstick off but the natural pink of them was better. He couldn't take his eyes off them, actually, and those teeth. Pretty-ass teeth that were small and neat, like she had worn braces once upon a time. He felt like a stalker the way he was annotating every detail of her face.

She pulled a full laugh from him with that one. If only she knew.

"Yo, baby, you asking for problems," he warned. "This ride got a height requirement. Got to get your weight up first, Ms. Charlie. Goodnight, bird."

"Bird?" she repeated, brow bent. She had been teased for years for being small and skinny. She had heard it all coming up as a kid. It had made her defensive and had made her bite real viscious because people stayed trying her with their bark. She had learned that people normally backed down when she stood up for herself.

"Chill, killa," he said. Amusement forced a vague smile onto his lips. "I don't want no smoke. Songbird. It's a compliment. No disrespect," he said.

Her face softened.

"Night," she said, retreating.

He waited until she was inside her door before he pulled off into the night.

Charlie entered her place and her Bulldog, Bails, automatically came to her feet.

"I missed you, Bails. Such a good boy. Mama loves you," she cooed, bending to rustle his blocky head. He rested right at her feet. He was a lazy boy and she was doing too much for his grumpy taste. She giggled as she bypassed him, sighing at the relief she felt. This was her solace. To anyone else, it was chaotic, but to her it was perfect. She had lived with a lot of mental noise around her for a long time. This place was hers and hers alone. Eclectic in taste, none of her furniture matched. A royal blue couch was the focal point of the room. She walked the path to her room, hurrying upstairs, bypassing the basket of clean clothes she had been telling herself she would fold for a week.

Tomorrow, she promised herself. Another lie, but hey it sounded good.

That was the beauty of living alone. Her own rules applied. Charlie shed her dress along the way to her room, leaving it in the middle of the floor as she headed for the shower. She turned on the water but instead of stepping inside, she pulled open the drawer, removing her portable Beats Pill and the vape pen she kept there. Charlie pulled her hair in a top knot and stood in the mirror in her panties and bra as she pulled the smoke into her lungs.

She felt instant relief. The anxiety, the fear she lived with daily, instantly floated outside of her body. Charlie connected her phone, pressing play.

Alina Baraz matched her vibe, and she took another hit.

Charlie sang to the mirror, pointing to herself and vibing before turning to the shower. She stepped one foot inside when heavy knocks halted her. She startled, turning toward the open bathroom door and looking out into the hallway like someone would magically appear. Her heart raced as she grabbed her silk robe, tying it before going toward the door.

She stood on her tip-toes, peeking out of the peephole and she stalled. Demi stood on her porch. She frowned and pulled open the door.

He held up her wallet and Demi gave her a flat smile. She could tell he was a little annoyed by her carelessness. Certainly, he had better things to do than to double back to play delivery boy. "Thanks. I would have tore my house up looking for that in the morning," she said.

She stepped back and motioned for him to come in. This time, he didn't decline, but as soon as he crossed her threshold, he froze. The clutter felt like a brick to the face. The house smelled like incense and her. The scent that she had left behind in his car, her body scent, and whatever she used in her hair lingered in the air like she sprayed the same thing day after day. His mind felt overloaded. From the clothes on the couch to the scattered clippings from the pile of Essence magazines on the coffee table, the paint easel she had in the corner with paint and brushes scattered on the floor beneath it, and the crystals that lined her windowsills, Charlie's place had no order. It wasn't dirty but it was chaos. His shoulders instantly bricked, filling with tension. Demi didn't do clutter. In his life, in his space, in his home. She was the definition of everything he avoided. He couldn't even gather his thoughts as his eyes bounced around her place.

"You coming in or no?" she asked, eyes low. The lingering. The uncertainty was blowing her high and she was seconds from calling it a night. The song played from her bathroom as he deadpanned on her.

"It's not life or death, Demi. Just being hospitable," she said.

He stepped inside.

"I was about to shower, one sec," she said. "Make yourself comfortable." Bails had moved to her couch and Charlie shooed him off, before picking up the basket of clothes and moving them to the floor to make room for him to sit.

Bails walked right up to his feet, nestling against his thousand-dollar sneakers and Demi's fucking skin crawled.

"He's harmless. A big, spoiled, baby," Charlie said. "I'll be right back."

Demi opted to stand. He for damn sure wasn't sitting where the dog had been. His eyes followed her as she walked up the steps.

The minutes ticked away as he tried not to be invasive of her home, but every inch of her place told a story about her life. The lace panties hanging out the basket told him she was bold, sexy even, the type of woman who wasn't afraid to wear red lingerie. The plants growing wildly on the window sill told him she was a nurturer. The bills piled up on the coffee table told him she was in no position to turn down the money he had offered him. She was gone all of fifteen minutes and he had learned a lot about her in her absence. As soon as he laid eyes on her, his mind forgot it all. She came back wearing sweats and a cropped t-shirt that was so small it lifted slightly, revealing the bottom of her breasts.

She pulled on her vape pen.

"You want to hit this?" she asked.

"I'm good," Demi answered.

"You want a drink?" she asked. "I think I got Henny or something."

"That'll do," he said. It wasn't his favorite, but he would need it if he was going to stick around.

Why the fuck am I sticking around anyway? He thought.

She led him to the kitchen. To his relief, it was spotless. She handed him the bottle and grabbed two glasses. "Follow me."

She led him upstairs and into her bedroom. More clothes. His eyes took in the ten, half-filled water bottles on her nightstand.

She pulled back the curtains and revealed a balcony door.

He was relieved that she opted to be outside. Her place made his chest tight, like he couldn't quite breathe amongst her organized chaos. He watched her grab the source of her music and then she led her way outside.

Demi followed her out onto the balcony and somehow the mess outside felt like an oasis. She had plants everywhere, a boho rug covered the floor and a pallet bed rested in the corner with plush designer pillows on top of it. White Christmas lights were strung above their heads and around the railings and a bookshelf had been affixed to the brick of the building.

"It looks like a chapter from your mind out here, Bird," he said.

"We sticking with this bird thing, huh?" she asked.

He snickered.

"Charlie," he corrected as he leaned against her door, propping one foot behind him. She sat on the bed and reached for the bottle, pouring two glasses.

"Bird is fine," she smiled. "And... yeah. My mind looks

something like this on the inside." She noticed he was still standing.

"Are you going to stand there all night?" she asked, snickering a bit. "You're very serious, aren't you?"

"Nah, man, I be cooling," he said, opting for the chair facing her.

She passed him his drink.

"So, where are you from? You said not around here, so where?" Charlie asked.

"Cali raised me; the D pays me, though, so I'm around that way for now. I'm just in Flint handling some business," he said.

"You look like you're too good for us Flint folk. Giving off real big energy, Demi," she said, chuckling, eyes sparkling in a way he didn't realize dark eyes could. They were so dark they were almost black. They sparkled like she was always on the verge of crying, only her smile told him she wasn't. Emotion just lived in her. It filled her home so much so that she expressed it through painting and crystals and shit. He wondered why she was so full-on feelings and if they were good ones or bad.

"Say, man, you wild," Demi answered, blushing. Demi didn't smile but the nigga was showing teeth as he chuckled at her.

"To the big business that lured you to town. Lucky me," she said, holding up her glass. He tapped hers.

"If I knew Flint made 'em like you, I would have come sooner," he answered.

"Oh, that's good. That one right there is the one, my

nigga!" she laughed as she sipped her drink. He laughed. It felt so foreign. Demitrius Sky was deadly. It was known that life didn't live in him. It ended in his presence, but she was pulling his baritone out of his closet and filling the air with it like he didn't have skeletons in there with it. Who the fuck was this girl?

He sipped his drink. "Did you always want to be a singer?" he asked.

"Who said I wanted to be a singer? I sing. It's in me, not on me. I can't wish to be that because I'm already that. I've been a singer since I was a kid. I just love it. Love hearing a song that describes exactly how I feel and making it my own. I don't give a fuck about nobody else feeling it or liking it. Attention is never the goal."

He nodded. "That's real shit. Most women crave that shit. Attention."

"I'm not most women," she said, taking another sip.

"I believe that," he said, nodding and loosening up as he drank too. The song played in the background. He found it odd that it was on repeat, but it was her house. House rules applied. If she wanted to listen to it on a loop, then that would be the soundtrack for the night.

"Even if you didn't, it would still be true," she said, shrugging.

Demi's dick jumped. She was so sure of herself. The confidence was phenomenal. It wasn't just a stage persona. It poured out of her.

"What do you do? What's your passion?" she asked.

"I get by," he said.

"In other words, mind my business. Noted," she said. He wasn't a giver of information. He made people earn it, but after the way she had dug deep with her reply, he felt like he was robbing her. Demi had walls. Rules. Lots of them. Letting people in wasn't something he did often but he could tell she was offended.

"I made some money in the streets, invested it in a few businesses. One of which is a record label. I'm a silent partner in Dynasty Music Group," he said.

"Dynasty Music?" she questioned in shock. "You own it?"

"It ain't a big deal. Just an investment, but I know some people who would love to get they hands on a voice like yours. You ain't on no autotune shit, you're fucking gorgeous," he said.

"Am I?" she asked, genuinely stunned at his description.

"You questioning it?" he asked, snickering.

"I mean, I've just never heard anybody say it like that," she whispered. "I'm not like... normal. Niggas like you usually see the girls with the man-made bodies, the lace fronts. Me and my little locs ain't pulling nothing. I'm legit the awkward black girl. I like my weed, my plants are my best friends and my books. I love a good book. Niggas don't be checking for girls like me."

Demi licked his lips. If only she knew the way her entire aura pulled at his dick. His manhood was begging him to take her down. She was stunning. Her skin glowed in a way he had never seen. She was luminating from her hair to her nude toes. His attraction to her was more organic than any bad bitch had ever been able to produce.

"Sound like peace to me, but no lie, you on that stage is masterful. You don't got to do nothing else. No dancing. No fucking naked-ass costumes and shit. No backup. Just sing. That shit transported me to a whole 'nother world," he admitted. "Ain't nothing awkward about that shit."

She was breathless at the way he spoke about her. There was appreciation in his tone, like he had discovered a piece of art that moved his insides around.

"So, if you want to sing, like for real, I can make a call," he said.

"I don't want that, but thank you," she answered.

He nodded and lifted out of his seat a bit to go into his back pocket. He pulled out a card. "If you ever change your mind."

She took it and placed it on her windowsill.

"I won't, but I might use the number still," she replied.

"Yo, anytime you feel like singing a nigga a song, you put that number to use," he said.

"You know I legit never invite anybody on my balcony. Not even Stassi's ass because she talks too much and she be fucking up my vibe," Charlie said. "But you're amazing company. You made a bad night better."

"Why was it bad?" he asked.

"Long story," she whispered, turning solemn. He saw her light dim as she finished the drink and looked out at the courtyard below them.

"The sun don't rise for four more hours. We ain't got nothing but time," he said. What the entire fuck? He had somewhere to be and here he was committing hours to a girl he'd just met.

She looked up at him, stunned. "Morning? You think I'm letting you stay 'til morning? A man who just told me he all up and through the streets. You think you resting your head at my house?"

"It ain't like that, man," he said, scoffing, dismissing the kingpin fantasy she was building in her head, but fantasy was reality when it came to Demi. He was getting major paper, both legally and illegally. One hustle financing the other and that hustle legitimizing it all. She didn't need to know that, though.

"So, you really think I'm a one-night stand type of girl?" she asked, laughing. She was fake offended because the way her pussy was pulsing in his presence, she knew all he had to do was say the right thing and that's the exact type of girl she would become.

"I ain't say that," he said. "Girls like you, with your sage and your whole earthy shit you got going..."

"Earthy?" she snickered.

"Yeah, the whole, natural, Erykah Badu vibe you got. Women like that ain't on no one-night shit. You gon' make a nigga earn it."

She fought her smile. All this damn smiling. Him. Her. Just a level of comfort two strangers shouldn't feel.

"What's your favorite color, Bird?" he asked.

"So, we're back in the safe zone, asking shit that don't matter? Okay, I'll play," she said. "Blue."

"Blue?" he frowned.

"What's wrong with blue?" she laughed, hitting her vape pen.

"What's right about it?" he asked, frowning.

"It's the color of the sky," she said. "So, I get like anxious and my whole body just kind of betrays me sometimes. I start overthinking, I have a hard time breathing, and I just kind of lose it a little. When I get like that, I smoke, and I put in headphones. I go outside and find grass. Doesn't matter where I am. I take off my shoes so I can feel the ground beneath me, you know? Then I lay down and I look up at the sky and it's so blue. It's like the prettiest blue ever. And I sing and I feel better. So, blue is my fav."

"Damn, blue it is," he conceded.

"What's your favorite color?" she asked.

"Blue," he answered, licking his lips and lifting the Hennessey to his mouth to hide his amusement.

"Seriously?" she laughed. "You're impossible." She shook her head. "Making fun of me and shit."

"Nah, I wouldn't do that. You cool as fuck. Like the most interesting mu'fucka I don' met in a long time," he admitted.

"Same," she replied. They stared at one another, but awkwardness tore their gaze apart and Charlie looked down. "So, you're favorite color?"

"Blue, nigga," he answered. "I like what you like. Whatever you like."

"Niggas be so full of shit," she cackled.

The song she was playing restarted and he pointed to the speaker. "How many times you gon' listen to this song?"

"Probably for a few days straight," she admitted.

Anybody else I'd be gone by now
Does it really matter, all that really matters
Second I'm with you, all my love pour out

"Who is it?" Demi asked.

"Alina Baraz," Charlie answered.

He nodded, pulling out his phone and adding the song to his library. She hummed the words and pointed at him.

"Don't do that," he groaned.

She laughed. "Sing to you?"

"That shit, man, you're dangerous," he said, rubbing the back of his neck.

"All that really matters is youuu keeppp showingggg uppp," she sang, moving toward him and touching his face.

Demi tensed, grabbing her wrists so tightly that Charlie's eyes widened, and her breath hitched. She pulled her wrists from his grasp, standing to her feet and looking at him in confusion.

"What just happened?" she asked, alarmed, her heart racing.

Demi stood too, overwhelmed. "My bad. I ain't mean to grab you like that. I just don't... the touching. I don't like to be touched."

Charlie blinked a confused stare at him as her face scrunched. "Like, ever?" she asked. "What do you mean you don't like to be touched?"

She was so confused. Charlie was the most touchy-feely person in the world. It was her love language. She had to feel shit. To be visceral. Even in school when she had a hard time comprehending, she had to create visual models of math problems and shit to make sure she could understand them.

"I just don't," he stopped, knowing it sounded odd.

He hated to be the weird nigga. With his rules. With his restrictions, but she had touched his face and it felt like he wanted to scrub his shit off. "I just don't like the shit, man."

Charlie squinted so hard at him while shaking her head then she snickered a bit. "That kind of makes me want to touch you more."

She reached for him and he moved his head. "Don't play, man," he said.

"Wow," she said, laughing. "This is really a thing. Like, OCD?"

Demi sucked his teeth and looked off to the side because he was annoyed that she was amused. She was playing in his face and another thing she didn't know was that he had a temper problem. She was flirting with it.

"I just ain't with the touching and I like shit a certain way," he said.

"Okay," she said, eyes sparkling with something like she was fucking blazing his ass inside her head. He could see the jokes she was withholding as she tried her hardest to be respectful.

"Ain't nobody say shit about your looney-ass talking about taking off your shoes and laying in the grass," he said defensively, face twisted up. He was salty and Charlie had to fold her lips to stop from laughing. She was a natural antagonist. A fucking Leo.

"Yup, you right. We all got our quirks," she said. She lifted her hands. "I won't touch." She moved back to the bed. "You want to come over here? Promise to keep my hands to myself. I want to show you something."

He was stubborn, so he stayed where he was for a few minutes as silence enveloped him.

"Please," she added.

He moved then, joining her on the bed.

Charlie laid down. "Lie next to me," she instructed. He repositioned himself and laid back. Side by side they stared at the sky. The moon glowed over them and Charlie reached one manicured hand to the sky, spreading her fingers. "It feels so close but it's literally millions of miles away."

"Yo, this shit is wild," he said, noticing her view. The entire sky lit up with stars.

"It's beautiful," she whispered. "Too bad you don't like to be touched. I would have fucked you out here."

He laughed so hard that it infected her and then they settled into a comfortable silence.

He laid there until her breathing was so peaceful, he was sure she was asleep. He thought about leaving but laid there, looking at the stars and breathing to the beat of her heart for another two hours before he lifted from the air mattress.

He grabbed the throw blanket and placed it over her. She was fucking beautiful. He turned the volume down on her speaker and paused, looking at her for another beat before leaving.

Demi opened his phone and pressed play. The song Charlie had played on repeat oozed through his speakers. He pulled his pistol from beneath his seat, placing it in his lap, and pulled off. He was four hours late, distracted, and completely thrown off by the incidental vibe he had stumbled upon, but business was still business. It couldn't be completely derailed. What could have been taken care of hours ago, would now be handled in the middle of the night. He had never allowed himself to become so distracted. He put his head back in the game, turned the radio off, and restored his gangster, a bit relieved that his interaction with Charlie was over.

CHAPTER 2

The club was silent. Dawn did the club no justice. As the sun cast an orange hue through the dirty windows, Demi waited patiently, staring at the empty stage. It was too small of a stage for Charlie. Her voice. Her face. Her aura. Everything about her was big. He was surprised the stage could even hold her. He had met her hours ago and here she was invading his mind when he was supposed to be focused on other things, heinous things.

Something that was supposed to be taken care of the night before had been put off until morning and that uneased Demi. He was a surgeon about his business. Precision and punctuality were important. When niggas got distracted, they usually made mistakes. He knew this. He had beat this into the heads of his team for years and still here he was playing fucking Mariah Carey lyrics back in his head.

Her voice filled these walls even when she wasn't there.

The doors of the club clanged as they opened and he heard footsteps echo as he leaned over, rubbing his goatee as he waited.

The owner of the club, Frankie "Big Bands" Banks, stopped walking as soon as he saw Demi.

"Demi, man, I got what I owe," Frankie said.

"You sure? Cuz I was told you weren't paying me shit and that I needed to come see you if I wanted my paper," Demi said. He pulled on the heavy herringbone chain that rested against his white t-shirt. "I try to show you niggas love out here, man. Try to be fair, but you ungrateful motherfuckers always got to try me. Apparently, niggas think cuz I ain't out here mobbing no more that shit sweet. That's the problem, when you get rich. Niggas think you go soft. Since when you ever known me to be that?" he asked.

Frankie and Demi had come up in the streets together. He knew more than anybody that Demi didn't take disrespect well.

"I got the bread, man," Frankie said.

"You should. You running my shit through this club, you ain't slick, nigga. Business ain't that good in this bitch. You pay me on time every time," Demi stated. "Or I'ma send somebody to come see about you, homie. Don't play with my FUCK-ING MO-NEY." Demi was still seated, rubbing his hands, squeezing his fists as he looked up at the man over a stern brow. He was really trying to practice some self-control.

"Man, we can just go to the office. It's in the safe. I don't want no problems with you. Shit went left with your man because he came in here disrespectful. It's all respect between me and you, though, Demi. I was always going to pay you," Frankie said. He was now singing a different tune.

Niggas so fucking scary. Stand on your word, Demi thought, as he recalled how his man had come back to him with a version of events that was filled with disrespect.

"You running 'round this bitch feeling like the man cuz you pack this little-ass shit out every night. I heard you was saying sum'n different. Something like, 'that nigga, Demi, can suck my dick, I ain't paying him shit,'" Demi stated calmly. "That wasn't you?"

Frankie's eyes doubled in size. "Ya man putting some extra on it. I told *him* that shit, man, it wasn't nothing against you. I would never disrespect like that. We been square, my nigga. It ain't like that."

"Take me to the safe," Demi ordered. He stood, hiking up his pants as he followed the man to the back office. He was in a mood now. Charlie's voice was getting smaller and smaller now.

"It's in the closet," Frankie said.

"Nigga, open that shit. I ain't gon' hit you in the back. Any nigga I ever closed the casket on looked me in the eyes before he left this side," Demi stated. "But you better be smart."

Frankie reluctantly turned his back to Demi. There was a pistol in the safe. Demi was sure of it. So, he kept his hand ready on his waistline. It was nothing to pull the trigger. In a gunfight, he would always come out on top.

Frankie put a hundred thousand dollars on the desk.

Demi walked over to the desk and eyed the money on top of it.

"Do I need to count my money?" he asked.

"It's all there," Frankie said.

"I got better things to do with my time than chase a nigga on some street shit, Big Bands." His level of irritation couldn't be hidden. "You disrespect anybody we send up in here that's the same as disrespecting me. I don't care if it's the mailman."

Without warning, he grabbed the letter opener from Frankie's desktop and viciously stabbed it through Frankie's hand. His scream was deafening as Frankie grabbed his wrist with his uninjured hand. Demi gripped the back of the man's neck, slamming it down to the wooden desk.

"Next time, you lose your life," Demi said. His calm didn't match his crazy. The place he had stabbed, dead center, missing the fragile bones between Frankie's middle and ring finger, hitting soft cartilage only, no bones, was like target practice for Demi. A flesh wound. A deep one, one that would teach a lesson, without disfigurement. It was more blood than pain because Demi was sure shock acted as an anesthetic. "Clean your shit up and give my money to that pretty-ass girl you got singing in here. Every payment is to go to her from now on. The first time you short her..."

"I won't be!" Frankie wailed, holding his bleeding hand as he held it up while shaking uncontrollably from the pain. He was leaking blood everywhere.

Demi knew his money wouldn't be a problem again. Both he and Frankie knew that he had gotten off easy. Demi was known for his murder game. He had a reputation for two things: getting money and being heartless. He had killed without remorse for much smaller offenses than the one Frankie had committed.

The barking that broke up her sleep made Charlie groan in complaint as she tried to hold onto the dream she had been indulged in.

"Okay, okay, Bails. Mama's coming," she whispered to herself as she climbed up, glancing up at the sky and then down at the evidence of last night's events. When she saw the stack of money beside her, she gasped. "What the fuck is wrong with him?" she said. Ten thousand dollars for a song, and her company apparently, was the going rate. Charlie picked up the money and his card before rushing inside.

"Come on, boy," Charlie said as Bails followed her inside. She put the money in her nightstand and then plopped down on her bed, tapping his card against her palm, biting her lip as she thought about calling him. "What you think, Bails? To keep or return the money? That is the question," she said. She dialed the first three digits of his number and then stopped.

"He'll call," she said to herself. Her ringing doorbell pulled her to her feet and Bails led the way to answer.

Charlie knew who it was before she even pulled open the door.

"Only you would lay on my doorbell, you asshole," Charlie greeted, stepping aside to let her sister in.

"Bitch, my hands full as fuck. It was either lean against the doorbell or drop breakfast all over your porch."

Stassi handed a bag of groceries to Charlie as they made their way to the kitchen.

"Why do you look like you been freshly fucked?" Stassi said as she put the bags on the table.

Charlie frowned. "I don't know what you're talking about." Charlie's words denied what her face revealed.

"Then why you looking like you looking? Like good dick just snuck up out of here through the back door?" Stassi asked.

Charlie pulled the contents from the bag and her guilty smile made her sister's mouth drop.

"Charlie!" Stassi exclaimed. "The guy from last night? The random? You slept with a nigga on the first night?"

Stassi and her assumptions. They seemed to come one after the other these days. Charlie knew she didn't have the best track record with men, but she did have some standards in place.

"Relax. You always got to take it all the way. I didn't sleep with him. We just talked," Charlie said. "He was..." Charlie paused and scoffed as her mind ventured to the night before. "...weird," she finished.

"Weird?" Stassi questioned.

"That's the only way to explain him," Charlie replied as she pulled the mixing bowl out of her cupboard.

Charlie stood in her kitchen in boy shorts and her midriff shirt, mixing pancakes as she thought of calling him.

"He left his card," Charlie said.

"Doesn't mean you have to call," Stassi said.

Of course, she would say that. It was the opposite of what

Charlie wanted to do; it was just like Stassi to be judgmental.

"But would it really hurt to just call?" Charlie asked, skeptically.

"You like him?" Stassi asked, shocked. "What happened to your plan, Charlie? You know, focus on yourself, heal? You're just now starting to get your shit together."

"What are you talking about?" Charlie said defensively. "He was company for one night. You act like I'm marrying him or something, Stassi, damn."

"I'm just making sure you're okay. You don't have to jump right back into something just because you're lonely. Just slow it down."

"I'm not afraid to be alone," Charlie said, irritation lacing her tone. "And who made this rule that you have to be alone to heal, anyway? What if you find someone that accelerates the healing?"

"Niggas like the one you were with last night do more damage," Stassi said. "Trust."

"I'm not talking about him. I can't speak to who he is and I'm never vouching for a nigga I don't know cuz a nigga will have you defending him knowing he foul. I'm just saying in general." Charlie poured the pancake batter onto the electric griddle, making six perfect circles. "I don't have to seclude myself to love myself better. I got this. I don't need you down my back watching my every move. Just be here."

"Alright, Charlie," Stassi said skeptically. "You remember what happened last time..."

"I'm not that same girl," Charlie snapped. "If you knew me then, you don't know me now. Shit ain't the same."

"Well, if you're not the same, toss that nigga card in the trash and focus on you," Stassi urged. Charlie put down the spatula.

"You know what? Just so I don't have to hear your mouth." Charlie grabbed Demi's card and dropped it in her trash can. "Happy now?" she asked, resuming her pancake duty.

Charlie flipped the pancakes as her nostrils flared. She was 24 years old and Stassi was only two years older than that. She didn't need her sister preaching to her about shit she couldn't change. If Charlie hated nothing else, it was to be judged. "And, bitch, scramble an egg or something. I ain't your damn personal chef. This is sister's brunch and you the one with the damn culinary degree, so get to cooking something," she snapped.

Charlie and Stassi had spent every Sunday like this for the past six months. Reacquainting, reuniting, after many years had kept them apart.

"What about you? Who you entertaining these days?" Charlie asked as she pulled a bottle of champagne from her refrigerator. One orange juice, one pineapple.

"Nobody, girl. This damn business is my boyfriend. I feel like all I do is cook and eat. I can never find a date because I'm always covered in food, looking crazy. Let me tell you how I met this nigga in the grocery store. Fine-ass fucking man named Day. I'm walking through there with a damn apron and flour all over me because my egg delivery didn't come in this week and I ran out in the middle of baking this girl's birthday cake. So, boom, I shoot to the store and bump into the finest fucking man. Nigga legit smelled like money. Like he in there high as fuck, smelling like kush, looking for sunflower seeds cuz he got the munchies. Nigga legit walked up on me, talking about can you show me where the nuts and shit at?"

Charlie giggled. "I mean, you do keep that damn apron on all the time."

"Bitch, I don't work in no fucking grocery store! I mean, don't get me wrong, ain't nothing wrong with working at the grocery store, but I shouldn't be walking around looking like I know what's on aisle 2!"

"So, what did you say?" Charlie asked, her eyes smiling in amusement.

"I cussed his ass out," Stassi replied, sipping her mimosa.

"And he hired you after that?" Charlie asked, eyes wide. "How you parlay that to a job?"

"Girl, so he looks me up on Instagram. I mean, like right there on the spot cuz I was going in on him, talking about I'm a business owner, yada, yada, right?" Stassi paused to take a bite of the bacon Charlie had just finished frying. "So, he liked what he saw, and he booked me on the spot. Cash App'd me the deposit and everything. It's a fifty-thousand-dollar job. Some showcase at his company."

"Oh my God! That's so good!" Charlie was genuinely ecstatic for her sister. They never competed. Even as kids. When one won, they both celebrated; no matter how much their mothers hated it. They had refused to put the step in their title. They were sisters. Not by blood, but by love.

"Soooo... you got to come with me," Stassi said.

"Stassi, no! Don't nobody want to come to work for free!"

"Come on, please, Charlie? You don't even have to do anything. I just need you there for moral support. This guy is a big deal. You can just come and vibe out. I just don't want to walk in alone," Stassi said.

"I'll help," Charlie said. "But you owe me."

CHAPTER 3

Charlie walked into the empty club and the sound of the band warming up sparked excitement in her soul. She carried her guitar at her side, but she sat in the back in obscurity as she allowed the band to finish their set.

She hadn't been singing with them long. Before she had picked up a mic at Karaoke Thursdays six months ago, she hadn't even known them. The bass guitarist, Justin, had heard her sing that night and had offered her a gig on the spot. She had been singing every Saturday with the four men ever since. Charlie loved it. She loved everything about singing to live music, in front of drunken crowds, as the sensuality of her voice brought out the sensuality of them.

They were playing a live rendition of a Summer Walker joint and it was the drums for her. Her heart thudded with every high-hat and she swooned. There was nothing like soul-filled music. It was her first love. She remembered writing down the lyrics to Lauryn Hill's album as a kid while singing the songs, matching her sultry tone. It was how she had learned to sing. Matching the voices of her favorite singers and then eventually discovering a voice of her own as she got older. No matter what she had been through, through her father leaving, through the death of her mother, through lonely and misunderstood teenage years, and through years of being mistreated by men, music had never left her side. That notebook with song lyrics from songs she wanted to learn only grew.

Charlie emerged from the shadows as Justin played a solo on his guitar at the end. The way he played took her breath away. His hands seduced the strings with expertise. Fitted jeans, Ray-Ban sunglasses, and a beanie hat in the summertime, he was an artist if Charlie had never seen one.

"It's a shame for someone to be so talented," she said, smiling as he finished, and she stepped onto the stage.

"I say that every time you sing over these strings, Charles," he said. "You want to lay some vocals over this sound?"

Charlie smiled, grabbing the microphone, and fell right into the rhythm of the song. She had been singing it in her head anyway, so she knew exactly where to come in.

"What an addiction, so high a cost, gambled it alllll just to be lost, but no loveee lost, no bridges burned, you live and you learnnn I learned from my hurt," she sang. Eyes closed and she let the band play for a bit before she added. "Waste of timeeeee my loverrrrr..."

"Wrap it up, clubs closed for the night!"

Charlie's eyes popped open as Frankie walked into the room. His hand was wrapped in gauze and medical tape.

"What happened to your hand?" she asked.

He looked down at it and up at her. "Nothing, don't worry

about it. Club is closed 'til next weekend. No rehearsal, no nothing," he said.

"Weren't the inspectors just in here last month?" Justin asked.

Frankie nodded. "They pop up when they want to. We got some wiring issues I got to take care of this week. I'll still pay you for your set, but the club's doors stay closed," Frankie informed.

Charlie frowned but didn't contest it as long as she was getting paid. She didn't miss his energy, though. He was talking fast and trembling a little. She didn't think he was giving them the full story but she wouldn't question it. It wasn't her business to know.

"Charlie, let me holler at you in the office," he said.

Charlie nodded and followed him into the privacy of his office.

He handed her a small tote bag.

"Tell your boyfriend I won't be late again," Frankie said. "Make sure he knows."

"My what?" Charlie asked, frowning in confusion. She opened the bag and blew out a sharp breath at the money she found inside. "Frankie, what is..."

"Just tell him," Frankie said, practically yelling as he sat at his desk, struggling with a pack of cigarettes. His nerves were bad. She didn't miss his shaky hands.

"Tell who?" she shouted in exasperation. "I have no idea what you're talking about."

"Demi. I don't want no problems with that nigga. Just take the money and give it to him. He told me to give it to you. I'll have another twenty-five by next weekend."

Demi?

"I can't take this. I don't even know him!" she protested.

"He said to give it to you. He was specific. Just take it and close the door on your way out," Frankie said.

Charlie took the bag and rushed to the table where her guitar and tote bag sat. She unlocked the guitar case and put the bag inside.

Her hands shook a little bit, and she didn't know why. It was just a feeling. Like this money was bad. Like the man who had given it to her was worse.

Did he do that to Frankie's hand? What is this money about?

Justin placed a hand on her shoulder and Charlie startled.

"You good?" he asked.

"Yeah, umm... I'll call you. Maybe we can go over next week's set at my house since the club is closed?" Charlie proposed.

"Yeah, that's a date, just hit me," he said. "You need a ride?"

"No, thanks. My car's out front," she said. "But you can come by in about an hour," Charlie said.

"Bet," Justin said. "I'ma run by the crib, grab some food, then come through."

Charlie walked out, rushing over to her old, raggedy car. The old-school, blue Corsica was nothing fancy, in fact, it was falling apart. Rust at the bottom of all four doors, evidence from the many winters it had survived.

She hopped in and started her car. She couldn't get to her house fast enough. She practically sped the entire way. She hadn't stored Demi's number and she had thrown the card in the trash.

"The one day I want to take my trash to the dumpster," she mumbled as she pulled into her apartment complex. She parked, racing over to the dumpster that was now full.

"Damn it!" she said, stomping her foot in frustration. "Stassi's punk-ass," Charlie fussed, needing someone to fault for throwing the business card away in the first place. Charlie fought the air. "Son of a bitch," she mumbled as she gripped the sides of the dumpster, grunting as she lifted herself onto the side. She sat on the edge, staring down at the mountain of trash beneath her. "This motherfucka."

The sound of a car horn startled Charlie and when she turned and saw Demi parked next to the dumpster, standing outside his open car door, one hand on the roof as he stared up at Charlie in perplexity, she lost her balance falling into the pile of trash.

"Aghh!" she screamed, landing in something wet.

This would happen to her. The nigga had literally caught her in the garbage. Charlie shook her head and planted her face in her hands.

"Demi?" she called out, wincing in embarrassment from her throne of trash.

"Yup," he called back, laughter in his tone.

Charlie grabbed the edge of the dumpster and peeked out over the side. He was so damn fine, standing there looking up at her, and Charlie shrank in embarrassment, lowering back down.

Just throw the whole day away, she thought.

"You want to tell me what you doing, Bird?" he yelled.

"Nope! Nothing I can say makes this moment any better," she said, finally climbing out, struggling to gain her balance as she slipped all over the trash.

Demi cringed, wiping his hands down the top of his head. He would help but nah. He didn't do shit like this. She would have to clean this mess up on her own. His skin was crawling just looking at her.

"Yo, you got some kinda bullshit..." He fingered his cheek to motion to the spot where something white marked her cheek.

She hopped down, feeling disgusting, as she wiped the spot on her cheek.

"You're probably hella grossed out right now," she said.

"Emphasis on hella," he answered. "What you doing out here?"

"I threw your card away," she said, shrugging in defeat.

Demi bit down on his bottom lip and nodded. "You feeling the kid that much where you diving in a fucking dumpster to get at me?"

"The kid?" she teased, laughing. "Oh, you're real cool, speaking about yourself in third person."

He snickered. "Now's not the time to talk about cool, Bird. You're covered in baby shit and old sour cream."

Charlie frowned and flicked goop off her fingertips. "Come in. I need to shower, but I have... umm... just give me a minute, please?" she asked.

"Take your time," he said. "Take a nice, LONG, shower." She chuckled as she watched him pull into a parking space.

Charlie retrieved her bag and guitar case and then led him inside. Bails barked instantly as soon as Charlie stepped in the door.

"Hey, Bails. Hey, baby boy," she cooed. Always so eager to see him.

"Five minutes," she said, rushing upstairs.

"Nah, Bird, you gon' need a few more. I'm not going nowhere, wash ya ass," he said.

Demi sat on the couch, eyeing Bails as the dog inched near him. "The fuck on, man," he said, body tensing. Bails only inched closer to him, until he was sitting directly at Demi's feet, head leaned onto his palms, big, emotion-filled eyes looking up at Demi.

"This fucking dog shit," Demi mumbled. He sat there, going through his phone as he heard music floating from the second floor and the sound of the shower running. He was glad she took her time. He would be more comfortable with her that way. She tended to like to touch, and at least he'd know her hands were clean.

The knock at the door lifted Demi's eyes and he looked back toward the stairs. The second knock lifted him from his seat. He climbed the stairs, headed to her bedroom. Of course, she showered with the door open. The silhouette of her body through the frosted glass door burned into his mind but he didn't look long, averting his eyes out of respect.

"Yo, Bird, somebody at your door," he said.

"Can you answer it? It's probably my friend. I'm almost done in here," she shouted.

A third knock and this time her doorbell. Whoever it was, was persistent.

Demi swaggered to the door and was unprepared for the man who stared back at him. In one hand he carried a brown paper bag that reeked of cheap Chinese. In the other hand, he carried his guitar.

"Not who I expected to see at all. Charlie here?" Justin asked.

Demi recognized him from the night before. He stepped aside and Justin walked in as Charlie rushed down the stairs. Of all the things Demi could have focused on it was her toes that stuck out to him most. A different color on every toe, Demi thought her feet looked like Skittles. He would bet his bottom dollar on it that they tasted like Skittles too. That pussy too. Demi's mind was in the gutter. He knew it because he had never thought of putting his mouth on a woman before that very moment.

"Justin! I... Ummm... I'm really sorry. I should have called you. Can we reschedule?" Charlie came out stammering, explaining herself, with a towel wrapped around her body. Demi felt a tug in his chest as he stared at her, body still dripping from the shower, her locs pulled up in a high ponytail.

She was so comfortable in her skin. In front of him in her skin. Hell, in front of Demi in her skin. Was this just her or was this nigga special? Was Demi special? Before Demi could stop himself, he was speaking.

"Say, man," he said. "I'm up. I'll get with you another time."

His irritation wasn't missed.

"Wait. I need to talk to you about something," she said. "Can you stay a bit?"

"So, fuck the songs? What about the set?" Justin interrupted.

"Plans changed," Demi said, staring at Charlie from across the room.

Charlie stared back. She didn't know if she was turned on or pissed at him for answering for her. It was all in his stance. He was arrogant. Certain. Like he knew that he was really holding back from what he wanted to say and that she should be grateful that he was even being this civil at all. "Umm... yeah, I'm sorry, Justin. I'll make it up to you," she said.

"Probably not," Demi interrupted, again.

"Demi!" she exclaimed.

Justin frowned and shook his head. "Yo, Charlie, for real?" he said.

"I swear I'll call you later. This is just kind of important," Charlie explained.

"Wow, Charles. I didn't think you were that type," Justin said, sucking his teeth and turning for the door.

"What type is that, my man?" Demi asked.

"Demi..." Charlie intervened. She stopped him. From what? She didn't know. Maybe the same fate that she was sure Frankie had suffered at his hand because while she hadn't seen it, she was sure he had done it.

Demi bit into his lip and turned toward her kitchen,

pulling open the refrigerator and pulling out a bottled water like he lived there. Charlie turned back to Justin.

"I promise I'll make time to rehearse the set," she said.

"I'll see you at the club," Justin said, heading out.

Charlie didn't quite know what to say, so she let him leave. She would diffuse the situation with him later. She turned to Demi.

"What is wrong with you? That is my friend," she said, scoffing, pissed at herself that she found herself offering clarity.

"Yeah, okay," he answered, coolly.

"He is!" Charlie argued.

"I said, okay," Demi repeated, with a calmness that took her temper up a couple notches. "The nigga want to fuck you, though."

"And you got all that from the one day you've known me," she said sarcastically.

It reminded them both that they had just met. This was a lot for two people who were practically strangers.

"Look, here's your money," Charlie said, stalking over to her guitar case to retrieve the bag. She opened it and held it out for him. "I don't know what you have going on with Frankie, but don't involve me in it again. Did you do that to his hand?"

Demi stared at the bag like it was infected. "I wouldn't put you in no bullshit and I don't know what you talking 'bout. I'm just trusting you to hold onto that for me. Did you count it?"

"It's not mine to count," she said.

"Count it."

"Nigga, do I look like a bank teller?" she asked.

Demi leaned onto her countertop and put his face in his hands... big hand... tattooed hand... she wondered who he trusted enough to let touch him to do them in the first place... Then, he scratched the top of his head, before lifting irritated eyes to her.

"You look like you don't mind how dirty money is. Can you just quit arguing with me about everything and count the shit, man?"

Charlie was stubborn but she rolled her eyes and opened the bag, pouring the contents out onto her coffee table. Her hands flicked through the bills and when she was done, she looked up in shock.

"It's a hundred thousand dollars, Demi. I can't keep this for you," she said.

"It ain't a big deal. You got it," he said.

"You don't even know me like that to be trusting me with your money," Charlie said, frowning.

Demi pulled his bottom lip into his mouth and looked off to the side and then separated her blinds with his finger, peering outside. Always aware of his surroundings. "You gon' steal from me, Bird?" he asked, finally placing his eyes back on her.

Charlie flicked through the thick knot of bills. All hundreds. Who carried around all hundred-dollar bills?

"Probably," she smirked, shrugging.

This fucking girl. Demi laughed. Always so lighthearted around her. He dug back into his pocket and pulled out another knot. "That's on you. Now, you ain't got to dip into the stash," he said.

Charlie plucked it from his fingers. "Guess not," she answered, smiling. She shook her head in disbelief. "This is nuts." She didn't know if he was crazy, if she was, or if they both were, but this felt insane. This sudden thing that they were dancing around, this impromptu invasion of him into her life. "Is this all you came here for or are you planning to stay?"

"I'm a little pressed for time tonight," he admitted.

"You should never come by when you're pressed for time," she said, shaking her head. "Cuz I'ma make you late. Now you can't leave."

She reached for his hand and she felt his palm go wet. Sweaty palms were a thing for him when he was uncomfortable.

The touching, she thought. She had forgotten just that quick.

She stepped close to him and smiled as he stared down at her. Brooding. Wound so tightly. Charlie placed her hands on the sides of his face, cupping it and he gripped her wrists.

"You're going to have to deal with it, Demi, because I like to touch," she whispered.

"Bird, you killing me," he said.

She wiped her hands all over his face and he grimaced, cringing, and nodding. "You think this shit funny, yo. I'ma fuck you up," he said, irritation lacing his tone. "You been touching that money and shit."

"Are you freaking out right now?" she asked.

"Fuck you, man," he snickered.

"I mean, you could clean up here. Stay here tonight," she offered.

"I told you I got somewhere to be," he insisted. Charlie reached for her towel and opened it, exposing pretty perky titties that made Demi's dick stiffen.

"Well, I had plans too, but somebody felt like he had the right to change them. So now, I'm changing yours," she said.

"I got to go," Demi said, voice just above a whisper as she stood so close to him that his skin crawled, and his stomach hollowed.

"Do you?" she asked.

It was Charlie's skin that pulled him in. She had scars all over her body that told a story of pain. Like her mother had lost control during childhood beatings. He wanted to ask questions but opted not to. He wanted to put his lips to those scars, but he opted not to do that too. He cleared the lump in his throat and swept a hand down his mouth as she backpedaled toward the stairs.

"Let me clean you," she said, smirking.

He took heavy steps her way, his pants hanging low off his hips as the thud of his sneakers echoed off her floors. His eyes met her ass and never left as she ascended the stairs. She didn't have much, just enough like a delicacy, some of the best shit to put on your tongue came in small portions. He was a look-but-don't-touch type of nigga and he enjoyed the visual as she led the way to her bedroom and then into her bathroom.

She turned on the shower and then came out of her panties.

"Take off your clothes, weirdo," she said.

She stepped closer to him, pulling his shirt over his head. The gun on his waistline was unexpected and she froze. He removed it and leaned to put it on her dresser.

The wifebeater he wore as an undershirt clung to his brown skin. He was the color of tree bark and the art on his body was phenomenal. Her fingers traced the ink. "How do you have these if you don't like to be touched?" she asked.

"Somebody I trust put them there," he answered, tone guttural, like temptation was building in his throat. She kissed the inked Bible on his chest, and she felt him stop breathing.

"Stay here with me, Demi. Don't disappear in your head." Her tongue wet his nipple and then she stood on her tiptoes to allow her tongue to trace up his neck.

"Mmm," she moaned as she tasted his skin.

The spot she kissed felt like it was burning. Love burns. Like she had placed an iron to his skin.

His throat was closing, second by second, as she made her way across his chest and down his abs. Demi was solid. Strong. His habit of five-star restaurants and thousand-dollar bottles of champagne had stolen the definition from what used to be washboard, but somehow, she still found those V-cuts as she undid his Hermes belt and unzipped his jeans. He stepped out of them and Charlie moaned when she discovered how his body reacted to her. Dick on brick, forming temptation in his black Tom Ford boxer briefs. It was only right. Expensive wrapping for premium dick.

She stood. She was all over him. Her hands leaving little, invisible pieces of her behind. She couldn't see them, but he could feel them, her germs, her essences... everywhere. Charlie was infecting him. He knew he would scrub his skin raw after they were done.

His gaze was deadly. He was unhappy about this invasion, about her persistence, but his dick told her he liked it too.

"You don't like this, do you?" she whispered, as she took his hands, lacing her fingers between his and holding them in front of her.

"You know I don't," he replied.

"Then why are you letting me do it?" she asked.

Fuck his hands, Charlie moved closer. He moved his face because she was fucking disrespectful with the skin to skin. Charlie turned his face back. "Because I fuck with you," he answered.

He was so stiff, like she was Medusa and her gaze turned him to stone.

"If we shower together, will that make you more comfortable? If you're the one who cleans me?" she asked.

"I'm fucked up, Bird," he said. "This is fucked up."

"And I still want to do this," she said. "Fuck me in the shower, Demi."

"I ain't a regular nigga. I fuck a certain way. I can touch you, you can't touch me. I don't like slow sex. I fuck rough. I got rules."

"I know how to take dick, Demi," Charlie said, breathless at the thought of what she was about to get herself into. She was nervous but she would never admit it. Did she know how to take the type of dick he was giving out? The way he made it sound made her question if she could. Would it hurt? "I break rules," Charlie whispered. "I want to break so many of your rules, Demi." She was all in his face, her lips decibels from his, so close he could have heard the thoughts in her head.

Charlie pulled his bottom lip into her mouth and Demi lost it. His hands around her neck and her back to the wall. Yeah, he was a rough-ass nigga.

"Stop, damn!" He jerked her and Charlie closed her eyes and her mouth opened. His hands shook. Did she scare him? Did this scare her? This was a different level of crazy.

Been up since six doing ritualsssss

She didn't know why she started singing. She could barely get it out between his hands. They were like cages trapping the breath in her neck.

Burning incense just to wish you well

It was working. His hold loosened.

Throw all my sins into wishing wellsss
Smelling your scent, I do misss you stillll

His forehead to hers and a growl he couldn't contain. Charlie's heart raced as she watched his unspoken struggle and she kept singing.

What kind of spell do you have me under

He pulled back from her, heavy breathing as he pressed his hands into the wall around her.

"You got to slow it down for me, Bird," he said, staring down like she had gut-punched him and he couldn't take the pain.

"Okay," she conceded. "I'll go slow. Just let me clean you, babe."

Charlie snatched intimacy from behind his guards. She was serious. She lowered and removed his boxers and then led the way into the shower. She removed a towel from her linen closet and held it up for him. "It's clean," she said.

He nodded and then she grabbed her soap. "It's natural so it won't make you feel like all the dirt is gone, but it is. I promise, okay?" He nodded and she lathered the towel. She washed him first then washed herself and when they were done, he pulled her to him.

He was comfortable in the shower. When their bodies were clean, he was at ease.

They stood chest to chest and Charlie turned her head sideways as he pressed her head into him. Her locs absorbed the water and he massaged her head, then pulling all her locs into his hands before wringing the water from them. She rested her head on his chest, listening to the rhythm of his heartbeat. Loud and fast. His pulse raced. She wrapped her arms around his waist as the water beat over them.

"This is the crazy shit that makes women insane, Demi," she whispered. "This is different. This energy…" Charlie paused to breathe; a deep, centering breath that slowed down her overwhelm. She didn't even want to like this man. She had a feeling that he was too much, too soon, but she also knew that she didn't want him to go away. "Don't start this if you aren't going to finish. Like, if you're going to be on some bullshit. If you're going to play games with me, just don't start, because this is different."

He rested his chin on the top of her head but didn't respond.

"I got to go, Bird," he said. Dick pressed against her belly. He was hard for her, and it felt so good that just the heat of his need touching her made her breath go shallow. His mouth was saying one thing, but his dick was arguing for something else. A debate. He wanted to leave. Dick wanted to stay. She was siding with Dick.

Charlie craned her neck, staring up at him. She was intoxicating and his struggle to not kiss her was potent. She rubbed her nose to his.

"I got to goooo," he groaned.

Charlie took a step back, out of the direct stream of water and it was like she freed his mind. She could see his relief. She was stuck. She didn't know how to get past this physical roadblock between them.

"Okay," she replied. "I hate that I make you uncomfortable."

It was hard not to be offended, even though she knew it had nothing to do with her. He had warned her, but damn she was standing in front of him with pussy so wet he could bathe in it, but her touch was a turnoff.

Demi reached for a towel, wrapping it around his waist and

following her into her bedroom. He hated that his stomach tensed at the sight of Bails.

Charlie noticed his change of mood and followed his eyes to the bed. Bails was snuggled up right in the middle. She was speechless. She didn't know what to say.

"It ain't you," Demi stated.

"Yeah, that much is clear," she scoffed as she slid into her robe.

"What are the rules?" she asked, sitting on the bed. "I want to understand you."

"Your hands can't be everywhere, Bird. You're just fucking all over me. I got to think about every place you touch, and the shit makes me feel like hurting you," he admitted.

"Hurting me?" Charlie asked, her voice broke, trembling, and for the first time, he saw fear in her. The only reason he knew she was shaking was because he noticed details, almost every detail of every person he encountered, and the hem of her robe was vibrating.

"You need to leave, Demi," she said, eyes prickling.

He nodded and leaned over onto his knees, his strong arms tensed, the traps around his neck pronounced as a vein appeared in the center of his forehead.

"Now," Charlie said.

"No," Demi answered.

"This is my house, get the fuck out!" she shouted, trying to appear strong, grandstanding, yelling like her voice did anything other than make his heart flutter. Even in anger, the shit sounded like a song.

"Demi, please, just leave," she said, drawing in a deep breath as she opened her legs and leaned forward a bit while anchoring herself against the bed, gripping the sheets tightly and trying to find her peace.

In. Out.

She couldn't breathe.

Why would he say that? Why would he want to hurt her?

It was the ultimate trigger and Charlie felt like she was suffocating. Like his hands were wrapped around her neck and squeezing.

"If I could leave, Bird, this would have never started," he said, somberly.

"You can't say shit like that to me. About hurting me. What does that mean? Do you hurt women? Do you hit women?" she asked.

He blew out a breath so heavy it was the hurricane that forced her back to meet her bed. Charlie placed hands over her face and stared at the ceiling, but it only made her feel trapped. She sat up, abruptly, and rushed through her house, down the stairs, and out her front door.

Air. The fresh air helped. She was down the porch steps in seconds and in her grass, on her back. Eyes up. The stars. The sky. She cried out like that view was oxygen and she had been deprived.

She appreciated the way her heart slowed until she felt his hands under her body, picking her up.

She clung to him as they went up the steps, past her junky-ass living room, back up the stairs, bypassing her dog-infested bed and straight back to the shower. Their comfort zone. He turned the water on and Charlie didn't speak as he put hands around her, trapping her between strong arms as he leaned into the wall.

"I ain't gone hurt you, Bird, but you got to be careful with me. Shit ain't gon' be what you used to," he said. "It ain't gon' be normal."

"I don't want normal and what I'm used to hurt worse than anything I've ever felt," she whispered, tears mixing with the water spraying over them. "I want different."

"Then slow down for me. I'ma get there but let me wrap my mind around you first. Be patient with me, baby." He wasn't asking and she wasn't denying him of the order. She nodded and he pinched her chin, gripping it between his fingertips.

He kissed her and the fucking growl he made while doing so made her river flood. He was doing this for her. Going past the limit, giving her connection because it was the love language she understood, but his shoulders were like bricks. Charlie moaned as he parted her thighs and then without warning, he was inside her. They went from no touching to being one body.

"Is this okay?" she panted, mouth falling open as his tongue invaded her lips.

"No, Bird. This is fucked up," he grunted, as his wide dick pushed into her.

"Oh my God," she moaned.

She didn't think twice about a condom because no way was this weird-ass man dirty. He was too particular to not be safe. She was sure this was killing him. That he was counting her germs, probably keeping a note in his head of all the places he would need to sanitize on his body after they were done.

Demi was too good at this to be so selfish. He fucked her against her shower wall, delivering inches of bliss as he split her walls. Inches. Demi delivered inches, both wide and long. She felt all his frustration as he hit it. He pulled out and teased her clit, pulling moans from her soul as she sank her teeth into his shoulder.

"Demi," she whispered, hanging on tightly, like the ride was moving too fast. He gripped her ass with one hand and her neck with the other, fucking her so good that Charlie wished she was able to run from him. He was so deep she was gagging on the dick. She felt him in the depths of her soul until neither of them could take anymore.

"Fuckkk," he said with bass. "Oh shittt." He pulled out, leaving her legs too weak to support her as he pressed his forehead to hers.

He was quaking, body literally shivering from the encounter. He didn't know if she was made of magic or if he was just completely in over his head, but her touch lingered. He felt her everywhere. Charlie had pulled an orgasm from him that started at his toes and spread over every inch of him, inside and out, until he had erupted. Demi had indulged in plenty of women; none had brought him to a nut like this.

"Are you okay?" she asked, voice unsure, small, unusually so because Charlie gave big energy. He could tell he had thrown her off, made her uncertain of how and if she should be handling him.

"Give me a minute," he said.

Charlie nodded. He was trying to be normal, but she could see the abnormality in him.

This nigga is fucking odd, Charlie thought. She slipped out of the shower, leaving him in the bathroom alone.

Demi's fist bawled against the tile wall once he was alone.

"Fuck, man," he spat, gritting his teeth, temple throbbing. So much conflict swirled in his chest. He had crossed a line. So many lines, but it was too late to turn back. He should have never let her get in his car, never discovered where she lived. This was bad. This was out of fucking control. He was out of control. He cleaned his body and then located her cleaning supplies and cleaned the shower before stepping out of the bathroom. Charlie sat on the bed anxiously, dressed in his shirt. He tensed. It was shit like that. Her opting to wear his shit, leaving invisible Charlie pieces on the fabric. She was going to drive him crazy.

"This was too much?" It was rhetorical because she knew the answer already.

"The dog," he said. Charlie looked behind her to the dog resting on her bed. Of course, he didn't like dogs.

"The sheets," he continued. "They're the same as last time."

It hadn't even been three days.

Oh, this nigga is pyscho.

"It's little shit, Bird. That will have my mind running for days. The clutter. I just need my life organized," Demi tried to explain.

He had even cleaned her entire bathroom before emerging. Demi was a man who required order.

"You can't organize your heart, Demi," Charlie whispered. "I can do some things to make you comfortable, but I'ma make mess of your heart."

He nodded, biting into his bottom lip, face destroying in indecision and turmoil. "I know."

"I can't not touch you," Charlie said. "I need to be the exception."

Demi stood before her with beads of water dripping from his strong body. "I don't fuck face to face. I ain't fucked nobody without a condom ever and I don't put my tongue in wet places. I would say you're the exception."

"Can we revisit the tongue in wet places rule?" she asked.

He snickered at that and she blushed. "Com'ere," she whispered, patting the spot beside her.

He sat beside her, and Demi turned, lifting her left thigh onto the mattress so she could face him.

"Will you stay?" she asked.

He nodded.

"Yeah," he whispered. He didn't even hesitate. He wanted to hop in his car and push 90 in the 70 zone just to put some distance between them, but there was an urge to be in her space. To smell her. Her locs. To inhale the scent of her hair because the shit smelled like freshly cut flowers and he breathed deep when he was around her.

Her smile was blinding. Worth it. She stood. "Come on, Bails, Demi don't like you, baby boy," she said, pouting as she picked her dog up and put him out the room. He whimpered on the other side of the door and Charlie laughed. "You're fucked up for making me put my best friend out," she said. She went to the linen closet and pulled out new sheets.

"My bad, Bird," he smirked as she pulled off the old sheets. She changed the linens, tossed the water bottles, and sprayed the room down with Lysol before opening the windows. She went to the sink to rewash her hands and forearms and Demi was appreciative because the fucking dog was a real thing.

"I'm clean, you're clean," she said as she climbed into the middle of the bed, sitting up on her knees.

Demi walked over to her and Charlie made her way to the edge.

He placed his face in the groove of her neck, kissing her shoulder. Progress. They were making progress. The shit felt so dirty, but it was the most enticing filth he had ever discovered. Muddy puddles. Charlie was like the muddy puddles that kids loved to jump in on a rainy day. Liberating, completely senseless, but the best fucking time. He would watch those kids when he was younger, having the time of their lives, smiling bright as their laughter infected the warm scented air. He never joined in the fun until now. Charlie was his muddy puddle.

Charlie climbed beneath the covers and held them up for him. He hesitated but joined her. Demi eased behind her body, wrapping one hand around her waist, spooning her, burying his face in her wet hair.

"You've got to breathe, Demi," she whispered.

"Fucking I can't," he whispered back.

She sat up, yawning, and nodded. "Okay." She scrambled across the bed and reached for her guitar. "Relax."

"A tornado flew around my room before you came, excusssseee the mess it made, it usually doesn't rain innnn Sunny Demifornia, much like Charliezonia," she sang, changing the lyrics, pulling a scoff from Demi as he sat back, both arms folded behind his head and watched her play. She laid down, cozying underneath his arm as she strummed the strings. Frank Ocean's song had become her own and her version was better, at least to Demi.

"My heart won't get you dirrrty, boy, let's ball, cuz I'm thinking 'bout you. Oooo, nahh, nahh, nahhh, I want to touch up on you, oooo, noo, noo, nooo, rub my hands up on you, please, boy, tell me that you will, let me, let me..."

Charlie had changed the entire song and her voice regulated his pulse, slowing it, taking the anxiety out of his mind effortlessly.

"Or do you not think so farrrrr, aheeeeeeaddddddddd, cuz I've been thinking about forever, with your weird-asssss, yeahhhhhh."

She felt his chest rumble as he laughed. Such a deep, throaty sound. It made her heart fill and her lips spread east to west as she tried to contain her own... Smile. He made her smile. How this man had ended up in her bed was anybody's guess. His timing was all off, but somehow, he was filling a hole in her heart.

She stopped singing and just kept playing lazily, her fingers stroking the chords from memory as Demi's body relaxed.

"Charliezonia, huh?" he asked.

She nodded. "That's our place. A clean, safe place where we don't think. We just exist and do whatever we want with one another," Charlie explained. She was playing the guitar effortlessly, not even thinking or looking at the strings. The impression she was leaving on Demi was one that he wouldn't be able to erase.

"Sound like it might be my new favorite place," he said, caressing her thigh gently with the back of his knuckle.

"It's completely sterile there by the way," she said, cracking a joke that made his entire face heat in embarrassment. She laughed.

"I'm thinking 'bout you, do you think about me still? Do you? Do you?" She leaned forward, placing her lips on his, not missing one chord as she forced a kiss. Demi's dick stiffened and his skin crawled. This woman, whom he had just met, confused him. Body, mind, and soul. She was violating him, ignoring rules, doing what she wanted. Whatever lived inside her mouth was now inside of his and it was an erotic exchange, unlike anything he had ever felt.

Charlie did this often, strumming the songs of her heart in the middle of the night, but tonight she had an audience, and a good one he was. She felt the tension be put to rest when he finally fell asleep and she stopped all sound, gently placing the guitar on the side of the bed. She placed a pillow between them because she wasn't sure if cuddling under him all night would make him uncomfortable, and before she laid down, she looked at him for a long time, just staring. He was so rough around every edge, the kind of edge you cut yourself on if you didn't walk around it just right. Like the corner of a bedframe. His handsome features had never looked so relaxed. The permanent dent that normally creased his brow was gone and Charlie felt full on him, full on the uncertainty of them and it both electrified her and terrified her. She listened to him breathe until hers slowed and her eyes closed. Peace was rare for them both, but together, somehow, they had found it. This night, lying under one another, they had discovered it and it felt glorious.

CHAPTER 4

It wasn't the rise of the sun that pulled Demi from Charlie's bed. It was the rise of his conscious. He lifted from the bed and Charlie stirred.

"No, babe, nooo," she groaned, eyes closed, reaching for him, hands fucking everywhere. His skin burned, but his heart thundered as she pulled him back. His fists melted into the bed around her body as he hovered over her. She rubbed her eyes like a big-ass baby, fists going to work as she yawned and then she looked at him through the dark. Her eyes in the morning time were magnets of darkness that had gravity on her side. They pulled him, bringing him from reality back to Charliezonia. The loose hair that curled around her golden locs were feather soft as he took the darkest side of his finger to her face. How easily Charlie chased intimacy. He saw it all over her. Her comfort. Her willingness to indulge in a game of emotional hide and seek with him. He was hiding. She was it. He was desperate to find home base. "You were going to leave without saying bye?"

She took his breath from his lungs. Stole his words. He just stared at her. He cleared her locs from her face but paused.

"Touch me, Demi. I don't like when you think about it but don't do it," she whispered.

She put so much conflict in this man's chest. A man who didn't think twice about pulling triggers thought twice about his every interaction with her.

He caressed the side of her face and her eyes closed.

"Lower, Demi," she whispered. His fingers made her squirm as he traced her nose all the way to the tip, then manipulating her lips.

"You the shit, Bird," he said, tone guttural, almost groaning as she felt his body responding.

"See," she whispered. "I won't hurt you."

The seconds ticked away as he hovered there.

"My chest feels so tender with you," she admitted. "It's like you tore everything out and I'm waiting for you to put something back in."

He broke every single rule when he stole her lips, trapping the pout of her mouth between his teeth and then bullying his tongue inside her mouth. So much passion existed in their interaction. It was hard to fathom that 24 hours prior they hadn't even known one another's name. If this was what a one-night stand felt like, he could only imagine a lifetime of her. Some man would have the pleasure to call her his forever, not Demi, but somebody would.

I'll kill that nigga, Demi thought, going crazy, overthinking, because he didn't even know this girl and already, he was possessive. She tasted so damn good.

He was on top of her, and when Charlie reached up to touch his face, she felt him stop breathing. He tried not to react, but the rigidness of his body was a guilty tell. Her body felt his send silent alerts to his every extremity, steeling him. She had never met a man so guarded. It only made her want him more.

"You're kissing me, Demi," she whispered, smiling slightly. "And touching me. Like I'm yours. Like I'm you. Half of you."

"You are," he answered.

Charlie sucked in air as he kissed her chin and then moved to her neck, onto her breasts. Her nipples tightened as he wet them, teased them. It felt so damn good and her sex flooded. She tensed when he kissed the scar between her breasts. She had tattooed over it, but it was still visible, and her every insecurity sprouted with him focusing there.

"What happened here?" he whispered, coming up to look her in the eyes.

"I don't like to talk about it," she answered.

He frowned. "Whatever happened, it ain't gon' happen again. Everything I love is safe," he said. Her heart stopped. How was he doing this? Making her feel this? Saying shit like this? After only one night. Demi was promising her something— protection. An act of service. A confession of love. Informal and premature, yet still true. He felt it. She did too.

"I'm going to change your whole world, mark my words," she said, blushing.

"Don't count on me, Bird," he said. "Take what you can get from me while you can get it. Whatever it is. Money, opportunity, whatever I'm giving, you rack it up while it lasts, but keep your expectations low."

"No expectations. Got it," she replied.

He reached down and parted her, exploring her with his fingers.

"This pussy good, baby," he said, replacing fingers with dick. The way he pushed into her made Charlie's back arch off the mattress. Backs weren't supposed to incline like that, but good dick did it every time.

"Mmmmm," she moaned. His stroke was deep. Deep as fuck. The loooongestttttt strokes she had ever received and her head craned back every time he hit bottom. He bit her chin.

"You gon' let me keep this shit, Bird? This my pussy?" Demi groaned as he hit her in circles. Charlie's hands went to his back and then to his ass, pressing him into her completely. She felt the hardness of him pressing into her clit.

"Fuck!" she screamed.

"Tell me, Bird," he growled. It was fitting because he was an animal in bed.

"It's yours, Demi, it's yours," she whispered.

"Then cum all over this dick ,Bird. Hmm?" he said, gritting his teeth.

"I ammmmm, Demi, I'm cummingggggg. Wait for me, Demi. I feel it, aghhh!"

Demi murdered her pussy, coming straight up on his knees and gripping her at the crease of her hips, slamming her down onto him. "Cum. On. This. Fucking. Dick," he said. Demi beat it like she stole something. Beat it like a case. Beat it like a bitch beat her face. Demi knew how to make a woman feel like a woman. He was on an archeological dig to unearth the history of her sex and Charlie was leaving the evidence of her existence all over him. He had that pussy creaming. Demi played with her clit like he had seen her play her guitar, strumming her love, mastering her strings, as he admired the juices coating his dick as he went in and out.

"Shit!" she cried.

"You making a mess, Bird. Look at this shit," he said, biting down on his bottom lip. "Fuckkkkkk."

Round two was a beautiful tie, conceding to one another, giving into fatigue as he collapsed on the bed beside her.

"You want to shower? I can change the sheets," she whispered, turning to him as she laid on one shoulder.

"Nah, Bird," he said, eyes lowering. There wouldn't be any creeping out before morning. Not tonight. Whatever will he had mustered to leave, she had just stolen.

"But you don't like it. I touched you," she said, voice small, exhausted.

"You just gon' do the shit again, so I might as well keep you on me. I'm tired over here, man. Like fucking exhausted. You make a nigga feel like he ain't slept in years," Demi said.

"What do you mean?" she asked.

"As soon as I walk through the door it's like I can't wait to close my eyes. You got a real comfortable vibe about you, Bird. Your house feels like a good place to sleep," he explained. He didn't close both eyes often. Demi was always on point, always anticipating his past in the streets coming back to haunt him. He never relaxed, except here, for this one night. He was more relaxed than he had ever been. He didn't know if it was because no one knew where he was, or about Charlie, or if there was something special she was doing to make him feel that way, but his guard felt useless in her house.

"So, sleep, babe. If my house brings you peace, you can come here to sleep. Whenever you need to."

Demi looked at her and lifted one arm, so she could ease beneath him. She was hesitant.

"You sure?" she asked. He was so damn funny acting. So damn picky, particular about where her hands touched before touching him.

"It ain't the house, Bird. It's you. I'm sure."

Demi felt something cold and wet and it stirred him from his sleep. He opened one eye and Bails laid cuddled beneath him, licking his cheek. He damn near fell out the bed, trying to scramble away, knocking over the lamp on her nightstand as he hopped from the bed.

"The fuck, man," Demi snapped. "Yo, Bird, this fucking dog!"

Bails laid down on the bed staring up at him with those glossy, big eyes.

"Fucking look at me like that, man. We gon' have to come to an understanding around this motherfucka," Demi bitched as he took heavy steps toward the bathroom, slamming the door before climbing into her shower.

He practically scrubbed his skin raw as he stood beneath the stream of water. He was pissed, grunting, and growling his complaints as he used damn near a whole bottle of soap to get clean.

"Should have took my ass home," he mumbled. "Goddamn dog."

He washed his body until the water ran cold, and when he emerged from the bathroom, he paused, noticing the bed had been made with fresh sheets, Bails was gone, and there was a Macy's bag on the floor.

The smell of food was in the air and Demi stood there, hair on his chest, bare feet soaking the floor, rubbing his semi-toned abs as Charlie appeared at the door.

"Bails versus Demi. Bails-1, Demi-0?" she asked. "You okay?"

He nodded. "What's this?" he motioned to the bag.

"You've been sleeping all morning. I thought you would want something clean to put on when you woke up. I know you rock your Gucci and shit. I just ran up to the mall and got you clean drawers and a Nike fit. So you don't have to wear last night's clothes," she said. "The mall is a mile away. It's not a big deal. You hungry?"

Demi rubbed his head. "You bought a nigga an outfit?" he almost laughed wholeheartedly. He had heard something similar in a Beyonce song one time. Had he fucked her that good? To where she wanted to buy him a short set? The thought was sweet. He fucked with it.

He reached down for his pants that laid on the floor and dug in the pockets, pulling out more money. He peeled off what he was sure was way more than what she paid and put it on the nightstand. He went to the sink to wash his hands before reaching for the Macy's bag.

"Thank you," he said.

"Of course, and you don't have to pay me back, Demi," she said.

"I'm not paying you back. I'm just making sure you straight. This real cute, Bird. The fucking and clothing and feeding and all that, but you ain't never got to go through no trouble for me," he answered as he dressed. Grey sweatsuit, drawers, socks, t-shirt. Yeah, he was appreciative as fuck because the hour-long drive to the crib in day-old clothing would have tortured him.

"There's nothing wrong with letting people make sure you're straight sometimes, Demi. Taking care of the people I love isn't trouble," she said, sitting beside him and handing him a plate.

"Love?" he skipped right over everything else she had said, sitting the plate down on the nightstand.

"I didn't mean it like that," she said, lowering her eyes to her plate and picking up her fork to feed him eggs. He didn't open his mouth.

"I haven't eaten off the fork yet, boy," she said, giggling.

He took a bite and nodded. "You're a liar," he replied.

"About what?" she frowned.

"You ate off the fork," he said, grabbing his own plate. "I taste you with my eggs."

She blushed so damn hard.

"I'ma get used to you. It just takes me a minute. Your touch, your smell, your taste," he said.

"Glad you're making plans to do that," she replied.

"You gon' have to choose, though. It's me or the dog," he snickered.

"Nigga, my dog! The fuck!" she shouted.

He laughed hard at that and took another bite of his food before standing. "I got to go, but I'ma be back for you. I need a little more of that," he said, reaching between her thighs and grabbing her pussy like he owned it, playing with her clit through the fabric of her panties. "A nigga got to earn another short set."

Her eyes were soft, and her lips pressed together in a smile as he reached for his keys, money clip, and the left-over roll of money. He picked up his old clothes and folded them, but her heart fluttered when he left them sitting neatly on the end of her bed. He intended on coming back. She was smiling so big on the inside but playing it as cool as she could.

"Text me your number, Bird," he said. It was a shame. After doing what they had done, he didn't even have it.

She nodded and then he left, taking her heart out the door with him.

CHAPTER 5

Guilt was a passenger in the car as Demi sped South on I-75. Wale beat through his speakers as the night's events played through his head. One hand on the steering wheel, seat leaned back, head nodding slowly to the beat as he played with the hair on his chin. His mind was clouded. Filled with a pretty song and Charlie's face. He hated it. He had been around many types of women being in the game and the music industry, but there was an authenticity about Charlie that affected him. His phone buzzed and Demi answered.

"What up, boy?" Demi asked. Day Night. His best friend. A man who had stood shoulder to shoulder with him in the dead of winter, pushing product, and a man who had stood shoulder to shoulder with him on the red carpet of the Grammy's. They had truly come up together and stayed down. Best friends was an understatement. Brothers was more like it.

"My nigga, Lo, been hitting the studio all night. Fuck you was, nigga?!" Day asked, amusement lacing his tone. Day could hear the weed smoke choking him as Demi tried to talk and smoke simultaneously.

"Caught up, bruh. Had this lil' business to handle, nothing major. I'm headed her way now. You calling to pass messages now, nigga? What up?" Demi asked slightly annoyed.

"You get that joint I sent?" Day asked. "That shit ready for radio, my nigga. Just need a lil' pretty bitch on the hook and it's out of here."

"Let me play it and I'ma hit you right back," Demi said.

"Yup," Day said.

Demi hung up and opened the email from Day, ignoring the notifications for missed calls as he pressed play on the track that was waiting for him.

Demi knew it had legs when his head fell into a nod to the music. Three minutes and 25 seconds of pure artistry pumped through his custom speakers. He called Day back right away.

"My nigga, yo that's fucking out of here," Demi said. "Def needs a feminine vibe on the track." His mind went to Charlie. "I might have somebody new for it. Let me get to the crib. I'll hit you about it later today. That paper, though... it's been taken care of."

"I knew it would be. Niggas think cuz I'm on the radio I ain't getting busy no more," Day stated.

"You not, I will, though. Either way, it's taken care of," Demi stated.

"My mu'fucking bro, man," Day said. "Later."

Demi hung up and took the exit that led to his home. When he pulled up, pride swelled in his chest. Four thousand square feet of luxury awaited him. Tucked in the suburbs of Detroit, Demi lived amongst Michigan's elite. He pulled into his four-car garage and sat behind the wheel. Charlie had overdrafted his heart. It had only taken her a day to disrupt his entire life. He was playing with fire. As he exited the car and pushed into the interior of his home, he knew he was risking it all.

"Daddy!"

The sound of his eight-year-old son running his way full speed let him know he was risking too much.

"DJ, my man," he said, picking his only child up and tossing him over his shoulder. "What you got going on, huh?"

"Not much! Playing Roblox! Want to play?"

Demetrius Sky Jr. was a perfect blend of his parents, some called DJ his twin but Demi saw his mother most, but that spirit was his through and through.

"Yeah, set it up for me. Where ya mama at?" he asked.

"She's in the den," DJ said.

"A'ight, give me a minute, bet?" Demi said as he made his way through the house. A woman's touch was all over every inch. Lauren had done a beautiful job, not only choosing but filling the house with love and in one night, Demi had poured it out, into another woman's cup, filling it up, while poking holes all through the relationship he had been in for fifteen years.

He found her in her home office. Her back was to him as she spoke on the phone while pacing the carpet.

"The vendor for the linens is short on stock, so we need to find partners to make sure we have enough to cover all the tables at the reception. Oh, and can you check on my bottles of champagne? We'll need 300 bottles. They were due last week. They still haven't arrived," Lauren said. She smiled at Demi when she turned to him, holding up a finger to put him on hold as she ended her call. "Okay, well, keep me updated. This is a big account for us so we need to make sure this wedding is perfection." She hung up and leaned to sit on the edge of her desk. She was so damn pretty. Onyx-colored and short hair that was so fine that she only had to wet it and gel it to the back. High fashion. Gabonese with some Congo blood in her, by way of Louisiana, she was filled with melanin and culture. A stint at Clark Atlanta had put a pinch of hood in her.

"Hey, baby," she said. "I was beginning to think you forgot where you live."

"You know my job ain't got office hours, Lo. You know better. What's with all the calls?" he asked.

"What's with you not calling? You normally do if you have to stay out," she said.

Demi deadpanned on her. "I'm not questioning you, Demi. I know the life you live and the things you do to keep a roof over our heads. I'm just saying. Respect me. You always have. I was just worried," she said.

Demi nodded. "You don't got nothing to worry about, Lo," he said.

Lauren crossed her arms and stared at him.

"You seem different," she said. "You good?"

"Whatever ain't good I keep outside this house. I always have," he said.

Demi didn't know if it was his conscience or her intuition, but he felt like she was picking him apart, disarming his lies, one by one until she got to the truth. He had cheated. He never had until now. Not even during their college years. It had always been her, but things between them had gotten so routine that he could predict the next year of his life with accuracy. He knew the positions that they would fuck in. He knew what meals he would come home to. He knew what candle scents would fill their bedroom. He finished her sentences; they knew one another so well. He loved Lauren. Dearly loved her. Respected her, but somewhere along the way, he had fallen out of love with her. Or perhaps he never really had been *in* love with her, but the love and loyalty, plus the connection of a baby had been enough to carry them through the years. Until last night. The mistake he had made eroded his stomach. If she ever found out she would be devastated.

She lifted from her seat and walked toward him, standing directly in front of him. She was used to his rules. She wasn't like Charlie. She knew better than to touch him and Demi sighed, a bit relieved because his guilt would have allowed him to let her and he didn't think he could handle any more physical contact.

"I love you," she said.

"Love you," he replied. "I'm going to shower."

"I'll run your bath. There's food in the oven for you."

It was shit like that. She was a woman. His woman. He knew he needed to do a better job at appreciating what he had. Normally, he was accomplished at that. Making her smile. Rooting for her wins. Being her support. Her protector, but last night he hadn't protected her at all. Not from his selfishness. Demi felt like less than a man, as his son's video game blared in the background, making the soundtrack of their lives. This was his home. This was his family. He hated the song, Charlie's song. "My All." His all. She felt like his all. It felt like she expected him to give his all and damn it if he didn't want to, after only one fucking night. Witchcraft. Charlie had to be a fucking witch the way she had him running those lyrics back in his mind. The damn song was interrupting the sound of Roblox. Lauren looked at him, forehead creased in a look that he was sure was skepticism.

"That's not what you left the house in," she said, surveying his change of clothes. Women didn't miss shit, especially not this woman.

"Since when you don't know the type of business I'm into, Lo? A change of clothes ain't nothing new," he said. "Relax and stop overthinking. A nigga been solid with you, I'ma keep being solid with you."

He meant it. He drowned out Charlie's voice, but inside he really wanted to go back to Charliezonia. The place she had sung about. Their place. He wouldn't though. 15 years versus one night. He'd be a damn fool. One night couldn't stand a chance but still, it had been a good fucking night, one he couldn't seem to get off his mind, even as he stood here in front of his girl.

Lauren seemed pacified with that. Her face softened and she walked by him, stopping before she walked out of the room. "Are we good Demi?"

"I'ma always make sure we good."

He found his son and took a seat beside him, grabbing the remote control.

"You ready, dad?" DJ asked.

Demi opened his phone and clicked on the unread message Charlie had sent. He put his AirPods in and pressed play on the video she had sent.

He found her simplicity extremely complicated. Her hair was all over the place, destroyed from their time in the shower. She did little to tame it, opting to pull it up by a red scarf, leaving locs cascading out of the top of her head like pineapple leaves. Just disorderly. Charlie was a spur of the moment, throw on anything, who cares if it's wrinkled, type of girl and all those things, all that chaos drove him mad. Ying and yang. Day and night. They were completely opposite, but the pull he had felt when in her presence made it hard to delete this song.

"Since you stopped me from rehearsing," she said, as she reached for the phone, coming near the camera, her hand swallowing the frame as he counted the lines on her palm as she adjusted her phone. She positioned it and then sat back, giving him a visual of her.

Her fingers to those guitar strings and the fucking melody that came out of her was hypnotizing. He listened to her sing for 1:42 seconds before his son interrupted.

"Dad, come on!" DJ said.

He clicked out of the screen, sliding his phone in his pocket as he grabbed the remote control and focused on his son.

Charlie was temptation. He had fought temptation through every part of his come up, avoiding women who could destroy what he had built with Lauren. Putting last night behind him should be easy, but as he thought of her, even in this exact moment when he should have been enjoying time with his son, he knew that letting go of her would be the hardest thing he had ever done. Demi had been touched.

CHAPTER 6

Stassi pulled up to the brick building and parked curbside as she hopped out of her car.

"You're late."

She heard the baritone behind her and she looked up to find Day climbing out of the black, big body Benz. Black Jeans and an open hoodie, revealing a fitted white t-shirt beneath. He certainly wasn't dressed for the occasion.

"I'm not," she said. She was but she couldn't let him know that she had destroyed the fondant on the cake she was currently making twice before getting here. She was supposed to be earning his business. This was supposed to be a meeting where he could see her in action, all professional, composed and orchestrating a corporate event so that he would feel good about hiring her company to handle an event of his own. So far, it had been a disastrous morning. "I actually emailed you letting you know we had a thirty-minute delay." A lie, but she knew a man like Day wasn't paying attention to emails.

"I must have missed that memo," Day said as he met Stassi at her trunk as she opened it. She reached in and grabbed the cardboard box that was inside, passing it off to him.

"Put potential customers to work. Got it. That's how you run your business?" he said, smirking.

"You look like you can handle it," she said, giggling as she grabbed her overflowing tote.

"You got your whole life in there or something?" Day asked.

Stassi smiled. "Literally everything," she replied. "So, I've been planning this event for six months. It is a wedding, but I've learned that the reason for the event doesn't matter. I've handled both corporate and personal events. The process is pretty much the same."

"It's a wedding?" Day asked.

"That's why I told you to dress up," she said.

He glanced down at his street gear. "You can stay out the way, it's fine," she said.

Stassi's dress clung to her curves as she pulled her heels off her feet and put them in the tote, replacing them for crystal slides that would allow her to maneuver around the event easier until start time.

"This way," she said.

"Yo, that dress," Day said as he followed her, eyes where they shouldn't be.

"Is not the focus," she said, blushing as she opened the door. As soon as they stepped inside, it was like they were transported into a fairy tale. "So, of course, this theme isn't your vibe. This was what the couple wanted, but I can transform any space in any way you want."

"Nah, I'm familiar with what this looks like on a normal day. This shit dope. You did all this?" he asked.

"I did. Me and a team of very creative people who work with me," she said.

"Stassi! I can't tell you how happy I am to see you!" The manager of the event space said, approaching her with relief in his eyes. "The kitchen is a disaster! We're missing the lobster for the bisque. It was supposed to be flown in this morning, but it isn't here yet and one of the damn servers dropped the top layer of the cake. It's completely destroyed. I don't know how to salvage this."

"What?" Stassi hissed.

"I know, I know. What do you want me to do? I've called every baker in town," he said.

"Calm down, just lead the way," Stassi said, her mind spinning.

Stassi and Day followed the panicked man through the venue and into the kitchen. Stassi took the box from Day and sat it on a countertop.

The kitchen was in a panic. A line of chefs attempting to prepare 400 custom orders for the arriving guests.

"You have an apron?" she asked. She was passed one and she turned and put it on Day.

"Yo, fuck you think this is?" Day asked, laughing. "I ain't getting paid to be here."

"Oh, you're definitely not getting paid," she said. "But if you want to see how I make sure my clients' events go off without a hitch, this is how. I put aprons on thousand-dollar dresses, and I do whatever I need to make sure shit gets done. I've got exactly three hours to pull off a miracle, so yes, you're helping."

Day rubbed his chin and eyed her curiously.

"Yeah, a'ight," he conceded. "What type of cake anyway? You got a picture or something? What's the flavor?"

Stassi frowned and pulled out the rendering of the cake. "This is the cake. Lemon with custard filling on top. Now, can you help me please?" she asked.

Day nodded, picking up the picture and annoying Stassi's soul because what the hell would looking at a picture of the cake fix.

"Yeah, I got you," he said.

Stassi tied up her hair into a top knot and then slipped the apron over her head. She moved around the kitchen like the chef she was. She thanked God she had chosen to learn desserts too. Day was patient as she ordered him around. He was measuring, whipping, cracking, spreading ingredients all over the place and Stassi was grateful.

"How long you been a chef?" he asked.

"Like two years, but I've been cooking all my life," she answered.

"It shows," he said, as he leaned against the counter, arms folded across one another, watching her work. "You locked in on it like you love it."

"That's because I do," she said, looking up, smiling. "But wedding cakes are not my specialty, and this is hella pressure. This bride is super particular."

"It'll work out. Day of the wedding I'd think the last thing the couple would be concerned about is the fucking little-ass cake on the top," he said.

"You'd be surprised," Stassi said. "This bride is hell and I don't exactly have everything I need here to replace her $15,000 cake and I've been running my own full-service event company for so long that I haven't seen a kitchen lately. I always have my lead chef handle the kitchen, but he doesn't bake."

Stassi finished the cake as Day distracted her with conversation. Surprisingly, she was grateful for his presence. What would have been panic otherwise was lessened because of him.

"So, what's it like being famous?" she asked. "Did you always want to own a record label?"

"Nah, I wanted to sell dope, but every little boy got to eventually become a man, so this was natural progression," Day explained.

"That's kind of terrible," Stassi said.

"It's life," Day answered. "It's real. Every rap nigga ain't fronting. It's a few of us who create from the real. Most of these niggas in this music shit just play gangster. They ain't about it for real," Day answered, smirking.

"You sound proud," Stassi said.

"You sound bougie," he shot back. "You must have come up with that silver spoon. I don't know nothing about that."

"I guess we're from two different worlds," Stassi said. Day nodded, biting his lip and staring at her for a moment longer than awkward. His glower flustered her as she iced the cake.

"What are you looking at?" she tittered nervously.

"Just looking," Day said lazily. He hopped down off the steel table he used as a seat. He removed the apron Stassi had tasked him with. Stassi dusted her hands on her apron and then took it off.

"The wedding should be over. Come on," she said.

Day followed her out to the main ballroom. It had taken her two hours to bake a cake from scratch. The couple was an hour into the reception by the time she showed her face. Couples took to the dance floor, dancing to love songs.

"Are you going to ask me to dance or are you too tough for that?" she asked.

Day rubbed his chin and looked out at the crowd. He was underdressed and stood out like a sore thumb, but still, he took her hand and led her onto the dance floor.

"Nah, nigga used to earn his stripes by slow dancing with bougie-ass girls like you at the parties back in the day," he said. "Before niggas was getting any kind of pussy, slow grinding was all we had." He chuckled and Stassi blushed, shaking her head, giggling too because she knew it was true. She remembered giving teenage boys free feels to R. Kelly as he sang about feeling on your booty.

"Is that right? Just sell us bougie girls all the dreams and break our hearts, huh?" she teased.

> *Let me knowwww- Let me knowwwwww*
> *Oohhhhh, ohhhhhhh*
> *Let meeeee knowwwwww.*
> *Let meeeee knowwwwww.*
> *Let meeeee knowwwwww.*
> *When I feellllll, what I feellllll.*

"Hell yeah, back then," Day admitted. "A nigga was just

looking to rub up on something and earn his respect. Today, I'm just trying to act like I'm good enough for a girl I'm pretty sure is out of my league." He grabbed her hand and pulled her smoothly into his arms.

Stassi blushed as she placed her hands on his shoulders while Aaliyah serenaded the room.

"I'm not out of your league," she replied, a demure smile showing off those cheekbones her mother had blessed her with.

"You don't give yourself enough credit," he answered.

They swayed to what sounded like an angel as classic Aaliyah described Day as a positive and motivating force within Stassi's life. His hands went from her hips to one on her upper back as he pulled her close, the other to the nape of her ass.

"You smell good like a motherfucka," Day whispered as they swayed.

"Hmm," Stassi whispered, her eyes closed as she rested her head on his shoulder. "I was thinking the same thing."

It was his body for Stassi. His strength. She felt like she was wrapped in a fortress, protected and her breaths were so light she felt like she was filling with air every time she inhaled. Like she could float away.

When he extended her hand and turned her around, she smiled. He held her from behind as they two-stepped. Stassi reached behind her, her fingertips gracing his face.

Should you ever feel the need to wonder why
Let me knowwwwwww, Letttt mee knowwwwww

"Yo, a nigga ain't danced with a pretty girl since I was 15 with whack game," he said.

Stassi laughed as he buried his face in her neck.

"Got to come back from behind all that hardness and be soft sometimes," she replied.

Stassi turned to him, snapping her fingers. "A nigga can get with soft," Day said.

"You're good at soft," Stassi whispered.

Before she could say another word, his lips were on hers. The man was an entire vibe. With his expensive cologne hypnotizing her, his body pressed against hers. He tasted like Backwoods and Jolly Ranchers because he kept candy on him. A green apple-flavored tongue had her captured and her panties soaked.

"Day, I'm at work," she whispered, pulling back slightly because she was too absorbed in this dance, this kiss. Her head swirled. "If we're going to work together, I can't do this."

"You're about your paper, I respect it," Day said. "If that ever changes..."

"It won't," she answered quickly. "It can't, Day. Women don't have the luxury to date without thinking about it. Like, I can't just throw myself at you, can't enjoy your company and allow you to put me on too."

"And you're choosing business over pleasure?" Day asked.

"I always choose business over everything," Stassi said.

"I got a problem with that, lil' mama," Day said, smirking as he took a respectful step back. "I respect it, though. I want to introduce you to Lauren Sky. She puts together all my company's events but she's in high demand, so she's been outsourcing a lot of her work. She's been looking for a partner to expand her shit. She does everybody shit. The whole industry fuck with her. I can connect you."

"Thee Lauren Sky?" Stassi asked. "She is goals! She does all the planning out in L.A. for Emmy weekend and the Grammy's. She does major productions!"

"Yeah, sis official, but the way you kept your cool with the cake and executed this wedding, I think y'all can benefit from partnering. I'll set up an introduction and tell her to bring you on for all my company's events. Starting with the talent showcase we do monthly," Day said.

"Wow, yes. I'd love to work with her and on your events, Day," she said, nodding. "I really, really appreciate the opportunity. Thank you!"

"Not a problem, beautiful," he replied. "I'ma break out of this wedding. I'll have the lawyers draw up an agreement."

"I'm sorry to interrupt, Stassi, but the new cake is here." Stassi looked at one of her line cooks and frowned.

"New cake?" she asked.

"It was always handled," Day explained. "I just wanted to see how you worked under pressure. I'ma get with you."

He walked out, weaving through the fancy crowd as Stassi watched him in shock.

"Package the one I made, and have it sent to him," she said.

She would have to work hard to keep things professional between her and Day. He was handsome, powerful, and hard to resist. The taste of his lips still lingered as she watched him push out of the ballroom. She would love to get to know him better but not at the expense of her reputation or her career.

CHAPTER 7

Charlie stared at her phone. Her mind was twisted in confusion, or perhaps it was clarity, a knowing that she didn't want to admit. She was such a stubborn girl that it was hard for her to admit that she had gotten played. Again. Charlie had been a sucker for a man, again.

"Story of my life," she whispered, shaking her head.

It had been a week since she had slept with him.

Damn, why did I sleep with him? She thought. *Leigh was right.*

The words that stared back at her from the open text added insult to injury.

CHARLIE
Hey just checking on you.

She had tried to keep it cool. She hadn't even wanted to send that, but the silence was killing her. The message had been sent two days after he had left her house, and here it was five whole days after that and still nothing. If that wasn't hint enough, it should be. She felt like she was going a little crazy because what she had assumed that night, everything it had felt like, was unlike anything she had ever experienced before.

Maybe I misread the shit. I clearly misread him.

She couldn't get rid of the sick feeling in her stomach. She hated to be stupid for a man... again... after she had told herself another nigga would never... another nigga had. Demi had, and even though she barely knew him, it hurt. Bad. Cheapened by an expensive night, Demi had maxed out her emotions and left her body in debt.

It had always been her problem. She fell for men too easily. Trusted them too soon. Demi and his crazy had sucked her in as soon as he had overpaid to hear her sing.

Charlie couldn't help the text she sent him next.

CHARLIE
Wow.

That was all she had for him. Disappointment and shock because she hadn't seen this coming. Not expecting a response, she clicked out of the screen and then grabbed the keys to her car, heading out the door.

Rehearsal was a must. She had avoided it all week. She wasn't sick in love. It wasn't that serious to her. She had only known Demi for 24 hours. He had shown up in her life like a flash of lightning only to disappear just as fast, but she was in her feelings. The pride of a woman was a motherfucker and she had injured herself. She had allowed too much, too soon and she knew that when women did that, they normally didn't control the tempo. Charlie felt foolish and she dreaded facing Justin. She had allowed Demi to be terrible to him. That should have been her indication that he wasn't shit. She had learned to judge a man by the way he treated ordinary people, not those he loved.

Her nerves frayed at the edges as she drove to the park where her band sometimes played. A little place where families went on Sundays. Michigan didn't have many sunny days, so when it was warm, the park was the place to be. Charlie loved to sing. She would sing anywhere. So, putting a fedora on the ground and singing as the sweet air kissed her lungs was a vibe. A preference, in fact. It wasn't about the tips. It was about creativity. About the freedom because freedom was important to her these days.

When she arrived, she called Justin's phone. It had never felt awkward between them before. It was what she appreciated about him. They just enjoyed the time they spent together, enjoyed the music, put on a good show, and let the energy flow downstream. It was when you tried to get water to flow upward that things got tricky. Unnatural. She and Justin's chemistry was effortless. A dope-ass musical marriage. Every singer had one. The Babyface to her Toni. The Jermaine Dupri to Monica. The Tommy Mottola to Mariah. Justin was a musical genius, and their sessions took away all the bad things in her life. She had been stuck in a rut for a week. This was much needed.

"What up, Charles? I see you. I'm parked in the back," he said. Charlie lifted her eyes and saw him flagging her down. She parked next to him and exited the car.

"Where's everybody else?" she asked, grabbing her guitar from the back seat.

"Big Matt got his kid last minute. Brent can't make it," he informed.

"Should we reschedule? After the week I've had I'm so okay with that," she admitted.

"Nah, it only takes two to catch a good vibe, Charles. Besides, my strings miss you," he said.

Charlie smiled. "Can't lie. I miss those strings too," she said. Justin was the most skilled musician she had ever heard. He read music because he was classically trained, but the way he played his guitar wasn't trained at all. It was straight from the soul.

"We over here with it," he said, leading the way. They walked beyond the play area where screaming kids ran by, passing the normal bench they usually posted up at. When they arrived at the fountain, Charlie stopped walking.

"What's all this?" she asked.

"Just a vibe. I thought you might like it and an apology for being an asshole with your boyfriend the other day," he said.

A red and white checkered picnic blanket rested on the green grass and a woven picnic basket sat on top. A bottle of champagne in a bucket. A bouquet of flowers sitting next to that.

"He's not my boyfriend," she corrected. "And about that. I'm sorry if I was flaky with you."

"No apologies, Charles. Let's pretend like it didn't even happen. Eat some food, sip a little bit, and play because I could tell when you pulled up that you really need to play," Justin said.

Charlie was relieved that he didn't make a big deal out of things. "Is it that obvious?" she asked.

"I just notice your heart when it's heavy," he said.

Charlie was taken aback. Did he? Notice that? Had he noticed it before? Because it was her solemn that had made her want to sing in his band in the first place.

Charlie scoffed.

Justin sat on the blanket, grabbing the bottle of champagne and then resting his elbows on his knees as he popped the cork. The bubbly flowed and he moved to let it flow out onto the grass some before grabbing a plastic flute and filling it for her.

Charlie came to her knees, sitting down her guitar case and accepting the drink.

She sipped the champagne, feeling it fizz in her chest as he grabbed his guitar. His fingers knew those damn strings so well.

He kept the tempo by tapping the wood of the instrument while playing perfectly.

"I love this song," she said.

"Want to try something different? Add it to the set this weekend?" he asked.

"This weekend? I have to learn the chords, Justin! I swear y'all just like me to stand there and look pretty. I'm more than a bar singer. I actually play too," she fussed.

"Nah, you're not just that. You're much more than that," he said, smirking as he made music of the afternoon air.

"You say I'm tripping, bullshit. You're the one that make me do shit," he sang.

He never sang but he could, and he did it so well that it caused the hair on the back of her neck to stand up. She nodded her head, sipping the champagne.

"True love is absolute. What more can I sayyyy, you make me this way." Charlie joined in, making up a harmony that complimented his tone. It sounded completely different than the H.E.R. track it originated from, but that's what music was about, transforming songs into your own.

"Yo, you're ridiculous with it," he said.

She shrugged.

"What's up with you and ol' boy?" he asked.

"Absolutely nothing," she answered. "And I don't want to talk about it. Men just ain't shit. Like, you can be so receptive to their flaws. So understanding to the weird-ass shit they got going on," she said, shaking her head as thoughts of Demi ran through her mind. "And somehow still be treated all kinds of fucked up. I'm sick of niggas."

"Nah, just say you sick of the ones you're choosing," Justin said.

Charlie shrugged as he passed her a wrapped sandwich. "Maybe. Maybe it is my tastes that get me in trouble," she said.

"Just saying. Don't write us all off because a few mishandled you," he said.

She pulled the sandwich from the sandwich bag and laughed when she saw the peanut butter and jelly sandwich inside.

"Simple shit, Charles. Don't laugh. Bet you haven't had one since you were a kid."

She took the sandwich from the baggie and took a bite. Every taste bud in her mouth exploded.

"It's legit fire," she chuckled. "I was going to complain but it's probably the best thing I've tasted all week."

"See," Justin said. He winked at her. His cool demeanor fit him perfectly. Attractive in a leather jacket-wearing, ripped-jeans-sporting, take the doors off his Wrangler kind of way. Justin was a vibe all his own. A very different vibe than what she was used to, but she couldn't deny that their chemistry was smooth. It was so easy to get lost in a world of music and lyrics with him. He was the first person she connected with when she had come back home six months ago. She had walked into the bar looking to waitress and had interrupted their entire rehearsal. They didn't have a singer at that time. Just good music and good vibes, and a guitar that rivaled the late great Prince. She had walked away with that waitress job, but singing after hours as she cleaned and they played had led to her singing with them full time. After everything she had been through, it felt like she had finally found a place to belong. "It ain't much that beats a peanut butter and jelly. It reminds you of your mama. It's comfort food. Everybody mama used to make these joints."

"All facts, Justine," she said, smiling. Her mind went down memory lane. "There were a lot of days when PB&J was all my mom could afford to feed me and I never got tired of them. She used to cut off the crust and eat that part and let me keep the middle."

"Your mama was a smart lady," he chuckled. "The rough edges are the sweetest parts." She grew quiet as she looked off toward the crowd in the distance. The air was thick. Like it was a summer day in New Orleans and humidity laced the air. She could barely get it to her lungs.

"My mom's dead," she said. "They say she died of a stroke. I think she died of a broken heart."

Justice grabbed his guitar. "You want to sing it out?"

Charlie sniffed, and nodded, erasing her feelings. "Yeah," she answered, knowing exactly what he meant. Only a musician could get rid of a feeling through song.

Charlie stayed out in the park with Justin until the sunset and somewhere between the bumblebees and lightning bugs, she forgave herself for the one-night stand. As they headed toward the car, Charlie turned to him. "Thank you for today. For the distraction and for being cool enough to not hold a grudge about the other day."

"It's already forgotten, Charles," he said as he opened her car door. "Time for an upgrade. This thing has seen better days."

"It was my mom's," she said. "This was home a lot of nights."

"My bad, Charlie, I didn't know," he said.

"It's fine. Just saying, I'll never get rid of it. It's one of the very few things that I have left that remind me of her," Charlie said.

"We all have our attachments," he answered.

She sucked in a deep breath and then slid into her car. Justin put her guitar in her back seat.

"I'll see you later. Thanks for the picnic," she said.

He knocked on the top of her roof as a form of goodbye before she drove off. It wasn't quite chemistry and it wasn't quite loneliness. Friendship. Justin gave her friendship, and it was one she appreciated.

CHAPTER 8

"Remind me what I'm getting again for coming to this thing with you?" Charlie asked, as she stepped out the car and handed her keys to the valet of the five-star hotel.

"My undying love, sis," Stassi answered, laughing. "We should have self-parked this ugly-ass car, though, Charlie. You got me pulling up looking poor."

"It's work, right? Does it matter how we pull up?" Charlie asked. "Take care of my baby, here. She's my prized possession." Charlie pointed at the valet, warning him but her smile was endearing. "It's old and ugly but it means the world to me, and if it doesn't start right away, just give it a little gas."

The older man smiled and accepted the key. "You got it," he answered.

Charlie's black, lace bralette left nothing to the imagination, but her thin figure made it less seductive and more high fashion. Her skirt was black and skin-tight, with two slits that rode up so high her red thong showed when she walked.

"This looks like a big deal," Charlie said. "What did you say this guy did again?"

"It is a big deal. If I nail this tonight, I'll likely book five more jobs before I even leave," Stassi said. They stepped inside the hotel and headed into the ballroom, bypassing the crowd as they headed for the kitchen.

"Let me just make sure my staff has this in order and then all I have to do is make sure everything goes smoothly," she said.

"You're not working the kitchen tonight?" Charlie asked.

"Nah, she's working the room tonight, meeting a few people," Day said, walking up to them, interrupting. Charlie didn't miss her sister's blush and she can't say she didn't understand. Day was just one of those men. He commanded the room, the type to make you misplace your words midsentence. Charlie felt the urge to pat her pockets in search of them because his sudden presence had certainly stolen her moxie. He examined her first, then swayed his gaze toward Stassi.

"You and your friend showing out at my event," he said.

"My sister. This is Charlie. Charlie, this is Day," Stassi introduced. "He's the man of the hour. Dynasty is his company."

Charlie's stomach fell out of her. "Dynasty? Like, the music group?"

"Yeah, and I'm not exactly the man of the hour. I'm a partner at the label. Let me introduce you to my man. He was super impressed by the setup, said we got to get you on the team so we can use you for future events. Told you I'ma put you on," Day said.

He turned and cupped his mouth with his hands. "Yo, D!" he shouted.

Charlie knew before he even walked over to her who would come. Demi approached and Charlie's stomach knotted. He was freshly faded, lined to precision, but he looked royal. A blue so dark it almost appeared black rested against his skin as he wore the Yomi dashiki, tailored pants, and Gucci loafers.

Is he African? She wondered. *Would explain the dick.*

She had never seen a more regal man. Black and blessed. His weird-ass was pre-occupied in his phone as he headed their way. He didn't have to look up because everyone moved out of his way, some vying for his attention as he passed. He lent it to no one as he sipped his drink. Charlie was frozen. She didn't know if she should flee or stay. He looked up at her and she saw her presence affect him. Shock and a bit of appreciation flashed across his face as he took in every inch of her body before coming back to her face.

"This my man..."

"We know one another," he said.

"Not really," Charlie said. "Not really at all." Charlie turned to Stassi. "I'm going to get a drink. Let me know if you need me."

Charlie started to walk away but Stassi was on her heels. "Is that-"

"Yup, that's his bitch-ass," Charlie said before Stassi could even finish her sentence. "Nigga is alive and well, so he chose to fuck me and then ghost me." Charlie couldn't put enough distance between her and Demi.

Stassi had to grab her arm to get Charlie to stop. "Hey, we can go if you want. My team can handle this."

"No, I know how important this is for you. The networking is worth more than the commission. I'm cool. I'm just keeping my distance. Go ahead. Do your thing. I'll be taking advantage of the open bar."

"Are you sure?" Stassi asked.

"I'm positive," she said.

Stassi nodded and then glanced back at Day who was absorbed in conversation with Demi.

"You say the word and we out," Stassi said.

"Handle your business," Charlie stated. "I won't be the reason why you miss this opportunity. I'm good."

Stassi gave her arm a squeeze of appreciation before making her way back through the crowd. Charlie could feel him staring and when their eyes met, she rolled hers away.

Bitch-ass nigga, she thought. She glanced his way once more but quickly retreated when she discovered he was still staring. *Fine. Ass. Nigga.*

She was grateful when he kept his distance, but his eyes never left her. Every time Charlie searched the room for him, he would already have her in his crosshair. It was like he was touching her. His eyes left a fingerprint behind. A grace to her neck. A kiss to her lips. Damn, a flick of her clit. How did he have this much power over her? Charlie was soaking wet as her heart stampeded, she was winded as an unbelievable anger and wanting filled her. God, how her body ached. She had only had him once but it had created an addiction. Clearly, she had done the same.

He didn't even try to look away. One hand rested on the front of his slacks because she knew his dick was trying to pull him to her. Like a metal detector, it was screaming for her because Charlie felt it. Her pussy clenched and she had to force her eyes elsewhere. How could she resent and desire a man all at the same time? Demi needed to stop giving out good dick, if he only intended to do it once, because Charlie now wanted it again and again. He was surrounded by people. Artists on the label, other executives, women, his circle. So many important people around him, clamoring for his attention, and he gave them all a moment of his time, but those eyes always ended up back on her.

"You look real uncomfortable over here."
Charlie turned her focus to the man who approached her. He handed her a champagne flute. Charlie took it but didn't drink from it. She didn't know him well enough to trust what might be in it.
"Just enjoying the vibe," she answered.
"You are the vibe. It's a lot of people in this room, but you're the one," he said.
She frowned and then laughter escaped her. "That is so terrible. Like, seriously, why do you niggas do shit like that? Tell obvious lies just to make conversation," she said, shaking her head.

The man laughed and shook his head. "Damn, baby, you going hard on a nigga. I been trying to figure out how to start a conversation with you for 20 minutes and you ain't making it easy. I'm embarrassed as fuck right now," he said, snickering as he sipped the bubbly.

"I'm embarrassed for you," she laughed. For the first time all night, she didn't feel uptight. "All you have to do is say hi and maybe provide a name. I'm super simple."

"Hi, I'm Sin," he said, holding out a hand for her. "And you're beautiful, and I apologize for the extra shit."

Charlie placed a delicate hand in his and he caressed it with his thumb as they shook.

"I'm Charlie, it's nice to meet you, Sin," she replied. "See, wasn't so hard, was it?"

"Easiest shit I've ever done," he answered, staring so hard that it made Charlie blush.

"Yo, nigga, take a walk."

Charlie heard the lethal tone of voice as it came up behind her and she almost choked on the champagne she was sipping as she turned to him. Demi stood over her shoulder, so close to her body that she could feel his dick pressing into her ass as he placed a subtle hand to her hip.

"My bad, Demi. I ain't know this was you. No disrespect, family," the man said. "It's all love."

"More walking," Demi said. He wasn't with the conversation. He was like a dog with a bone — territorial as fuck.

Charlie spun on him. He had some nerve. He had all the nerve. The audacity of this man.

"Who do you think you are?" she asked.

"Nobody, Bird. I'm a nobody-ass nigga for handling you the way I did, and I know I got no right to be tripping on you, but I'm fucking tripping. You in here with your titties all out. Got these red fucking panties on," he said, backing her against the bar and leaning to whisper in her ear. "Damn, Bird."

Charlie shook her head in disgust.

"You gon' make me kill something in here tonight," he said. "Niggas eyes been on you all night, thinking about what it would be like to fuck you. That's what you wanted with this outfit? For niggas to shoot they shot right in front of me? They can do that. They can shoot they shits with you, Bird, as long as they ready to shoot with me too, cuz I got all the shots, Bird. All the bullets in the world behind you. Out here being fucking fast, man."

He had never been so irritated with a woman. His temple was throbbing, his pulse racing, with anger, in jealousy.

"Fast? Nigga, I'm grown," she said, face twisted in irritation.

He looked her up and down, down then up, and then fixated on her throat. He wanted to wrap his hands around her throat and squeeze a little. His dick bricked just thinking about it. What was it about this girl that made him lose his discipline?"

"You real grown, Bird," he agreed.

"I didn't know this party was for your company. I don't have time for this. I would have never come," Charlie said, shaking her head as she shifted in her stilettos and looked away from him. Charlie stormed off, heading out of the ballroom and into the hallway, anywhere that was away from him. She needed some place where she could breathe because, in his presence, she just couldn't quite inhale, all her breaths were leaving her.

"Yo, Charlie, give me a minute; let me talk to you," he said as he followed her. Her entire being had thrown him off. Hers was the last face he had expected to see tonight, but it couldn't be unseen. Twenty-two days of discipline, of erasing her texts, of watching the video she had sent him again and again just to get a fix, had all been flushed down the drain at one glance. She looked beautiful, not in the overdressed, stunt on these niggas type of way that every other woman present did... but in Charlie's way. In a, I don't give a fuck about nobody in this bitch so I'm going to wear whatever, fuck a dress code type of way. She was fucking beautiful.

"Oh, now you want to talk? Now you got some shit to say? You been silent for weeks but all of a sudden you an orator, my nigga?" she asked, a little louder than she intended, getting stares from the stragglers that lingered in the hallway.

"Aye, clear this shit out! Get the fuck in or out!" he barked on the guests that lingered in the hallway, desperate for a moment of privacy with Charlie. His temper flared as she kept walking. He knew he had no right to be mad but hell, she was mad, so he was mad too. They were mad as fuck together, because damn if Demi didn't just want to do everything she did, wherever she did it, however she did it. He had no business in this hallway with this damn girl, pleading for a second of her time. Demi didn't beg anyone. People normally begged him; women, especially women, normally begged to be in his presence, normally begged for dick, for money, for trips and he always declined. He had a woman at home, a good woman, but Charlie made him weak.

"Stop following me you fucking weirdo," Charlie spat as she pushed into the women's bathroom, the one place he couldn't follow. Just as she suspected, he halted. Not because he wasn't allowed there but because his OCD wouldn't let him take another step. Public bathrooms disgusted him.

He had a feeling she knew that. It enraged him. Charlie and her fucking boldness, her disregard for his rules. He wanted to kick the damn door in but instead, he backpedaled to the bench across from the door and sat. He wanted to walk away, but he had pictured her in his mind too many times over the past few weeks to let her get away. This couldn't be a coincidence that they had crossed paths again.

When 15 minutes passed, he knew she was stalling him out. He pulled out his phone and sent her a text because while he had deleted the number, his obsession with her had committed it to memory. Self-preservation. It had to be. He knew he would need that number one day because no way should he know it, but his brain wouldn't let him forget.

DEMI
Bring your shitty-ass out the bathroom.

CHARLIE
Bring your weird-ass in the bathroom.

He put his phone in his back pocket and grit his teeth so hard his jaw hurt. He stood and walked into the bathroom, suffocating instantly. The banging of the door as it hit the wall startled Charlie as he crossed the room, pressing her back to the wall and bracing both hands around her body as he bowed his head. A struggle. Demi was having a mental battle. Against the fucking germs he was sure was in the air and now all over him, against his conscience, against the mental battle he desperately wanted to win against Charlie.

"You playing with me, Bird," he said.

"The way you played with me?" she asked. "Get the fuck away from me, Demi. We don't have shit to say to each other."

Charlie tried to push by him, but he wasn't budging.

"Move, Demi, before I scream," she warned.

"If you were going to scream, you would have done that by now," he said.

Charlie was so annoyed that she did the only thing she could think of. She mushed him, rubbing her hands all in his face like she was smashing a snowball. Demi lost control, wrapping one hand around her neck, and hemming her up. His face felt like battery acid had been poured all over it.

"You done lost your fucking mind," he said sternly. His hold on her tightened as his nostrils flared and he stared into her eyes. Without warning, he let go, storming out of the restroom and leaving Charlie inside with tears in her eyes.

CHAPTER 9

It took Charlie half an hour to gather herself and even as she emerged from the bathroom her hands shook a little. Men who got physical with women terrified her and Demi had done more than a little yoking up. She could sense his danger. He was a live wire, one that would electrocute her if she touched it, and he both terrified and enthralled her. She opened the door to the ballroom of the hotel and searched the room for Stassi. She wouldn't ruin her night. Her sister had worked hard for this. Pulling it off meant more business in the future; so although Charlie was over it and ready to leave, she couldn't bail. She found Stassi in a booth, tucked away with Day whispering in her ear. Charlie made her way across the room. She slid in next to her sister, plastering on a fake smile.

"You okay?" Stassi asked, leaning over to whisper.

Charlie nodded.

"They're about to start a showcase," Stassi informed.

"A music showcase?" Charlie asked.

"Introducing the new artists we signed to the rest of the company," Day said.

"You know Charlie sings..." Stassi said.

"Is that right?" Day asked.

Charlie frowned and waved off the attention. "No, not really," she said, shooting Stassi a look.

"What? You do," Stassi whispered.

"Stassi, stop," Charlie said.

Charlie hated to be put on the spot. This event was full of important people. They were going live all-over social media. Charlie wanted to be as far from the stage as possible.

"I'm saying, though, gorgeous? I'm always in the mood to hear some heat if you got it," Day said, his lazy drawl making Stassi swoon. "Or are you one of them studio singers? The kind that need a production and the auto-tune and shit, cuz if that's the case, don't waste my time. I got enough of them."

"She's not some fad singer, Day. She can really sing," Stassi defended.

"I tell you what," Day said. "Your sister get up there and blow it down and I'll contract you for our quarterly showcases. If she fuck up, you got to let a nigga slide for the night."

Charlie couldn't even contain the laugh that came from her.

"Bet," Stassi said.

"Bitch, you putting your pussy on the pass line?" Charlie asked, eyes widening. "Stass!"

"What?!" Stassi defended. "I'm going to win; and I mean, if I lose, I ain't mad at it!"

The snicker that left Day's lips infected the table.

Day lifted his hand and motioned for a man that stood by the stage. It was like he was a puppeteer. He and Demi. The grand orchestrators of every other man around him. Demi said walk, niggas walked. Day said come, niggas came.

I wish I had a brain-ass nigga, Charlie thought.

Salutations in the form of handshakes like they were exchanging something on the sly.

"Add Charlie here to the program. She up next," Day said.

"You want to just slide her in? What about the DJ or the band? They ain't..."

"I pay you to figure it out," Day said. "If I figure it out for you, I no longer need you, do I, bruh?"

"She up next. What's your name, sweetheart?" the man asked.

"Charlie," she answered. Her nerves were immediately on edge. She didn't want this. It was one thing singing in a lowkey bar to ease the weight on her soul, but to do it like this... In front of all these important people... These industry tastemakers? Charlie was too exposed, but she didn't want to let Stassi down.

"It's showtime, baby girl," the man said.

Day grabbed the champagne bottle out of the bucket and popped the cork, pouring a flute for Charlie. "Liquid courage," he said.

Charlie took the glass up with her on the stage.

"Why did I do this? I swear I'm going to kill her," she said

The guy handed Charlie a microphone as she climbed onto the stage. The lights were hot, or maybe she was just hot, maybe she was melting under the microscope that was the cameras that flashed before her as the room looked at her through the lens of their phones. Nobody was really watching her live. They were watching their screens. Filters. They were filtering life and getting it secondhand instead of just being in the moment and watching her. It was kind of sad.

"I'm going to need a stand," she said into the mic."

Mr. Figure It Out looked like he wanted to say no, but he moved to get it and handed it to Charlie.

"Hi, everybody," she said, her nerves ate her alive, and her voice shook. She was better at singing in public than speaking.

She shook her hands at her side. "My name is Charlie," she introduced. She didn't know why she had done that. Her name was the last thing these people wanted to know. None of the other showcase artists had bothered, but then again, they had been properly introduced.

"What song to sing?" she asked herself aloud as she adjusted the microphone stand, lowering it to fit her body.

"I'm a little nervous, y'all," she said. "Can I get a guitar? Is that possible? And a chair?"

"We don't have all that, this ain't ya concert, beautiful. Pretty girls always got requests, don't they?" the MC said in his own microphone, putting her on the spot and drawing a laugh from the crowd. Charlie was sure she turned red. She was so embarrassed.

"Get her whatever she wants."

She looked to the back of the room where the voice had come from.

Demi stood at the door, staring at her. He wore different clothes. This time, a black Nike sweatsuit and a black Gucci hat. He was so damn rugged.

When she was handed the guitar, it felt like someone had cloaked her in comfort.

"You got it, baby girl, we gonna follow you wherever you go. We got a real musician on the stage," the lead bass guitarist of the band said, making Charlie feel even better.

She nodded and began playing a simple chord.

"Y'all want to do me a favor and lower your phones? All I see are lights. I want to see y'all," she whispered. Demi stood, stone-faced, and she locked in on him. "When my mom was alive, she told me to focus on one person in the room. One face that makes you comfortable, and sing to that one person, no matter how nervous you are." Charlie found Demi. Despite her anger, he was the one person who she knew would appreciate her set. Her heart raced as anxiety put a tremble in her voice. She cleared her throat and took a deep breath as she began to sing. H.E.R., because she had sung the song a hundred times and it was one that she had mastered, nerves or not.

"Set the toneee when it's just me
And you alone, never lonely-
In the room, breathing slowwwly"

Charlie's long nails tapped the wood of the guitar, creating a mini baseline as she played simultaneously. H.E.R was always a good choice. Start small. She sat on that wooden chair, one spotlight shining on her, strumming the simplest chords as she went into the chorus.

"I feel so comfortable with youuuuuu."

Then her eyes closed, and he was there too. Usually, her mom joined her on stage, when she was nervous. She escaped inside her head and her mom would always show up. Tonight, it was Demi.

"Lay your head on my pillow say wooo hoooo," she sang.

The band joined her as Charlie went into a medley, changing the song effortlessly, skillfully as the guitar led the other musicians in the room naturally.

Ari Lennox.

"I've been smok-ing pur-ple azeeee, oooooo-
-all to forget abouttt youuu."

Charlie was a vibe. Whenever she got out of her head and got in her bag, pulling notes from her heart, she shined. She stood and put the guitar strap around her body so she could focus on the microphone stand, gripping it with both hands.

"Don't date these niggas 'til you're forty-threeee."

Charlie's fingers found her strings again and she changed the song. Frank Ocean.

Charlie felt like no one else was in the room. There was an invisible chain that connected them, had to be because she felt him pulling her to him and it took everything she had to stay on the stage.

She was so mad at him, hurt by the rejection of it all, embarrassed by his dismissiveness. She had opened her aura to him, let him bathe in her waters. Charlie had put her best shit down on that nigga and he had the nerve to not call her afterward. When she finished the song, the crowd roared in applause and the bass guitarist stood to give her a hug.

"Thank, y'all," she said before rushing off the stage. All the confidence that had filled her had deflated as soon as the music stopped. Stassi was still on her feet when Charlie approached the table.

"I secure the bag?" Charlie asked.

Day's brows were lifted. He was stunned. Amazed. "Fire. I don't think I've ever heard nobody sing like that. Bag secured. I'm a man of my word; but for real for real, I got a record deal for you tonight if you with it."

"Thanks, but no. That's not even close to what I want to do," Charlie said.

"It could be if you stop letting other people control your life," Stassi said, shrugging as she tried to urge Charlie to take the opportunity.

"Stassi," Charlie warned. She didn't like to be pushed. "I think I'm going to head out. You coming?"

"I've got to stay until the end, make sure this gets wrapped up correctly, but go ahead, girl. I can call an Uber," Stassi said.

"I'll have a driver get you where you got to go," Day interjected, as he glanced at Stassi for a second before shifting his focus back to the conversation taking place at the table. The atmosphere was loud. Dynasty Music Group was corporate, but it had been built up by two men from the streets, so the showcase was the hottest ticket in town. If you were somebody you were present.

"Call me when you make it home," Stassi said. "You going to Mommy and Daddy's anniversary dinner, right?"

"Hmm... Do I have to?" Charlie asked.

"Yeah, you have to," Stassi said.

Charlie nodded. "I'll think about it."

She pulled away and snuck through the crowd, choosing to go out of a side door instead of chancing running into Demi.

She dug through her handbag for the ticket to her car and then stepped out into the night.

"You keep it safe?" she joked with the same valet attendant who had greeted her hours ago.

"Safest in the lot, but you'll have to see Mr. Sky about the keys. He took them, ma'am," the man said.

"Wait, who? Who is Mr. Sky and why does he have my car keys?" she asked.

"Demitrius Sky. The owner of Dynasty Music Group, ma'am. He instructed me to leave the key with him and he would get them to you," the man said.

Charlie saw red. "This nigga..." She pulled out her phone and dialed his number only to be sent to voicemail. Even her house key was on that keyring. She couldn't even get inside her house until he returned it. Before she could even open her text messages, his name popped onto her screen.

DEMI
Room 7070

CHARLIE
Bring me my key, Demi. I'm not coming to your room.

Charlie saw bubbles and then nothing. He wasn't responding and she was pretty sure he wasn't delivering her key either. She was breathing fire as she stormed back inside, bypassing the showcase ballroom, and heading toward the main part of the hotel. As she took the elevator to the 7th floor, she wondered if she should have made him come to her. The bathroom. His hands around her neck. It all flashed through her mind, putting a pit in her stomach that was so vast it felt like it might suck her inside out. His gravitational pull was too strong. He was like a black hole and Charlie needed to keep her universe intact. When she got to the room the door was propped open by the security bar and she pushed inside. Demi sat on the couch, leaned over, legs planted on the ground, hands rubbing together like he was putting a play together in his head. Maybe he was. Maybe he was plotting on how to get her to drop her attitude. It wasn't happening. He had gotten ghost on her so fuck it, she was going to catch the hint and disappear too. She wasn't into chasing. Not after everything she had been through. If she had to beg a nigga for his time, she didn't want it.

"Where are my keys, Demi?" she asked, holding open the door.

"You ain't getting the keys to that raggedy-ass car until I say so, so close the door," he said.

"You drive me, Demitrius," she said, lifting her hands up in mid-air like she wanted to choke him while gritting her teeth.

He chuckled. "Demitrius?"

"Nigga, I know your name. I Googled your whole life after we fucked," she said, rolling her eyes.

Demi wondered how much she had uncovered. Did she know the true reason why he had gone M.I.A? He knew she didn't. His family wasn't online. Not on his social media, not mentioned in any interview. He moved that way for good reason — in case his past ever came looking for him. He felt like shit because he was relieved in this moment, relieved that his songbird didn't know what he was leaving out.

"You know? After you laid in my bed, after you were between my legs, in my shower, eating my fucking food. You might have forgot since you clearly ain't thought about me since."

"I swear you be talking hella shit, Bird," Demi said, blowing a breath of frustration out his mouth and leaning back on the couch, kicking one Lebron sneaker out as he rubbed the top of his head. "You don't know shit about shit."

"And I don't want to know. I don't even want to be here. Give. Me. My. Keys." Her tone was lethal. Charlie wasn't playing and he had already shown her that he was full of games.

"I want you to be here. I ain't supposed to want you, Bird, but I want you," he said. He sounded tortured and the pain she heard in him brought her resentment down a notch.

"If this was a week ago, I would have asked you why you haven't called, but after three weeks of staring at my phone wondering what the fuck happened that turned me into a notch on yet another nigga's belt, I don't even care. I can't care about what you want. It's about what I want, and I want consistency. You're not consistent. Fuck you," she said.

"Com'ere," he said.

She stood with her arms folded across her chest. She was stubborn and she wanted to glue her feet to the carpet, super glue them so she wouldn't follow his commands. When he held up her keys as bait, Charlie crossed the room.

"Shit gon' sound crazy, Bird, but I need you to put your hands on me," he said.

Charlie's heart ached. He was asking for her to torture him. He had just yoked her up in the bathroom for the very same thing and here he was asking for her to bring him pain. She knew it was all mental. The OCD was extreme and was a mental chain he had created in his mind. She didn't know why, but they existed. It had taken his all to let her in that first night; now, here he was again, unlocking his mental, fighting himself to connect with her.

"You humiliated me," she whispered, a tear sliding down her cheek.

"Nobody knows we slept together unless you out here telling people," he said, frowning because he wanted his business to be his business and if she was spreading it, he had an issue with that. The audacity of this nigga to think he owned the stories of her vagina. If Charlie wanted to tell it, she would tell it. She hadn't, but if she wanted to, she would.

"I know! I'm judging myself! I wasn't worth a call?" she asked.

He leaned forward and held his hand up to her exposed thigh. He thought twice before touching her skin, but he did it anyway. Then, his other hand gripped her waist and he pulled her down onto him. Her thighs spread over him and he lifted a bit, pressing his dick into her as one hand went to her ass, the other gripped her chin.

"I wanted to call. You're fucking trouble. Goddamn, you're trouble, Bird," he said. "I'm touching fire and I don't even give a fuck that it burns. What you call that? Huh? Cuz I call it crazy," he said.

"You hurt my feelings," she said. "I can't do this with somebody that can pick me up and put me down without notice. That one night made me want it all. I wanted more and you just seemed to go on with your life like it didn't even happen."

Demi's chest was ripped open. He could feel it. It was a hurt he hadn't felt before. It was a gutting of his entire being. She wanted his heart in her hands and she wouldn't stop until she had it.

"A nigga life been on pause since that night," he said. "Shit that made sense before don't make sense no more, Bird. I wanted to call. Me staying away was for you, cuz if I did what I wanted to do, I would ruin you."

Charlie put her hands on the sides of his face, and he pulled in air through clenched teeth. It was like she had poured alcohol over an open wound.

"I'm sorry if I hurt you in the bathroom earlier." The remorse in his tone was heavy and she nodded.

"I know," she whispered. "You can't make me fall in love with you and then punish me for it," she said. "Staying away from me so I can't touch you is punishment. It's not fair."

The air was so damn thick. It pushed on his chest as he palmed her face too. Forehead to forehead, he breathed heavy. CPR. He needed to be resuscitated. Demi was overstimulated and he just needed it to stop.

Let her go, nigga, he thought.

Don't let me go. Was the thought that countered his, running through her mind simultaneously. An unheard argument, a struggle for power. Neither knew who would win.

His hands didn't move. Her mind was stronger.

Say, man, what the fuck?

This was sorcery. She was ordering his steps.

Kiss me, Demi, Charlie thought.

His lips touched hers. He damn near growled as Charlie pushed her tongue into his mouth.

"I love you, Demi," she whispered, pulling back.

Fuck. Demi was mindfucked. Charlie was talking that talk... that talk that made niggas run for the hills, and he felt like a bitch because if he had panties, she would be finessing him out of them with only words. It was the need in her voice that made his dick ache. He believed her when she said she missed him. He knew that feeling. Even after one night.

This bitch crazy, man, he thought. He could see them six months from now. She would be busting windows out of his car and putting sugar in his tank. That had to be her vibe. She was saying I love you too soon, letting her pussy do the talking. He wanted to warn her but damn it if he didn't feel the shit too.

"You ain't known me long enough to love me, Bird. You don't know what you asking for," he replied.

"I don't care. I feel what I feel, and it was more than sex. Maybe it's stupid. Maybe I'm childish, but is it impossible? To find one person out of the seven billion people on the planet that just makes you feel shit in your stomach? A little sick. A little afraid. A little giddy. I been in love with you. Since the club. So, if you're not going to be around. If you can't stick around, or if you're going to disappear or if this is too much too fast, then let me know. This ain't normal. You're not normal but I like the kind of crazy I am when I'm with you," she admitted. "It's insane, right? To say that to somebody you barely know?"

Demi knew it was a slippery slope they were sliding down. His feet weren't rooted in the ground. Neither was hers. It was the type of impulsivity that would leave someone wounded. He had a family at home but with Charlie's hands on his face, with her breath in his lungs, with these thighs wrapping his waist and his dick hardening by the second, he pushed them to the back of his mind.

"Yeah, Bird, you a little crazy," he groaned. "But I'm a little crazy too."

He loved the fuck out of this girl. He had tried not to. He didn't like anything that didn't make sense. Demi added up situations from front to back and from back to front just to establish clarity, and in this position, he still came up short. There was no explaining the potency of this feeling. He barely knew Charlie, but he loved her.

"I just want you all over me, so if I got to go without you again, I can last longer this time," he said.

"You feel it too?" she asked.

The nod was all she would get. It was all he could muster. He couldn't vocalize what perplexed him. Demi was a man that relied on logic. Things had to make sense to him. This misunderstanding of emotion, this game of hearts made him feel irrational. It made him feel unsteady. The feeling of his racing heart hemorrhaging in his chest as it went wild, beating against the cage of his heart, trying to break free to run from her. Fear. Charlie was terrifying. The scariest dream that he didn't want to wake up from.

His strong thighs lifted them both from the seat and they kissed, long, deep, sloppy kisses that he hated but that she loved. She already knew where he was headed. The bathroom. The shower. The only place where her touches didn't hurt because her hands would be clean. He put her on the vanity and unhooked her bra. His hands held an expertise that made her nipples pebble in yearning. There was no fumbling with hooks, no clumsy fingers tripping up on the lace. He was skilled in undressing a woman. Never any like Charlie, though.

"Out here in this little-ass shit," he chastised, removing it. Charlie was so damn petite, she had just enough of everything to fit in his mouth. Portion control. Charlie was bite-sized, only enough for a quick taste. In order to savor her, he would have to have her again and again. He ripped the skirt, tearing the slit until he exposed her red panties, and then he tore through those too. Demi had a lot of beast in him. He tried to control it. Putting his murder game down calmed him some. He had worked out his mental angst in the streets for years, but Charlie activated a different part of his crazy. It was her voice, the way she used it, even when she was only speaking. That tone hypnotized him. Her clothes were evidence of the crime he was ready to commit. Attempted homicide because

Demi wanted to murder that pussy. He gripped the edge of the counter around her as he buried his face in her neck. His tongue to her neck because he couldn't help himself. He thought of everything that was on her skin that was now in his mouth. He tasted her perfume. His skin crawled and his dick bricked. Charlie was an infection. What the fuck was he even doing here with her? This was sick. Her little-ass walked all over every boundary he had ever created for people.

"I need the water, Bird," he groaned, lifting her, pressing her wet into his sweatpants because he was still fully dressed.

"Okay," she gasped, locking her legs around his waist and her arms around his neck. He opened the shower door, put her down and then stepped back, admiring her body. Charlie was everything opposite of what normally attracted him. She was soulful and thin, with a little bit of everything: a lil' ass, lil', pretty titties with bite-sized chocolate chip nipples that were begging him to take a taste, and a lil', pretty pussy that he was dying to kiss. He wouldn't because he didn't know Charlie like that and he had to vet her entire medical history before he went there, but he wanted to. He removed the gold chain from his neck and put it around her neck. She gripped the crown pendant. The diamonds fit her well. Just like that, she took possession of it and he wondered if her magic was in her touch because when she had touched him just like that, he had become hers. Like the necklace... it was hers now. It made sense. She was a queen. She needed a crown. She deserved riches. It made sense that her presence commanded him. Charlie may as well had been Medusa because he turned to stone in her presence, unable to leave until she allowed it...until she uncast her spell on him. Demi came out of his clothes. Heavy. Demi was heavy, everywhere. Reputation, pockets, dick. Heavy-ass, boss-ass nigga. He stepped into the shower and turned on the rainfall. The water fell over them and Charlie cringed.

"Guess I can expect you to fuck up my locs every time I see you. I just got a retwist!" she said, laughing as his arm wrapped her waist, pulling her close.

"Every day," he answered.

"Nah, that's impossible because that means you're going to pull up every day and we both know you like to go missing," she whispered as she zeroed in on his bottom lip. Charlie bit him and then soothed the pain with her tongue as she pushed into him.

"Every day, Bird. I'm tapping in with you every day, that's my word," he said, barely finding space for words between kisses. They stumbled, kissing, all over the shower and Demi had to free one hand to find a wall to brace them both. His other hand never left her ass.

"Yeah, a nigga love you, Bird. Love the fuck out of you, baby," he said. She pulled back in shock. She nodded. They now had an understanding. This was on some love shit and he was terrified. She could see it in his creased brow, but fuck it. They felt what they felt. It was too late now. Gas. Charlie hit the gas and lowered. If he loved her, she wanted to taste his love. It was hers. He was hers. She swallowed Demi and he grunted as he widened his stance and gripped her hair with one hand.

"Oh shit," he moaned. "Suck that shit, Bird."

Demi was a different type of lover. He handled her, keeping her pace for her as he wound his hips into her face. Charlie kept up like a champ.

Aggressive and particular. He liked everything in his life a certain way, including sex, but Charlie somehow pulled spontaneity from him. He had been hitting Lauren the same way for years, opting for doggy style because he could control her hands that way. He pinned them behind her back as he hit it every time. Charlie, he wanted to see. The burn of her curious fingers, even now as she reached up his body, sliding fingernails down his stomach, was a defiance of his rules. She gripped him, riding the mic, pulling her neck back and forth while rotating her wrist. His ass tightened as he gripped the other side of her face. "Fuck!" He was throbbing and he pulled back because he was about to explode, but Charlie didn't stop. "I'm about to nut, Bird, damn."

When she didn't stop, his head fell back. Lauren didn't do this. Hell, he wasn't sure Lauren could do this because he wasn't big on saliva being on his body, but she definitely wasn't swallowing. Charlie took in every drop of his soul and his body seized as his mouth opened as he came.

He was in deep with Charlie. He knew it when he had stayed the night at her junky apartment, but this confirmed it. As he washed her body, while kissing her lips, and whispering shit about love, he knew. His head was gone. In Charliezonia. That's where it was. Lost somewhere in her psyche.

He hoisted Charlie up with dick and strong thighs as she bounced all over him. Soap and cum washed down the drain as she screamed his name in octaves he had never heard. It was a street symphony, a sex symphony, his new favorite song. "Oh my God, Demi!" was his favorite lyric. Heavy breathing and more kisses. When she hopped on him, he pushed out of the shower, getting water everywhere.

"I missed you, babe," she admitted as he placed her on her feet and reached for a towel. He wrapped it around her body, then got one of his own.

"No bullshit, Bird, I listened to that video you sent me a hunnid times. I know every sound. Even the damn dog barking in the background at the thirty-second mark," he admitted.

She blushed and giggled sweetly. His pretty bird.

"Don't make me miss you again," she said.

"I won't," he guaranteed.

"Promise?" she asked. There was something about promising a woman something. It was like a contract. Like a signing away of your soul. A fucking mortgage to his heart. Charlie wanted the keys, and she was currently working on placing a lock on him.

"That's my word," he said, against his better judgement.

"You ripped my clothes," she said. "What am I supposed to put on?" she asked, laughing.

"I ain't done with your body, baby, you don't need no clothes tonight," he said. "I'ma fill your closet tomorrow, don't worry about it."

His phone rang and he retrieved it from the pockets of his pants.

LO

Lauren's name on his phone brought him crashing down off the cloud Charlie had him on. He set the call to voicemail, and just as he expected, her text came through.

LO
Hey, baby. I'm here, where are you?

Demi frowned and his stomach sank. He wanted to ask her what she was doing there. Lauren didn't come to showcases often. When she stepped out it was a big deal, but she had been working hard lately and his son had a demanding schedule, so she hadn't been in the mood to be arm candy for months.

DEMI
I had to step out. Business. Got to take a trip. I'll call you tomorrow and let you know what's up.

LO
What do you mean a trip? How long?

DEMI
*No phones. Go home. It ain't nothing to worry about. It's just a quick trip. I'm back Monday.
I'ma call you in the morning.*

Demi sensed her hesitation because she didn't respond right away. He knew Lauren was choosing her words carefully.

LO
K. I love you.

DEMI
Love.

"Everything okay?" Charlie's voice pulled him back, erasing his urge to leave, but his mind dwelled on Lauren. She didn't deserve this. He had never been this man to her. She had never had to worry about another woman. A part of him wished it had never happened, but as Charlie placed her hands to his back and he turned to stare in her eyes, he remembered why he was doing this.

"Yeah," he said, putting his phone on DO NOT DISTURB, then tossing it to the chair.

He took a finger to her scars. "What happened here?" he asked.

She seemed to shrink some, recoiling as she turned and rushed to the closet, pulling out the hotel robe. Demi shook his head.

"You gon' have to keep that off, Bird. They don't wash them shits," he said. "You don't got to hide your body from me and you don't got to talk about it if you don't want to."

"I don't want to," she confirmed. "Maybe one day but not today."

His nostrils flared at the sight of her eyes prickling with emotion. Whatever story those scars told was a painful one. Someone had hurt her badly. He could tell and it made him want to hurt everybody, anybody in her life that had ever brought her pain.

Charlie went to the bed and found solace under the duvet. "Come're."

The sight of her, under white sheets; sheets he had changed himself before she had come up, pulled him to the bed.

Her naked body was beautiful. Flawed. Marked up, but somehow, he had never seen anything quite as remarkable as Charlie. It was like the scars were the source of emotion in her voice. When she sang, whatever hurt had caused those scars floated from her mouth. She lifted the cover for him, and he sank into the bed. Under those white sheets, they built a home. A little teepee of connection and passion as Charlie covered his head.

"Want to tell me what we doing under here?" he asked.

"Blocking everything out," she whispered as she turned to him. Demi stared at her.

"You know all you got to do is say the word and anybody that ever hurt you can like not breathe no more. That's the type of nigga I am. That's who you fucking with. I want you to know that. I'm in this music shit, but that I ain't who I always been. I turn into a whole different nigga sometimes. I'm violent, Bird. I lose my shit sometimes. My mind don't always stay with me. I've done shit. I've hurt people..."

Charlie was trembling and her eyes stung as she stared in his eyes. It was like he wasn't even speaking to her, like she wasn't even there. She wondered if his mind had left the room in this moment. The way he described his temperament gave her chills. Being here with Demi was like flirting with death, like walking the edge of a cliff and praying the wind didn't blow too hard. She wanted to touch him but was afraid to. What if he snapped? Like he had in the bathroom... No, Charlie would keep her hands to herself. She swallowed the lump in her throat.

"Women?" she asked.

"Never women," he said. "Never children, but anybody else..." he stopped talking like the acts were unspeakable and they truly were. He shouldn't have even divulged this much to her, but this was his bird, his sweet Charlie. "I'll squeeze life out of a nigga body over you, Bird," he said.

Charlie's stomach ached. She was both afraid and turned on. There was so much passion between them. It wasn't even logical.

"Does that bother you?" he asked.

"You're weird, Demi. You're a lot. You're mean. Your temper is unreasonable. You're dangerous. Everything about you terrifies me," she admitted.

"Burn me, Bird," he said.

"Burn you?" The complexities of this man were so confusing.

"Your hands. When they are on my skin it feels like an iron. The shit hurts," he whispered.

"So why would you want me to touch you? That's horrible," she exclaimed. Suddenly, the teepee felt like a prison. Were they running out of air? It felt like she was trying to breathe through a straw, like there wasn't enough oxygen for the both of them. Demi made her lightheaded, like her mind was a balloon that he was filling with hot air.

"Do it, Bird," he said, closing his eyes.

Charlie sniffed away emotion and placed her hand on the side of his face. An instant grimace and she pulled back. *It really does hurt*, she thought, enamored by the complexities of a man so strange. She touched him again and pain wrote all over his face.

He put his hand over hers and then moved it to the center of his chest. His heart was racing so fast and beating so hard that her own heartbeat sped up in alarm. He made her feel so powerful.

"Demi." She gasped as her pussy bloomed, petals opening as she felt all the intensity that lived between them. Energy. Demi was pure energy.

"As long as my heart beating like this for you, you ain't never got to worry about nothing. You ain't got to be afraid of nobody. Just keep starting my fire, Bird. You make a nigga feel alive," he said.

Whatever had been lacking before he had walked into that smoky club was abundant now.

She nodded and he swiped away the tear that fell from her eye. He pulled her closer. Body to body, and then pressed her head into his chest before turning on his back, forcing her on top. She straddled him and they just laid there, his eyes on the ceiling, her head searing his skin.

He was overthinking and she was trying to convince herself to get out of this now, but neither moved.

Demi couldn't believe he had done so much with Charlie. He had hit her without even reaching for the condoms he kept in his wallet. His dick had played tricks on him for days after the first time. He had never inspected his shit so much in his life. Every time he went to pee, he anticipated a burn; not because he thought ill of Charlie, he just thought like that...of all the possibility of infection... of germs... of the shit other people never considered. It had never happened, but even still lying here with her so intimately after pouring out his soul and dismissing his child's mother, he thought of the way he had explored her body. All trust, no rubber.

What the fuck this girl got me on?

He didn't even know how old Charlie was. Didn't know her last name. Didn't know if Charlie was her real name or a nickname. Didn't know her birthday. He didn't know anything about her, and he had dipped in her raw. Twice. The way his dick was rising, he was close to making it happen a third time and the thoughts that raced through his mind wouldn't allow him to delay the inevitable much longer.

"Say, man," he said.

She lifted her head and rested her chin to his chest and those eyes, those eyes fucking captured him.

"Say, man," she repeated, a lazy smile on her lips as she climbed his body and planted lips to his.

"Mmmm," he moaned as she put her sweet tongue down his throat. Charlie took his tongue and sucked on it like she was sucking dick and his fucking dick begged him to go diving again. He reached down. *Stay wet,* he thought, amazed as his fingers graced the silk between her thighs, rolling her clit between his fingers, making her bite down on his chin. "Wait, Bird, wait."

"No, babe, whyyyyy?" she whined, going harder, kissing him deeper. Fuck! He had never been so ready to bust something down.

"Bird, wait," he said, avoiding her kisses and gripping her chin.

She huffed her displeasure.

"I want to eat your pussy, Bird. I want to taste you, baby," he moaned. Even the thought made his dick jump.

"Say less, nigga. Why we stopping?" she asked.

"I'ma need them papers," he said.

She pulled back. "What?" She frowned because she knew he wasn't talking about what she thought he was talking about.

"I need you to take a couple tests..."

Charlie grabbed a pillow and knocked him upside his big-ass head. "Fuck you, Demi," she scoffed as she climbed from the bed.

"Shouldn't be a problem unless it's a problem," he said, sitting up, and leaning lazily against the headboard. "Come lay down. I don't want no smoke. It's necessary, though."

"Nigga, we've fucked already. Raw. Twice! And if we counting rounds, you already got whatever it is you think I have, asshole!"

"I ain't accusing you, but can you blame me? You let niggas slide on the first night, Bird. I'm just being..."

"A jerk," she finished for him, as she walked into the bathroom. Charlie snatched up her torn clothes. She couldn't even storm out on him because he had destroyed her clothes and stolen her keys.

Charlie sat on the toilet, her leg bouncing as she tapped pretty, black-painted toes on the tile floor. The knock at the door pissed her off.

"Go away, Demitrius!" she said. He pulled the sliding barnyard door open anyway and Charlie sent the blow dryer flying at him. He dodged it and then looked behind him in shock before turning his stare on her. An extra roll of toilet paper hit him in the face and Demi closed his eyes, blowing out a sharp breath to stop himself from fucking her up.

"I said get out," she said.

"How old am I, Bird?" he asked.

She crossed her arms and avoided his tense stare. She didn't answer. Couldn't answer because she didn't know.

"What I like to eat? Who I be with? Where did I go to school?" he asked.

Silence.

"You don't know. We blew by all that shit. So when I ask you about the history of your pussy, baby, I ain't trying to insult you," he said. "Some shit a nigga can't just speed past. The way that pussy call my name, Bird, I got to taste it. I want to eat your pussy all night. Go to sleep and wake up and eat it again, but I can't skip that shit. The tests. I never have. Except with you."

She hated that she semi understood.

"How old are you, Demi?" she asked.

"Thirty-three," he said.

Her brows lifted. "I'm 24, Demi," she said.

"That's a problem for you?" he asked.

"What you want with a girl that's almost ten years younger

than you? You want to fuck up my head?" she asked.

"I ain't here for none of that," he replied. "Come're, baby."

She stood and walked to him. Still mad. Still embarrassed.

"You my baby?" he asked. She nodded, blushing as she stood on her tiptoes. His hand gripped her. She was so petite his fingers curved into the most intimate of places. "Young-ass. This shit gon' be a problem."

She nodded. "I'm not the young chick that you got an advantage over. I'm the one that'll wear you out. Fair warning," she said.

"Say, man," he said, chuckling. "My dick said that's facts."

She laughed as they swayed from side to side. They were the vision of a couple who truly enjoyed one another.

"Say you my baby, Bird." He stared down at her, stern gaze penetrating her mad soul.

"I'm your baby," she answered.

He crouched some to scoop her and then carried her back into the room, placing his lips to her neck. Charlie giggled. "I love you, Bird." Caking-ass nigga. Demi finally understood how niggas went soft around their women. Lauren hadn't been able to pull this from him. Charlie, on the other hand. Goo. She turned his big, rough-ass to goo.

"You better," she replied. He tossed her on the mattress and then turned to hit the speaker button on the hotel phone.

"Hi, Mr. Sky. How can I help you this evening?" the concierge asked.

"You hungry?" he asked, without looking at her.

"I want everything," she answered. "One of everything."

"You hear that?" he asked into the phone.

"Yes, sir. One of everything. It'll be up in about 45 minutes," the woman answered.

He climbed back in bed and Charlie bullied her way beneath his arm and clicked on the TV screen. He wanted to move her, but he knew she would only come right back so he ignored his urge for space and let her be.

Charlie watched TV and Demi watched her. She sang everything. All the commercials that came on, every jingle she hummed. He found himself muting the volume so he could listen to her on those parts, and when her girly-ass reality shows came back on, she snatched the remote to turn it back up.

"You're annoying, Demi," she said.

"Yeah, whatever," he replied lazily. He sat up and reached down into his pants to remove the bag of weed he had in his pocket.

"You want me to roll up?" she asked.

He looked back in surprise. "Say, man, young bitches so ghetto. Ass can't cook but can roll up," he said, snickering.

She sucked her teeth and rolled her eyes, before falling back on the pillow.

"Nigga, I can cook. I cooked breakfast for you!" she said.

"Oh yeah, your Charlie-flavored eggs," he replied, smirking. She crawled over to him, interrupting him, sitting right in his lap as they faced one another. She pulled the weed from his hands, freeing them and they went straight to her ass. Gripping, pulling her into his dick.

"Don't be feeling me up now, boy. You need test results. You need pussy papers. So that dick on hold until I get you what you want. I don't know you, remember?" she asked.

He watched her roll up and cringed a bit when she wet the blunt with her spit. She fired up and took the weed in like a champ.

Hood-ass. Charlie was the type of girl who could be his best friend and his bitch.

"I don't sleep with men on the first night, Demi. Before you, I was in a relationship for a long time and that is the only other man I've ever been with. You were the exception."

Demi was a natural skeptic but the sincerity in her eyes told him she was speaking truth. Being in her presence felt easy. It felt comfortable, like he could spend a thousand days doing exactly this. Coming home to this. After a long day, being greeted with pussy, Charlie-flavored food, and a blunt. He was exhausted. She drained him of everything, took his ego, his logic, and every drop of cum he built up throughout the day. She left him depleted like it was a lazy Sunday and they had fucked so much they couldn't climb from the bed afterward. He almost forgot that he was lying and sneaking just to be there. Charlie felt like the one, but how could she be when he had a whole life outside these doors?

"I fuck with you, Bird. The long way on every day of the week. Remember that, a'ight?"

"You remember that, babe. I'm not the one who will forget."

CHAPTER 10

Stassi was always the last to leave. It never failed. At every event she had ever arranged, she hung around until the very last guest departed. It was the perfectionist in her. She thrived on seeing a venue go from nothing to something, and then back to nothing again. She had always known she wanted to become a chef. She used to cook up meals in high school and sell them out of her mother's kitchen in Styrofoam takeout boxes just to make money. When she discovered that she could parlay that into a full-service event boutique, she had found her calling. Her business was new and small but growing by the day. This talent showcase was proof of that. What had started as baby showers and graduation parties was blooming into something so much more. It was her baby, and she was proud of it.

"The kitchen has to be spotless and make sure we're bubble wrapping anything glass. A lot of stuff broke at the last event during transit, so be careful," she instructed. A young boss. Stassi was finding her way and it felt damn good.

"Anastassia Grant." Day swaggered into the kitchen, giving a slow round of applause as he approached her.

"Did I do my job?" she asked, beaming because nobody could tell her shit. She knew she had done a great job; it didn't matter what came out of his mouth next.

"You did that," Day replied. "Time to settle up."

Stassi held out her hand. "Pay up, pay up," she said playfully. "Write me a big check with a lot of zeros."

Day snickered. "Your bank account been blessed. You can believe that."

"I swear I gave out my card to like 20 people. Thank you for introducing me tonight. You vouching for me really made a difference. I would never be in the same room with these types of people."

"What type is that?" Day asked.

"Privileged, I guess. Bougie even," Stassi said.

"Nah, everybody in this shit is the same. We all hood wrapped in new money," Day said.

"Ten-thousand-dollar handbags, red bottoms on every shoe, sounds about right," she said.

"Don't judge. Niggas ain't never had nothing so they want everything when they finally get it. When you see the tip I gave you, I guarantee you'll be up at Somerset buying yourself something shiny. Everybody come with they shit."

"Everything I have goes into my business. I could care less about a label," Stassi said.

"You a different kind of girl then, Ms. Lady. Tell me something. How a nigga impress a woman that don't like pretty things?" Day asked.

"Show her something different," Stassi answered.

Day narrowed the distance between them, tapping the

edge of the stainless steel table with his finger until he was inches away.

"You on your hustle, Stassi. I respect it," Day said. "But I'd be a lie if I told you I was gon' play by your little rules." He bit down on his bottom lip. Restraint. Thank God he was showing restraint.

Breathe, bitch, Stassi said to herself. Day didn't have even a little ugly on him. He was fine as hell and he smelled so damn good. Like liquor and cologne.

"I want to take you out, get to know you and shit," Day said.

D'Ussé. He had been drinking D'Ussé. He was so close she could smell it on his breath.

Don't even think about taking backshots from this brown liquor dick tonight, bitch. Don't do it. I bet it's big… Aht, aht, be professional.

The internal struggle taking place in her mind was ridiculous.

"Day, I can't," she replied.

"You're fired then," he said as he closed the space and leaned into her neck, kissing there, leaving goosebumps and a wet spot behind.

She whimpered; it felt so good.

"Day…"

"Hmm," he groaned as he sucked on her neck, kissing his way to her ear and then down her cheek until his tongue was in her mouth.

"We can't do this," she protested weakly. He lifted her onto the table, the steel kissed her bottom, freezing her as a chill shot up her spine and stiffened her nipples. Day slid her panties aside and Stassi grabbed his hand. Day paused long enough to speak.

"We stopping or going? Swear to God if you press play, I'll eat this pussy to perfection but it's your call. These your rules not mine. You want the dick or the opportunity."

The dick.

Her inner ho was out of control. Her mind answered first but thank God she spoke a different answer.

"The opportunity," Stassi whispered.

"Smart girl," he scoffed, taking a step back and lifting his hands in surrender.

"Smarter than most."

Stassi quickly hopped down from the table when she realized someone else had entered the room.

"What up, Lo?" Day greeted.

When Lauren Sky stepped out of the shadows, Stassi's heartbeat quickened.

"I really hope this isn't the girl you've been dying to get me to meet. Anybody who ends up getting fucked in the kitchen after their own event has no business being anywhere near one of my productions," Lauren said.

"Easy, sis," Day defended. "You said you couldn't make it."

"I changed my mind," Lauren said. "The showcase went well. Everything looks beautiful. Everybody who matters is talking about it. I'm sorry I couldn't come through this time." Lauren met Stassi's gaze. "It looks like you were in capable hands, though. Congrats. You did good work."

"Thank you. I appreciate it and it's nice to meet you. I've followed your work for a few years and love everything about you and your company. You're literally goals."

"You're sweet, hun, don't let this one corrupt you," Lauren said jokingly.

"There will be no corrupting," Stassi answered, blushing because she wasn't sure if she could resist Day if he kept pushing up on her.

"I'ma let y'all chop it up..."

"No, I'm not staying," Lauren said. "Anastassia, right?"

Stassi nodded, smiling because she couldn't believe that Lauren even knew her name.

"Just Stassi," she answered.

"I will definitely be in touch about bringing you on. This business is one of friends. Nobody can do every single event, but we look out for one another. I help you; you help me, and we build. Your work is good. I think we can collab on a few things. Maybe bring you on at my company for one event to see if the chemistry's there first? You good with that?"

"Oh my God, yes. Absolutely. I'd love to work with you," Stassi answered.

"Day vouches, so it's a done deal," Lauren answered. Lauren went into her handbag and removed a card. "Call me first thing Monday morning."

"I will," Stassi said eagerly. She could barely hide her excitement.

"Alright, bro, I'm out of here," Lauren said. Her heels clicked across the kitchen floor until she reached the door. She paused. "I'm looking for my husband. Have you seen,

Demi? He claims he had some emergency. Some meeting out of town? What you know about that?" Lauren asked.

Husband?

Stassi had to stop her mouth from falling open at the revelation. *That lying-ass nigga. Ain't no way Charlie knows he's married.*

"Oh, um, yeah. We had something come up with the execs at the distribution company," Day said. "Nothing to worry about though, Lo."

Stassi was amazed at how easily the lie left Day's lips.

Lauren lingered, staring at Day in the eyes but she didn't speak. She simply nodded before walking out.

"Demi's married?" Stassi asked.

Day finessed his chin, looking off as he blew out a breath of discontent. "First rule of being in this business," he paused as he deadpanned on her. "Mind *your* business." Day walked out of the kitchen, leaving Stassi with a conflicted soul. Her sister had no idea that Demi was married, but Stassi knew she couldn't tell her. If she did, she would ruin the opportunity she had been given.

She's not even serious about him. She just met him. I shouldn't have to give this up because of who she's sleeping with, Stassi thought. *I'll just convince her not to see him anymore. This is too big to turn down.*

Charlie stood behind Demi. Her arms were wrapped around his waist as she rested the side of her face against his back as he faced the hotel clerk.

"How was your stay, Mr. Sky?" the woman asked.

"Everything was good," he answered. "Thanks for going to grab my lady a few items. You get that tip?"

"I did. It wasn't necessary, but thank you," she answered. "I hope I'm not overstepping here, but you guys are a beautiful couple. I see a lot of people come in here and I've never quite seen love look like this. Enjoy your day, Mr. and Mrs. Sky. Come see us again."

"You hear that, Demi? Mrs. Sky," Charlie teased as he turned toward her.

"That name a little big for you, Bird," he replied. "You might grow into it one day. We'll see."

Her cheeks warmed as he placed his hand on the small of her back and led her outside to the valet.

They hadn't seen the sun for two days. With the blackout shades drawn, they had drowned in darkness all weekend. Weed, sex, and food. They had overindulged, ignoring everything and everyone except one another. Charlie felt like she was floating as they stood in front of the hotel. Demi's brow knitted as he responded to messages he had ignored for days. Charlie didn't care to power her phone back on yet. She wouldn't until she was in her car and out of his space.

"So, now what?" she asked.

That question jarred him, pulling his eyes up and to her instantly. He stuck his phone in his pocket.

"I mean, now that this is a thing. What happens next? Is it a thing?" she wondered.

"It's a big thing," he said.

Her car putted up to the curb and Demi frowned. It was old and the exhaust could be smelled from a block away. The loud tick of the engine told Demi it was something wrong under the hood, but he didn't want to embarrass her.

The valet hopped out of the driver's side and Demi walked Charlie around the car, tipping the valet guy.

"I got it, man," he said. "I'ma get with you, a'ight. I got to catch up on what I missed so I might be busy, but that don't mean I'm absent. I'm coming back to you, just wait to hear from me."

She was so hung up on his every word that she felt queasy a little. She could feel him finessing the common sense right out of her.

"You trust me?" he asked.

"I don't know you, babe. It bothers me that I'm in love with a stranger," she answered honestly. "It scares me."

"I don't want you to do nothing you don't want to. I don't want your fear, Bird. I can't do nothing with that," he replied. There was still a space between them, and Charlie knew it was intentional. She looked down at the inches between them. It felt like a canyon.

"You want to touch me, don't you?" he asked.

"I'm trying hard not to," she replied.

"Say, man," he said, a little lost for words.

"Say, man," she replied, just as lost.

"I'd like to head out without feeling the need to take another shower if that's okay with you," he said.

She scoffed.

"I'm in love with you," she said.

"You sure about that?" he asked.

Shock took over her face. "What's so unlovable about you? I know what I feel."

"If you're sure, then a nigga got to give that vibe back. That's the expectation. That's what you want to hear?" he asked.

"I don't want to hear anything you don't want to say," Charlie replied. "If it's not real, don't give it to me. I only want what's true," she said.

"Then you got it, Bird. What's true," he answered. "A nigga in love with you."

He said it so naturally that her eyes widened some before a huge smile melted over her face. "You love me, Demi?" she teased.

"Yeah, here you go," Demi grimaced. "Gone with your bullshit, man." He scratched his temple, unable to contain the stubborn smile that pulled at the corner of his mouth. Demi always led with his head. He was always calculating, always logical. With Charlie, he was leading with straight emotion. It didn't even make sense the way he was taken with this girl. "Get ya ass in the car, Bird."

Charlie obliged but didn't turn her feet inside. She smiled up at Demi.

"I never want to shorten it, okay?" Charlie said, grabbing at his hand and forcing him to bend over to be closer to her face. She kissed him. He didn't like it, but she didn't care.

"Whatever you want, Bird," he agreed. He feared she would talk him into anything her heart desired because he couldn't see himself telling her no to anything.

"I'm serious, Demi. Like, don't ever say 'love you' to me. If it gets to the point where we're so lazy that we have to shorten it to "love you" we can just end it because that's not enough. "I want to know your roots, Demi, not just the flowers. So, when life gets cold, our love won't die," Charlie said.

"All roots, no flowers," he responded. The valet pulled his car up behind hers and Demi tapped her thigh to get her to put them inside. "Let me know when you make it home," he said as he shut the door.

"Will do."

She pulled away and Demi gritted his teeth with bawled fists on top of his head before swinging at the air in angst. He was walking a fine line and he knew it was only a matter of time before things blew up in his face. He would have to figure out how to balance time with Charlie and time at home, because if he had learned nothing these past 48 hours, it was that not having Charlie wasn't an option. The problem was, he couldn't quite see his life without Lauren either. He knew it was wrong, but he promised himself he would try his hardest to make them both happy until he could figure out how to clean up the mess he had made.

CHAPTER 11

"Where were you, Demi?"

The words were the first thing that greeted him as he entered his home. In the 15 years he had lived there, the air had never been so thick.

"Where's D?" he asked. He ignored her question, partly because he didn't like being questioned, but mostly because he needed time to think of how he wanted to respond.

"DJ's with my mom," she said.

"I told you I don't like him over there like that if you not staying. Go get my son, man," he said.

"Where. Were. You?" she asked. Lauren was sitting on the couch with her feet crisscrossed beneath her and a bottle of wine sat on the floor. It was half gone. Kendall Jackson before noon meant she was emotional, upset. The last time she had drank in the middle of the day, she had lost an important client and been fired from the event firm she had been working at for years. Demi had fixed that problem easily. He had put up the money to start her own firm. He was a 50 percent partner and the investment had paid off lucratively. This problem. This heartache, he couldn't fix. He was the root, her root, and he had dug it up and planted it in Charlie's garden so that she could have a bountiful harvest.

"I told you where I was," Demi said.

"No, you gave me some vague bullshit about being out of town and promising to call, but guess who ain't heard from you?"

Demi sighed and put his keys on the table and then walked around the living room to sit in the chair across from her.

"You happy with me, Lo?" he asked. It was a genuine question. He had thought they were happy, before meeting Charlie, before feeling happiness in her presence. He had thought he and Lo were just fine. Now, well, now he didn't know what they were. Comfortable perhaps. Content in the familiarity of one another, but it wasn't happiness. It couldn't be because it was so different than what he had experienced all weekend. Charlie had that shit that made his heart hurt a little when she left him. Leaving her had put a fucking canyon in his stomach.

Lauren chuckled and shook her head. "You were with a bitch. Really, Demi? You were with a bitch? After all these years that's the type of bullshit you on, now? You couldn't just be like a normal-ass nigga and get this shit out in your 20s? You wait until you're 33 to start acting stupid?" she asked.

"Ain't no bitch," He only semi-lied. Charlie wasn't a bitch. She was different than any "bitch" Lauren would ever think to be worried about. She was the opposite of his type. A young woman, younger than anybody he would normally have the patience of dealing with. A beautiful soul that he was fortunate to even cross paths with. Nah, there wasn't a bitch involved at all. Charlie was a gift. A kickstart to his dull existence. He had been getting money too long. He had been in this routine with Lauren for years. Life was on cruise control and Charlie was like pressing the gas pedal all the way to the floor.

"Stop lying, Demi. I called the hotel. I asked for your room. They couldn't give me a room number, but I know you had a room there because they confirmed it," she said.

"You lost your fucking mind? Calling around for me and shit," he muttered. "I had ten rooms there. We had people who needed to be accommodated, Lo. You know the deal."

That seemed to deflate her anxiety some. It made sense enough. He was always accommodating some artist, some star, putting them and their entourage up in a hotel. The lie was solid. He saw relief in Lauren's eyes. He was grateful for it. This didn't feel good to him, holding hurt over her head. Lying. Giving what should have been reserved for her, to someone else. Demi prided himself on being a disciplined man, but Charlie had come along with her chaos and swept him up in her wild. Even the thought of her now in this moment made his chest ache. He wanted her. Demi wasn't used to craving something and then depriving himself of it. He couldn't. He wouldn't. So, he had to keep it one hundred with Lauren and end things. Damn, how could he end this after 15 years?

"You happy?" he asked.

"Demi, why is this relevant? Don't try to change the subject," she argued. "You're deflecting."

"I'm just asking you, Lo. This ain't about nobody else. Just me and you. Are you happy with me?"

"Yes! I'm happy, Demi! So don't use that as some excuse to justify whatever you did this weekend. Like you were doing it for me! Like you were setting me free! I'm happy with you!"

It wasn't the answer Demi wanted to hear and he hung his head and rubbed the back of his neck as stress crept up his back.

"Who were you arguing with in the hallway at the showcase?" Lauren asked.

Demi's chest seized but he was good at poker, the panic never reached his face.

"The girl in the hallway," Lauren kept going.

"Fuck you talking 'bout, man?" he asked.

"Why do you think I showed up? I heard you were arguing in the middle of the event with a girl, Demi," Lauren said.

"That was business," he said. Lied. Demi couldn't believe he was lying. People lied when they were afraid, and shit, maybe he was. Afraid of losing what he had known for so long. Afraid of hurting the woman he had practically raised. They were kids when they had met. She was his family. Yeah, he was scared as shit to lose that. The ringing of his phone and Charlie's name on his screen pulled him to his feet.

"Business," Lauren scoffed. "Is that business too?"

Demi couldn't stop himself from pressing the green button.

"Oh my God! Oh my God! Oh my God!" The sound of Charlie panicking pulled him to his feet.

"Hello?" he answered. Another scream and he was walking

toward the door. "Yo!"

Charlie was crying. He could hear the tremble in her voice and when she said, "I need help. Oh my God..." he grabbed his keys off the table.

"Demi!" Lauren shouted. "Are you serious right now?"

He hung up the phone.

"I got to go, Lo. I told you it's business. I'll be back tonight, and we gon' talk," he said.

Lauren's lip trembled violently. The end of their relationship was near. They both could feel it. It hurt. It was impossible to wrap their minds around because they never thought they would see this day.

"Stop the drinking Lo," he said, removing the bottle from the floor. "Go get DJ and bring him home. I'll be back."

It was all he could say before he rushed out of the house.

"Oh my God! Thank you so much for coming! I'm freaking out!" Charlie said as Justin hopped out of his jeep.

"Don't worry about it," Justin said, laughing. "Where is it?"

"I couldn't even get in my apartment because it's right by the door handleeee," Charlie whined. She wiggled her body and shook her hands because it felt like something was crawling all over her.

"Where your keys, girl? You're dramatic as hell," he said, laughing.

Charlie handed him her house keys and then stood behind him as he walked up her porch steps.

"Oh shit, this motherfucka is big," Justin said. He took some spare mail from her porch and used it to smash the spider.

Charlie's unreasonable fear dissipated.

The sound of bass pulled her attention and her heart stalled when she saw Demi's car pull up.

"Umm, thank you, Justin," she answered. "Just ummm. Thanks. I owe you. You saved my life."

Justin snickered.

"Yeah, Charles. You owe me, a'ight," he said, winking. "I'll see you at the club."

He walked off as Demi exited his car and approached her.

"What are you doing here?" she asked.

"Interrupting, apparently," he said, his tone deadly.

"Kinda, you are, yeah," she answered, a little irritated at the fact that he had an attitude. "I told you Justin is my friend..."

"You called my phone fucking hollering at the top of your lungs. I thought something was wrong," he said.

"I did what?" she asked. She grabbed her phone and noticed she had indeed dialed him. "It must have dialed you by mistake when I dropped my stuff. There was a spider. I was freaking out and..."

"That nigga was here with you?" he asked. "I just left you, now he here?"

Demi's disdain laced his tone and Charlie was taken aback by his passive aggression.

"No, I called him, and he came to kill it for me, otherwise I would have never gone inside again," she said.

"Okay, Bird," he said, turning back for his car.

"Hey! Don't walk away from me all mad. You're tripping," she argued, going after him.

He spun on her. "Do you know what the fuck I was doing before I came here? What I had to drop to get to you!" he barked.

Charlie's brows lifted. "I didn't ask you to drop shit! So, fuck you and whatever it is you're so pissed about missing!" she turned to walk into her house, but he grabbed her wrist, pulling her back.

She pushed him and pulled away, but Demi pulled her back. It was like holding onto an iron, but he didn't let her go.

He gripped her face so tightly that her jaws pushed in and her lips pouted as he stared intensely at her.

"You call me, you understand me?" he asked as he backed her up into her apartment. Bails came running to the front door, barking and tripping them up as they made their way inside. Charlie nodded and he kissed her lips. First-degree burn. His lips tingled a bit. "Call another nigga over here and see don't I fuck you up." A second-degree burn as he kissed her again.

"I was trying not to be clingy, babe," she said, her eyes stinging.

"Be clingy, Bird," he said, loosening his grip, but now she was tightening hers, around his neck as she gazed up at him. "Cling to me, baby."

Kiss three. Third-degree burns. He felt it in his body as his kiss took her down to her couch.

"He's just my friend, Demi," she said.

"If you want to keep him breathing, stop playing with me, Bird," Demi said. He was dead serious.

"You can't possess the wind, Demi. I blow where I want to," she said. "I have people in my life that were here before you and they're not going anywhere."

She was defensive, stern like she wasn't willing to lose anyone to gain him.

He gave her space, swiping a hand down his goatee as he thought about what she said.

"I don't want you to cut me off from everything and everybody I love. I just want you to be here too. I don't want to lose myself in you, babe. I don't want to be your everything. I don't want that much pressure from anybody. I just want to be something to you, not everything, not your whole world, just a piece of it," she explained. Demi was lost on the concept of doing this with her at half-mast. She wanted him to dial it back, turn down the heat a little. Could he? If he was going to half-feel Charlie, he could just keep Lauren. He already half loved her. Charlie was different because she made his whole heart work, she made it race, she made his skin burn. She touched him. "I mean, you have people, right? I would never tell you to get rid of your people for me," she said.

It was then and there that Demi decided not to leave Lauren. Charlie wouldn't even stop a random nigga from coming around for him and here he was having sit-downs with the mother of his child for her.

Fuck you doing? Get your head on straight, he thought. He stood, hiking up his pants.

"Yeah, Charlie. You got it. I'ma get out of here so you can call your *people* back. Do whatever you want to do," he said.

"Babe," she called after him as he stood. Demi was irritated at the innocence in her tone, as if he were asking too much, as if she were confused about why he was leaving. He ignored her and kept it pushing toward the door. "Demi!" He didn't say another word. He walked out and Charlie let him.

CHAPTER 12

Lauren Sky sat in the stands with her eyes on the 40-yard line as she watched her son's team practice their drills. She remembered not too long ago it had been Demi she had cheered on as he ran touchdowns for the University of Michigan. That's how long they had known one another. College sweethearts. Those days had been amazing. She remembered how good it had felt to be under his arm in the student union as they soaked up those college vibes. They had been so in love then. She was still in love, but Demi, she knew he had fallen out of love a long time ago. She had made the mistake of cheating when they were younger, and he had never quite forgiven her. He said he had. He had even gone on to marry her, but somehow, she knew he had only done so because she had given him a son. Demi was loyal like that. She had given him someone to love for life and a ring had been her reward for that.

Lauren loved her family more than life. They had tried for a long time to expand it, trying for a little girl, doing everything they could to have another baby. They had been through IVF and all, but nothing had worked and as DJ aged, they had grown further and further apart. They didn't hate one another. She was sure he still loved her, but their life had become one predictable routine. A routine she cherished, but one she could tell was redundant to Demi.

"DJ's looking good out there!"

She smiled as she watched one of the other mother's make her way up the bleachers.

"Hey, Alani. Yeah, he's been working hard. Eazy's taking to it pretty good," Lauren said. "He's such a sweet boy."

"That's my baby. I'm surprised he likes football at all. I made him try it just to get him off that game and get him out and interacting with other kids, but he loves it. All he does is toss around a ball all day with his daddy, practicing the playbook," Alani said, smiling.

Lauren admired the woman before her. Her smile lit up the entire field. She knew a woman in love when she saw one. She used to smile that way with Demi. She could see the difference in their relationships. When Alani and her husband would come to practices and games, they always sat close, cheering their son on and Lauren would notice the little ways they loved on one another. Whether it was a shared pretzel that Alani would feed to her husband or the way he would carry her purse. Sometimes, they would have twin toddlers with them, and they were just the perfect family. When Demi came, he stood at the sideline, cheering DJ on and chopping it up with the coach. He barely acknowledged her until the end when it was time to walk her to her car. Lauren had never compared her relationship to others, but she couldn't help but admire Black love when it was evasive.

"I'm glad. If he ever needs a friend to practice with, he's always welcome over at the house," Lauren said. "You too, I mean, if you ever just want to have a glass of wine..." she paused as Alani looked down at her bulging belly. "After the baby, of course," Lauren added.

"Yeah, we could arrange something," Alani added.

Lauren felt like she was being awkward, forcing conversation because normally she didn't say two words to anyone at these games. Besides hellos and goodbyes, she didn't interact with the other mothers. Commotion on the field caused Lauren to shift her eyes back to her son.

When she saw the tussle between DJ and one of his teammates, she arose from her seat. The coach's whistle blared as he rushed out to the field to break up the scuffle. Lauren wasn't far behind him.

"DJ!" she shouted.

"Hey, hey, hey!" the coach said, as he pulled the two kids apart.

"He's garbage, man! He dropping every pass, Coach Ny!" DJ shouted. "I'm sick of this dirt team!"

"Hey! DJ!" Lauren protested.

The coach turned to her. "I got it," he said. He turned to her son. "DJ, give me 15 laps," he said.

"This is bull..."

"Finish that sentence if you want to and watch what happens, DJ," Lauren said, pointing a warning finger at him.

He gritted his teeth and began the laps as the coach blew his whistle.

"Let's call it," he said, disappointment in his tone as his

eyes followed her son around the field. "A'ight, get in here, get in here. Keep it G on three..." The group of boys huddled together, joining their fists in the middle of the circle. "One. Two. Three."

"Keep it G!"

Lauren smiled because she knew the phrase meant, "Keep it Godly." He was a man of God. Ax ex-football star but also a pastor.

"I'm so sorry, Coach Ny," she said.

"You good, Queen," he replied. "He been different lately, though. A little aggressive. Everything good with him?"

Lauren shrugged. Her growing son had everything. He didn't even realize how privileged he was, but she and Demi worked hard to give it to him. They weren't always as present as they'd like to be because, in order to maintain the lifestyle they had given him, they had to work. "I think so," she answered. "I just feel like I can't keep up with these changing moods. Between him and his father..." She caught herself. She was talking too much.

"Yeah, well, I'll straighten him out on the field, don't worry about it," Nyair replied.

"Thank you," Lauren said, folding her arms across her chest as she watched her son run. "You really mean a lot to these boys. You're like a celebrity around here."

"That's old news, man," Nyair said, smiling sheepishly. "I ain't been in the spotlight like that in a long time."

"Yeah, well, us little people remember it," Lauren said as she kicked at the grass nervously.

Nyair smiled, rubbing the side of his face as his dimples deepened.

"I'm not that guy no more. That guy had a lot going on. I'm just trying to do sum'n different," Nyair replied.

"Different is good," Lauren answered.

Lauren had to force herself to look away. Nyair was a beautiful man but not her man. Her man didn't have two words for her these days. It made her seek something elsewhere. Here. In her son's coach. She had never felt so pathetic.

"How your old man doing? He usually pulling up for practices," Nyair said. She was grateful for the shift. She was sure he'd done it on purpose because the interaction was bordering on flirtatious.

"He's good. Just working," she said, making excuses for Demi's sudden absence lately.

"Yeah, well, tell him don't forget to put his work in at home. Money's good, but if you lose the shit you working hard for, it defeats the purpose," Nyair said. "He don't want to do that. It's a man's biggest regret," he said, voice changing ever so slightly, letting Lauren know he was speaking from experience.

"Demi's a learn the lesson the hard way kind of guy," Lauren said.

"That's too bad," Nyair replied, as he thumbed his bottom lip while staring at her.

DJ ran over to them, panting and out of breath as Nyair rustled the top of his head. "No more picking fights with teammates. You save the frustration for the field and you take it out in your routes, you hear me?" Nyair grilled.

"Yeah, Coach," DJ replied, chip still on his shoulder.

"So sorry about that. I'll have his dad talk to him," Lauren promised.

"It's all love, Ms. Lauren," Nyair answered.

"Have a good night," she said.

She put her arm around DJ, and he sulked as they made their way to the car.

"Why did you hit Chance, DJ? Isn't he your friend?" she asked, brow dipping because her son was brooding. She could see the attitude he was clinging to.

"He was acting like a baby. Doing more bragging about his stupid dad than playing ball. He was dropping every pass, Ma!"

"I don't care if he dropped a million passes, you know better than to put your hands on other people. I don't mind you defending yourself but I'm not raising a bully," she chastised. "What is going on with you?"

"Nothing," DJ answered.

She left it alone until they were inside her car, but the look of discontent on his face nagged at her soul.

"It doesn't seem like nothing," she said.

"Why didn't dad come? He said he was coming," DJ complained.

The reason for his foul mood became crystal clear. DJ was upset with Demi.

Their bad moods were caused by the same source. Demi was distracted. Missing dinners, missing practices, taking away time from them. She felt her son's discontent because, hell, it was her own, but she could never and would never add fuel to that fire. She would never turn her son against his father and use his discontent as ammunition.

"Daddy's working, DJ. You know he would be here if he could. Nothing's more important than you. You know that," Lauren said, reaching over to rub the back of her son's neck.

"Yeah, right," DJ replied.

Lauren felt helpless. There were certain things a mother couldn't give her son. She could love him. She could nurture him. She could kiss away his aches and pains and wish away his nightmares in the middle of the night, but she couldn't teach her baby boy how to be a man.

"Your father loves you," Lauren said. It was all she could say because she was burning with anger.

She held the steering wheel so tightly her hands hurt as she sped home. They pulled into the driveway and she threw her car in park.

"When your dad gets home, he's going to be talking to you about that attitude," she said. "I know him, and if you're honest about what's upsetting you, he'll listen. Okay?"

DJ nodded and climbed from the car. She hated the way his shoulders hung as he entered the house. Lauren didn't know what was happening to her life. It was like someone had snapped their finger and cast a spell of discontent over her home. Things were changing. Demi would never admit it, and maybe he didn't even notice it, but Lauren could feel it. The fact that it was now affecting her child made Lauren want to spark a war. She pulled out her phone and dialed Demi, FaceTime, something she never did but had the overwhelming urge to do today. When he didn't answer, every alarm in her body went off. Lauren would have to have a talk with Demi, and it was a discussion that she wasn't sure she was ready for because she feared what would be revealed.

"Hey, Dad. What would happen if you and mom got a divorce?"

The question stopped Demi in his tracks as he bypassed his son's bedroom. He turned and stared into the dark room, only making out the outline of his son's body as he walked inside.

"What's that now?" Demi asked as he pushed into the room, navigating through the dark to have a seat on his son's bed.

"You missed my practice. Chance said the only time his dad started missing his games and stuff is when his dad left his mom," DJ said.

"Tell that lil' nigga, Chance, to stop speaking on your people cuz his little-ass don't know shit," Demi said, slightly perturbed at the notion that was being put into his son's head.

"So you're not getting a divorce?" DJ asked.

"No, son. Sometimes a missed practice is just a missed practice," Demi said. He had borrowed time from his family to spend it with Charlie and he was witnessing the effects of it. "I will never leave you, DJ. You are my son and I love you. I will never not be in your life every day."

"And Ma's life too? Cuz you told me a man takes care of what he loves. So, you got to take care of us both, right?"

"Your mama too," Demi answered. "That will never be your concern. Quit letting other people put ideas in your head. You're a man, you think for yourself, a'ight?"

"Yeah, a'ight, Dad," DJ said.

"Give me some," Demi said, extending his hand and doing the handshake he had made up with his son when he was just three years old. "Get some sleep."

Demi pumped the bottle of hand sanitizer on his way out of his son's room, and as he did something as simple as rub his hands together, he wondered if Charlie would ever know him as well as Lauren. Lauren's entire life had been catered to fit Demi. She accommodated his needs, took care of him. Demi couldn't remember the last time he had touched a load of laundry or cooked a meal. He never even drew his own baths. Lauren was a nurturer. He wondered if his heart was leading him astray. If he was going through a fucking mid-life crisis or something. He was in his early 30s, but he felt every year. He was no longer the young, gunner, mobbing through his 20s, moving weight and getting rich. He was still getting rich, that much hadn't changed, but most nights he spent in bed, relaxing on thousand-dollar sheets, sipping a sidecar, and watching old episodes of *Shark Tank* while Lauren painted her toenails. That had become their routine. A successful, power couple that was seemingly legit despite his ties to the streets. He wondered if the thrill of Charlie was some kind of self-sabotage. Discipline had stopped Demi from falling victim to beautiful women over the years. Charlie had him moving completely out of character.

He came out of his shirt as he stepped into the room where Lauren sat in bed, headscarf on.

Take that fucking shit off, he thought, suddenly finding a problem with what wouldn't have bothered him before. He was the one footing the five-hundred-dollar salon visits every two weeks so he shouldn't have minded her preservation of his money, but Charlie didn't tie up her hair. She left it out and it had quickly become one of his favorite features. He wondered if this is what he and Lauren had been reduced to, the unfair judgement of comparison. His cologne infected the air as Lauren sat there, applying lotion to her arms and hands, legs hiked up beneath the covers, making a tent for her laptop to rest on.

Demi rounded her side of the bed. When she didn't look at him, he knew she was angry. He commanded her chin, and she maneuvered her face out of his grasp. He pulled her back.

Her breath was heavy. Her chest heaved.

"You shower?" he asked.

She nodded.

"We need to talk," she said.

"Turn around."

Her need for conversation became the back burner as Demi took over. His order was so low and rough, like he was angry, like he was ready to work out the aggression that had built up throughout the day on her body. She listened. Lauren always listened. It was one of the things he loved about her. Her compliance. She never made life hard for Demi. Her breasts met the bed, and as his eyes rode the arch of her back, Demi came out of his jeans. Lauren was familiar. He knew every inch of her body. He knew the smell of her. He knew the routine of her. He slapped her ass. Such a rough lover but Lauren moaned in response.

Demi reached for the nightstand, pulling open the drawer to find a condom. He was hitting Charlie without protection and he barely knew her. No way could he do the same with Lauren. It was insane. It was as if Charlie and Lauren's roles were reversed. Somehow, Charlie had become a priority in his soul. Lauren didn't protest. They had opted for condoms a year ago after a bad miscarriage had taken an emotional toll on Lauren. Ever since, she wanted to be careful. That was the excuse she gave but Demi knew that she was simply afraid to take another loss like the one they had suffered. He wondered if it was during that grief that they had lost their connection as well because there had been a time when he would never have stepped out on her. Oh, how times had changed.

"Oh my God," she whispered as he entered her.

Demi was the type of man you ran from in bed. His dick was lethal, and as he reached for her hands to trap them behind her back, he felt her legs trembling. He was too much for her, but she took it like a champ as he fucked her to a slow rhythm. He hated that the rhythm was of a song he had Charlie sing. He couldn't get her out of his head. Even in this moment, she invaded his thoughts. It wasn't even Lauren beneath him. He saw Charlie and his stroke deepened as the tip of him weakened, throbbing.

He bit down on his bottom lip to stop himself from calling out. Lauren had always been amazing in bed. Since he had met her during her freshman year of college, and had talked her out of her panties on New Year's Eve after a party she was too young to be at, and he was too gangster to be in. He had been inside her since and Lauren had been running from dick ever since.

Lauren came in minutes. He always outlasted her, and she became a lazy lover after she got hers.

"Oh my God," she moaned again. "Babyyyyy."

He hated that Charlie was in his head while Lauren was beneath him. Thoughts of how she clung to him in bed, hell, how she clung to him all the time because Charlie didn't give a damn about his boundaries. He came home to fuck his wife and remind himself that she was whom he should be loyal to. That whatever other nigga that was in Charlie's life was not his concern because his concern was here in this home, in his bed, sliding on his dick. It didn't work, however. Nothing worked. Demi had tried to get her out of his system. He had attempted to stay away, but distance only drove him crazy. Jealousy had sent him home to Lauren, but as looked down at Lauren, guilt seized him because he wanted to be somewhere else. Sex was just sex with Lauren. It was physical, and as he watched his dick split her river, he acknowledged that it was phenomenal, but sex with Charlie had been mental. It was so emotional it choked him. It was intimate and filthy because there was no controlling the room, there was no pinning of her hands. Charlie touched him... everywhere, inside and out. Now that he had experienced her, he wasn't sure if he and Lauren had ever done anything more than fuck. It was always about the orgasm at the end of the road. His OCD gave him a preference. He always chose to hit her from the back, so that her hands couldn't take liberty over his body. One night with Charlie and he had given her the key. They switched positions so many times he had lost count and her hands were everywhere, leaving fingerprints on his soul like he was made of glass. He was dirtied up and traces of her were all over him, even in this moment.

He put bawled fists into the sheets as his last strokes went so deep that they leveled Lauren.

"Demi, what you do to me," she moaned as he pulled out orgasm number two. It wasn't unordinary. Demi was masterful in bed. They were excellent together in every aspect of their lives, but it was a muted feeling, a comfort that had kept them steady over the years. She was the roots to his tree and Demi felt like shit for straying. She hadn't done a single thing to deserve it. He met her at the finish line and then disposed of the condom before moving directly to the shower. Maybe he could wash off his guilt. Maybe the water, the heat of it, could sterilize the wrong, flush his sins down the drain, but as soon as it hit his skin, he thought of her. The shower was like their bedroom. They had sex there more than the bed and images of her doing the same things for another man caused Demi to bite down on his bottom lip so hard he tasted blood.

Lauren entered the steamy box and he turned to her.

"You've been different, Demi. Something's changing and I don't like it. I don't want it. DJ got into a fight today at practice," she said.

"He did what?" Demi stopped washing his body as he locked in on her. His son had never been in a fight a day of his life. He wasn't even that type of kid, so the news rocked him. "Who the fuck touched my son, Lo?" he asked. His voice held no amusement. He had spent most of his childhood fighting. His son would not. He'd put hands on some kid's daddy to drive the point home before he allowed anyone to hurt his kid.

"He started the fight, Demi," Lauren informed as she dipped her hair under the stream of water.

"He did what?" Demi asked, angered at the thought of his son bullying someone else. DJ knew better. Demi had taught him better. He wasn't raising a punk, but he wasn't raising an antagonist either.

"He wanted you there Demi. He was pissed because you missed his practice. You're not checked into this family lately. What's going on with you?" Lauren asked. "It feels like I need to be worried. There's this nagging feeling in my gut and I can't ignore it. When it gets to the point where my son is feeling it, I have a problem with that."

Demi didn't blame her. In fact, he loved her for it. A mother who would stand up for his kid even when he was the enemy. He loved the fuck out of her for that. He took her chin between the tips of his fingers. Her eyes misted a bit, and he knew she was holding onto her pride, trying her hardest not to be weak for him, for anyone because Lauren prided herself on being strength wrapped in femininity.

"What is happening to us?" she whispered. "Do you not love me anymore?"

"I'ma love you until I die, Lo," he responded. It wasn't a lie. It would never be a lie. No matter who came into his life, she would never lose her value. Lauren was his family. Charlie had proven today that he was a casual choice for her. She had her options open. Demi couldn't turn his back on a woman who had been a constant in his life for one who considered other men over him.

"Then what is going on with you?" she asked.

"It's nothing. On life, it's nothing," he answered. On life. It was the one thing he based promises on when he wanted others to believe him because he knew how valuable life was. He had learned the hard way when a nigga he had beef with had put a bullet in his back. It had taken him three months to open his eyes. Lauren had given birth to his son while he was in a coma, and when he finally came to, she had demanded he exit the streets, or she would take his son and leave. He and Day started the LLC for their record label a day after he came to. He had never really turned away from the street, he had simply elevated, cleaning real street money with fake rappers who wanted to pretend to live the life he did for real. The record label was enough to make Lauren stay. It was a comfortable lie that helped cover his dangerous truth. Demi was an entrepreneur, not a made nigga. At least that's the story he let Lauren tell because anyone who knew the rules of the game knew that there was never an exit, never a clean break. Demi just learned to hide it. He couldn't say he didn't love her. He did. Her standard had saved him, had forced him to grow up. Yeah, he loved Lauren. Charlie had his attention. He had tried to revoke it, normally in anger. Demi was off it, impatient with women who defied him, but somehow, she got him to move in ways he never had before. Even still, Lauren was his family. Charlie was young and she had proved she was about the games. He wouldn't and couldn't abandon the woman who had been at his side from day one. His guilt was between them like a witness in the room.

"I ain't gon' miss another practice, a'ight? That'll ease your mind?"

She nodded. "For starters."

Demi had never been a have your cake and eat it too type of man, but in that moment, he knew he wouldn't leave his wife. He couldn't guarantee that he would let Charlie go either. She had sparked an interest that he couldn't shake. He didn't know if it was her vibrancy or if it was just her ability to make him not give a fuck, but Demi fucked with Charlie the long way. He had never put himself in a position to indulge in multiple women, but Charlie was young, and she was wild... free... she wasn't allowing him to lock her down. She didn't even act like she wanted to be his. To risk his entire life to have this new thing with Charlie was foolish. He knew it was. As he inhaled the familiar scents of the home Lauren had made him, he told himself he wouldn't abandon it... or her.

I got to put the brakes on Bird, he said to himself. *I got to keep it real friendly over there. I got too much to lose.*

Demi laid in bed, heart empty, head full. He preferred to process things in that way. With his head and not his heart. Logic overruled emotion and he was okay with that. Lauren laid beside him, the silhouette of her body beneath the white sheets was brilliant. She slept peacefully but Demi was wide awake. He held his phone in one hand, mindlessly thumbing through his timeline, praying that social media took away his real-life problems. It only led him back to them, however, because he found himself on her page. Her page simply read.

Let a real nigga live.

Stubborn. Demi was a stubborn-ass nigga. He fought an entire war in his soul to stop himself from smirking. He didn't want to be amused by it, but he was entertained. It was the whole doe-eyed, golden skin, golden locs vibe for him. Charlie caused hell for him just by existing. Her eyes captured him as he clicked on the first picture. She was the oddest girl. Most women wore the least, did the most, to grab attention but Charlie literally just threw shit on and shined. She never matched, her shit was always wrinkled, and her little chicken legs didn't have no meat on the bone, but damn if Demi didn't want to suck the bone dry. Even now, even when he was mad, the fucking blonde pineapple on top of her head, and her smoldering eyes made his dick hard. The little green light that glowed next to her name invited him to her DM.

Silent treatment was a punishment with Charlie. Icing her out was torturing him more than her it seemed. If her pictures were any indication, she wasn't thinking about him. Unwilling to extend the first form of communication and trying to honor the promise he'd made to Lauren, he left without sending a message. He clicked on her story and her voice hit his air pods. Charlie sang everything. She hummed all the time. Old nursery rhymes, radio joints, sometimes when people got on her nerves and she was trying to stop herself from snapping on them. She spoke in song and her entire story was an impromptu musical, something about the grocery store not having ripe avocados. She had made the grocery story her stage. She fucking warmed him. He hated it.

On my fucking nerves, man.

His thoughts were lies. He knew it. She was on his heart. An uncontrollable desire. He ran the story video back five times before frustration pulled him from the bed.

"Fucking girl," she grumbled, leaving the room, phone in hand, as he went to take a piss. He hated how his dick reacted at the thought of her. Heavy in hand, he relieved himself then washed his hands before making his way to the family room. When he saw the message icon appear in the upper right-hand corner of his page he opened it.

TheCharlieShow

Her name fit her because he was tuned the fuck in. The video she dropped in his inbox made his dick go brick. Her pretty yellow fingers on her pretty pink button. Demi sat up on the couch as energy coursed through his veins.

Goddamn, he thought.

Charlie fingered herself for him, focusing on her clit, playing in that pussy so deep that Demi licked his bottom lip.

Pretty mu'fucka.

His head was in the gutter. Whatever loyalties he had just professed went out the window.

"I know you want me, babe," she said. He did. "Rub your dick, Demi."

Demi didn't, but he was locked in on the screen. If she kept playing with him, he was coming to bust it down. Mad or not. He had a condition and Charlie was the cause and the cure. Charlie pushed into herself. Her middle and ring finger disappeared while her thumb circled the wettest clit he'd ever seen. Her labia was brown and shiny from her silky juices and that little button that was growing by the second was pink. Charlie had a pink Starburst between her legs and Demi was dying to eat it. Before he knew it, he was rubbing his dick through his hoop shorts.

"I miss you. I know you're mad at me but I like mad sex, babe. I'm so fucking wet for you, Demitrius," she moaned. The little pink vibrator that came into frame made Demi tighten his ass cheeks as he leaned back on the couch. With his hand around himself, he stroked as she placed it to her clit. She bucked as the little toy went to work, obliterating her button, buzzing on it, as she rubbed it all over her sex.

His thumb circled the head of his dick. Charlie had him on some other shit with her young antics. His blood was racing.

"Fuck, Demi baby, I'm cumming. I wish I was on that dick, Demi. Come give it to me," Charlie moaned. "God, I need it. Unnn... Demi!" She screamed as she caught her wave. The way her pussy contracted in the camera and her wetness glistened as it poured, Demi was pulled in. So hard he couldn't stop his hand from pumping his flesh as he clicked out of the app and FaceTimed her.

"I want you," she said as soon as she answered. "Look how wet she is."

Demi lost his mind. "You playing, Bird," he whispered. "Look what you got a nigga over here doing. Childish shit. I want to be in that pussy and you got niggas at your crib."

Demi showed Charlie his dick and she moaned. "Keep doing that," she said. "Baby, stroke it. God, Demi, I'm going to cum again. Just from hearing your voice."

"Fucking playing," he throated. Demi hadn't beat off in years. Lauren fucked him on the regular. He didn't have to, but damn it if this young-ass girl didn't have him out here like a fucking lovesick teenager.

"Let me see, Demi," Charlie ordered. He shifted the camera and Charlie moaned. "Demi, I'm right there. I'm so close. Take me there, babe. Fuckkk, Demi, I need youuuu."

Demi fucking erupted. The sound of her fuck sounds as she came all over her fingers made him explode.

She giggled and he groaned. He had never felt this much shame and behind that rested guilt, but damn it also felt fucking refreshing. Charlie was helium to his deflated existence. Air. Charlie was air.

"One second, Bird," he said, setting down the phone as he pulled off his shirt to use it to clean himself up. The way he had spilled out, you would think he hadn't had sex in months. It was just her. Charlie turned him the fuck on.

He picked the phone back up.

"Sex with you is amazing," she said, blushing as she put a hand up to her red face, smiling in embarrassment.

"Is that what you call it?" he asked.

"Phone sex counts," she replied. "I want to fuck you everywhere in every way, all the time," Charlie said. "So be ready."

It was the "be ready," for him. He had to chuckle as he shook his head in amusement.

"A nigga always ready for that," he answered.

This young-ass girl, he thought.

"Say, man," Demi said, voice low as his eyes darted to the hallway. Charlie made him reckless.

"Say, man," she repeated. "I'm in love with you."

He nodded. His conscious ate him alive because no way should he be feeling this, doing this, with her, after the promises he had made to Lauren mere hours ago.

"Yeah, Bird. It's safe to say, I'm in love with you, kid." Demi leaned over onto his knees and scratched the top of his head. Stressed. Demi was stressed. "This ain't good, baby."

She shrugged. "So, let's be bad."

CHAPTER 13

Lauren awoke to an empty bed and pulled herself from the sheets. Bare feet tested the temperatures of the hardwood floors as she searched for him. She knew where he'd be. The home gym at the crack of dawn was a routine. It was a necessity for Demi, because if he didn't work out his aggression, he'd be volatile all day. She knocked on the door frame, announcing her presence, admiring him as he gritted his teeth while bench pressing a set.

"You want breakfast?" Lauren asked.

"Nah, you ain't got to do all that. I'll grab something when I take DJ to school," he said.

Demi finished his fifth mile and then powered off the machine. He walked directly by Lauren, only pecking the side of her head before leaving her alone. She didn't know what she felt. Indifference maybe, but something about him made a pit form in her gut. She turned on her heels and followed him. A woman's intuition was a motherfucker because Lauren felt it in her gut that something had changed in the short hours that had passed since they had gone to sleep.

"Demi, is something wrong?" she asked.

Demi turned, pausing, as he stared at her from the other end of the hall. She could tell just from his disposition that something indeed was wrong. She braced herself. The dip in his forehead and the way an invisible weight rested on his shoulders, tensing his entire body, made her heart ache. Definitely something wrong.

"Just say it," she said, almost breathless.

"Lo, there's something I got to tell..."

DJ popped out of his room. "Morning, Ma. 'Sup, Dad!" he said. "Aww dang, you worked out without me?"

The interruption sent Lauren's anxiety through the roof.

"DJ, go get ready for school. You can workout at practice. You don't want to be tired for school," Lauren said.

"But Dad said he would help me condition!" DJ protested.

Demi rustled his son's head and pushed him back toward the gym.

"I got you, man," he said.

Lauren couldn't hide her concern. "Demi..."

"Don't worry about it. It wasn't important," he said. "We'll talk later tonight. You got a meeting, right? You got the new girl coming in. You mentoring somebody, right?"

Lauren nodded, hating that he was right. She didn't have time to figure out whatever was going on between them.

"Yeah. Can you stop by my office for lunch?" she asked. "I really want to talk. I want us to be okay."

"I'll pull up, a'ight?"

That settled her nerves some and she nodded before heading to their bedroom to prepare for her day. She and

Demi had been through many storms over the years, but she felt like the biggest one yet was approaching. She'd be damned if she let it blow down her home.

"Show me that punch you hit the kid with yesterday," Demi said as soon as he entered the gym. He bent down to grab the training gloves he had and tossed a set to his son.

"I thought I was in trouble for fighting?" DJ exclaimed.

"For bullying. A man gon' have to fight in his life sometime. When the time comes, I need you to know how. Put them dukes up, li'l nigga," Demi said, tapping the side of his son's head.

"Hold up! I wasn't ready!" DJ's protests pulled a chuckle from Demi.

"You think niggas always run up when you ready? It would be nice but it don't work like that. You stay ready so you ain't got to get ready, boy. Hands up," Demi schooled.

Demi put his pads on and lifted his hands. "Let's get it. One, two," Demi said. His son threw two rooted punches and Demi tagged his ass.

"Move them feet," Demi said. "You keep your feet stuck to the ground like that and you'll get knocked out."

"You ever been knocked out, Dad?" DJ asked.

"A nigga ain't never touched your daddy. Your daddy put niggas to sleep, homie. Now, let's go," Demi said.

He spent an extra hour training his son before showering and getting him to school. He was late, always late to school when it was Demi's turn to drop him off, but the lessons he learned along the way, no school could ever teach. It was their time. Father and son. Demi wondered if those times would be fleeting if he did what he was thinking of doing. Leaving Lauren.

Demi wasn't a cheater, at least he tried not to be. He took no joy in lying to women, especially his woman, and Lauren indeed held that spot. Some men got a kick out of deceiving a woman, out of making a fool of her, out of making them believe one thing when reality was the opposite, but Demi thought it was bitch shit. If a man could sleep next to a woman and lie to her, be disloyal to her, the woman who provided a home, he could do anything. Demi didn't trust niggas who didn't have a code, who hurt the person who loved him most. If a man could betray his woman, he could for damn sure put a bullet in his back. How he had become a betrayer of women, he didn't know, but he had to make a choice. Time wasn't enough to keep him with Lauren. Or was it? It should be. Consistency over years was better than passion in the moment, right? His dilemma wasn't easily solved. Conflict lived in him because he couldn't explain this sudden need for Charlie that had transpired in the blink of an eye. He knew the conversation couldn't wait. He didn't know if he needed a break or if he wanted to end it altogether. All he knew was that he was headed to see Charlie and if he did it without letting Lauren know where he stood, he would be digging a deeper grave for himself, one that he would eventually have to climb out of.

Stassi sat in the plush lobby, admiring the style of the office. She held her portfolio in her hands and tapped her foot against the plush carpet, a nervous habit.

Traitor. She was a motherfucking traitor. She had a growing pit in her stomach that had been present ever since the showcase. The fact that she was sitting there knowingly interviewing for a position with Demi's wife made her feel like shit. Charlie would never hold that type of information. She knew it, but Charlie also didn't have as much to lose. Stassi was elevating in her career, chasing her dreams.

Charlie's a mess. She's singing in bars for tips. She wouldn't understand what this means to me. This is a once in a lifetime opportunity. I shouldn't have to turn it down because of her drama, Stassi thought.

"Anastassia, Mrs. Sky is ready for you."

Stassi looked up at the assistant. Even she shined like money. Anybody attached to Lauren Sky eventually blew up and became their own brand. Stassi wanted parts.

She stood and rubbed the wrinkles out of her dress, the same dress she had worn for every important event in her life, praying that it brought her good luck. Stassi followed the woman to a conference room. Lauren sat at the head of the table and she was stunning in a Louis Vuitton dress that Lauren recognized from ogling the website.

"Hi, Anastassia, thank you for coming in," Lauren said, smiling.

"Thank you for having me, and please, it's just Stassi," she replied.

"Stassi it is then," Lauren replied. "Can I get you a mimosa or anything?"

"No, I'm fine, but thank you," Stassi answered. Butterflies danced in her stomach as she tucked her hair behind her ears. "I'm so honored to even be interviewing with you."

"Day speaks highly of you and he doesn't speak highly of anyone." Lauren laughed. "You're a challenge for him and anyone who challenges Day is someone I need to meet."

Stassi laughed.

"I take it that's your portfolio. I'd love to take a glance at some events you've done," Lauren said.

Stassi handed the folder to Lauren. "I don't have as much experience as you, but I have been building a pretty reliable clientele. The event that probably put me on the map is the Okafor baby shower. I was the co-planner on that event, and I've gotten a lot of business from the guests."

"Oh, yeah! I heard it was beautiful! My son plays football with Alani's baby boy. I've seen the pictures. Great work," Lauren complimented. "I'd love to bring you on. I pay a salary and offer a twenty-five percent commission on business you bring in. Of course, it's easier to bring in business under my umbrella because we have the reputation and established brand."

"I'd love to work here. You're not much older than me but you're so established. You're respected by all the celebrities. You're practically an influencer all on your own. I want that to be my brand one day," Stassi said.

"Well, you're on your way. You're doing something right to have Day call in this type of favor, but honestly, you didn't need him to. Your work speaks on its own," Lauren said.

Stassi had never felt this type of pride in her work. Her grind was beginning to pay off and it felt amazing. Lauren didn't even seem like a bad person.

I deserve this job. This has nothing to do with Charlie.

Only, it had everything to do with Charlie, and she was sick to her stomach because she knew one day the shit would hit the fan.

"Mrs. Sky, I'm sorry to interrupt, but you're needed."

Stassi looked up at the assistant and then over to Lauren. "Oh, I mean, we can cut this short. I know you're busy. Thank you for looking at my stuff."

"I appreciate you for stopping in. You're absolutely hired. Let's get your documents together with McKinley and you can start as early as tomorrow. She'll show you your office and explain the benefits package to you," Lauren said.

Stassi had never felt so accomplished. She followed Lauren back to the front and her stomach bottomed out when she saw Demi waiting for her.

If he recognized her, he didn't let on, but Stassi's eyes grew wide at first sight.

"Hey, baby," Lauren said greeting him.

The hand to her hip and Lauren's kiss to his cheek told a story of comfort, a story of intimacy.

Oh, you dirty-ass nigga, Stassi thought.

"Can we go somewhere?" Demi asked, hardly looking her way.

"Yeah, we can go to my office," Lauren said. "Hey, I want you to meet my new coordinator. This is Stassi. Stassi this is my husband, Demi."

When Demi finally met Stassi's eyes, she saw the shift, the slight inkling of recognition.

"We've met, right?" Stassi asked. "At the showcase."

Demi scoffed but didn't even acknowledge her.

"Handle your business then get with me," Demi said.

Stassi watched him walk out and turned to Lauren feigning confusion. "I'm sorry, did I say something wrong?"

Stassi shook her head. "No, Demi just doesn't like new people. The fame requires us to keep our circle close."

Not close enough if he's stepping out with my sister, Stassi thought. She was straddling a line and as she watched Demi climb into his car, she prayed her sister didn't get hurt.

The knock on her door pulled Charlie from her restless sleep and she frowned in irritation as she climbed out the bed. Bails was right at her feet, accompanying her to the door. He was too loveable to be a guard dog. He was emotional support. Her companion when she felt alone, but he followed her anyway like he would do something to this mystery guest for interrupting Charlie's sleep.

"Who is it?" she asked, irritated as the oversized shirt hung off her shoulder and stopped right beneath the cuff of her ass.

"Quality Pest Control, ma'am!"

Charlie pulled open the door, perplexed.

"I think you have the wrong house," Charlie said.

"Is Demitrius Sky here? He ordered the service. Said you guys have been having issues with spiders," the man said.

Charlie was speechless. It was thoughtful. A small deed that showed big intention. She smiled, scoffing.

"Umm... yeah, you can start on this floor. I'm just going to slip on some clothes, grab my dog, and get out of the way. How long will it take?" she asked.

"Not long. About an hour," the man replied.

Charlie turned on her heels. "Come on, Bails," she said, tapping her thigh for him to follow. She threw on jeans and a t-shirt, not caring that she was wrinkled, and brushed her hair into a ponytail. A quick swipe of deodorant, she brushed her teeth, then grabbed Bails' leash before giving up her apartment.

She stepped outside and her heart seized at the sight of Demi sitting on the hood of his car, feet wide and dressed in Gucci sneakers, Gucci hat to match, expensive denim, and a plain t-shirt. More jewelry than an ordinary day required. Presidential. His aura and his watch. Cartier shades and a fucking pinky ring that made Charlie want to ho for him. One man shouldn't be this damn attractive.

It wasn't on him. It was in him. He was attractive in a different kind of way. So damn rough around the edges, but somehow still corporate, still a boss, still an executive but the hood in him shined, no matter where he was. Demi was an ugly, fine-ass nigga. With his face tattoos and mean-ass stares. She knew he was still upset with her just from his body language.

She walked toward him, stopping on the sidewalk, giving him his space.

"So you're afraid of spiders," he said. "What else don't I know?"

"What do you want to know?" she asked.

"Your last name for starters," he said. "I called the damn exterminator and couldn't even give them that."

"Woods. Charlize Woods," she replied.

He nodded and finessed the hair on his face.

"I want to take you somewhere, Charlize Woods," he said. "While they spray your spot. You might need a little something other than that wrinkled-ass shirt, though."

Charlie laughed. "You don't like my fashion choices, huh?" she wiggled her eyebrows and struck a couple poses.

He walked around to his back seat and pulled out a bag. Saks Fifth Avenue.

"Go get dressed. Let me spin you around in my passenger seat for a minute, Bird," he said.

"What about Bails? They're spraying. He can't be inside my apartment."

Demi's grimace showed his dislike for her dog, but he knew she wasn't leaving him behind. "Man, at least get a towel or something. Damn dog gon' have all types of bullshit in my back seat."

Charlie beamed. "Give me a minute. Here hold Bails." She took the bag, and he took the leash, looking down at the ground and side-stepping Bails who instantly laid at Demi's feet.

"Dogs know who the pack leader is. He's submitting to you, babe. Embrace it," she teased.

It took Charlie twenty minutes to get herself together. A quick shower and high-waisted denim shorts, with a bralette, and a black blazer. Demi had even gotten St. Laurent strappy heels to match. Light make-up, her locs pinned behind her ear on one side and falling toward her face on the other, and Charlie emerged.

Demi pushed air from his lungs when he saw her. It never failed. Charlie always looked like she was sparkling, like her skin was made of untouched sand, and the sun was shining down on it just right.

"Say, man," he said, patting the left side of his chest like he was beating an old vending machine that had stolen a dollar from him. "You do shit to a nigga, Bird. You don't even be trying," he said, scoffing as he shook his head. He took her hand and held it up so that she could sashay in a circle. She was so damn thin that Demi wanted to pick her up, put her ass right on his dick. It was all he thought of in her presence, but he practiced self-control. "You steal a nigga soul." He admired every angle before snatching her toward him, causing her to fall into his arms. She giggled. Damn. How did her laughter sound like a song?

"I thought it burned," she said, surprised that he was initiating touch.

"I'm learning to let it," he replied. "I fucked up with you last night. You right. I was doing too much."

"I just want this to be healthy, Demi. That's all. I've had enough toxic shit to last a lifetime. I just want this with you to be different," she said.

He should have ended this right then. He couldn't give her healthy love because he belonged to someone else. Eventually, what Charlie thought was bliss would turn to hell, but damn it if Demi didn't want to hold onto what they had for a little while. Ignorance would have to be bliss because no matter what he told himself about creating boundaries with Charlie, she was determined to cross every one. She was on some love shit. He just wanted to oblige.

He bit his bottom lip and then led her to the passenger side. He held open the door and Charlie placed the blanket she carried down on the floor. "Come on, Bails. Daddy's taking us on a date," she said, smiling bright, forcing one of his own as he shook his head.

CHAPTER 14

"You never told me your favorite color," Charlie said. "You know mine, but you never said yours." Charlie liked details and when it came to Demi, she knew very little. They were accumulating big moments, sex mostly, and although that was good, she wanted to get to know him. The trivial things made the grandiose moments make more sense and as they drove up the highway headed toward Detroit, she chipped away at him.

"Black," Demi answered without thinking.

"Black? That's not like a real color," Charlie said, laughing. "That's the color people pick when they don't have a favorite color. It's like a default answer."

"Says you," Demi said. "That's my answer, though."

Charlie's heart fluttered as they rode down the highway, pushing 90 in the 70 zone, but neither cared. He drove like he did everything— fast... it was just the pace of their relationship.

"Black is so sad, though. Like it lacks life. They bury you in black, Demi!" she argued.

"My skin is black, Bird. My mama is black. A nigga heart was black too. It's a little gray now, though, since you," he admitted. "You coming in adding too much color in my space."

"Good," she answered. He heard the satisfaction in her tone.

"Favorite food?" she quizzed.

Demi slouched in his seat, thinking, always overthinking, even at the simplest question.

"I can't answer that yet," he said.

"What? How can you not know your favorite food?" she asked, frowning.

"I ain't had you on my plate yet."

Charlie had to turn her eyes out the window.

"Soon, though. I'ma taste it real soon," he added. The bite to his lip told her he could not wait, and Charlie blushed. He made her feel like she was 16 and this was her first crush. She didn't know if it was their age difference or if he was just out of her league, but Demi made Charlie feel like the prettiest girl in the world. "I bet it's good too." he added.

Her cheeks might as well had gone up in flames.

"You're so mannish," she whispered.

A deep laugh filled the car and her heart at the same time.

"What's the thing in your life that hurt you the most?" she asked.

The entire mood in the car changed.

Demi didn't answer this time. He turned up the music, her choice because Charlie just liked touching shit, his body, his buttons, mental and the ones in the car.

She didn't push because she knew she would also have to share her greatest pain. It was a bad question for someone to answer so soon. She backed off as her playlist filled the car.

She hummed, petting Bails' head which rested between her thighs, as Demi drove. Even his silence felt divine. It was like she had been his girl since forever. This was comfortable.

He lowered the music and she stopped singing.

"Nah, you keep going. I want to hear you sing, Bird," he said.

And so, she did. Humming lazily, as they sped south on I-75.

"If you can show me loveee somehow, we don't need to have a label," she half sang, half hummed. Demi wondered how she did it, how she mastered his emotion every time she sang. How lyrics to random songs fit what he was hiding inside his chest for her. Love with no labels. That's what they were. She didn't want them. He had expected her to.

What kind of bitch don't want to put a label on it? He thought.

It was then he knew Charlie had the upper hand. He cared. She didn't seem to. He was bothered.

They arrived at a high-rise Chrysler building in the middle of Downtown Detroit.

"What's in here?" she asked.

"Birds fly baby. Come on," he said. They exited and Charlie leaned her head against his arm, lacing her arm through his as she dragged Bails to the elevator. They ascended and her ears popped as the open-air elevator gave her a view of the entire city and the Detroit River.

"Wow," she whispered.

The wind greeted them as they stepped off and a helicopter sat on the roof.

Bails began barking at the machine and Charlie turned to Demi.

"I know you don't think I'm getting in that thing," she said. "I hate heights, Demi."

"Spiders, heights, what else? I'm trying to know it all."

Her heart was pounding, and he could see her fear.

"Trust me, Bird. I got you," he said. She nodded and fought the urge to throw up as she walked up the stairs to the helicopter. Demi smacked her ass as she climbed up, but Charlie was too afraid to feel anything other than annoyance. She swatted his hand and then turned to find Bails staring up at her.

"My man, you gon' have to put the dog up there. I don't fuck with the dog thing like that," Demi instructed the second pilot.

The pilot laughed. "No problem, Mr. Sky." The man handed Charlie her dog and Demi climbed up last. They put headphones on, and Charlie braced herself. Holding on to her seat for dear life with one hand and gripping Demi's wrist with the other. She felt the helicopter lift from the building, and she panicked.

"No, Demi, no, no, no, I don't like it," she said.

"Relax, Bird," he said. He placed a hand over the one gripping her wrist and then pulled her into his lap.

"Open your eyes, baby," he said.

Charlie pursed her lips, taking labored breaths.

"Trust ya man, Bird." He almost gritted his teeth after he said it. *Her man.* He was setting the expectation in her heart that he belonged with her. It was a pedestal that he wouldn't stand on long because his situation at home wouldn't allow it. He now regretted walking out of Lauren's office. Her eyes popped open and Charlie was in instant awe.

"Oh my God, Demi!" she exclaimed.

It was incredible. The wind in her hair, the powerful hum of the engine as the blades whipped above them. It was a rush like nothing she had ever felt.

"Can I burn you, babe?" she asked into the headset. The second pilot looked back in confusion as Demi pinched her chin between his fingertips and pulled her lips to his.

"That's some burn," the pilot said, his voice coming through their headsets.

Charlie laughed and Demi replied, "The very best kind, my man."

"I'm in love with you," Charlie said.

"So, act like it," he said. Demi was a grudge holder. The disagreement from the night before was still heavy on his mind. Her choosing of Justin over him. His willingness to choose her over his wife, but her not giving the same energy in return, unnerved him. He was perturbed that she had that much power over him so soon. Not even Lauren could change his mood so easily.

"So, you not gon' say it back?" she asked, jerking her neck back.

"I'm in love with you, man," he said, stubbornly.

"Then act like it, nigga," she snapped, climbing from his

lap and going back to her own seat. Temperamental. Demi and Charlie were finicky as ever. Fucking and fighting. A recipe for disaster.

Their tension kept them silent as the helicopter landed after an hour tour around the city.

Charlie looked out her window to see the catered table and personal waiter that had been arranged on the rooftop. She wanted to go soft, but she was with whatever vibe he was bringing, and he had an attitude, so fuck it.

She didn't even acknowledge the setup as he climbed out the helicopter. When he didn't turn to help her, Charlie's chest flared in rage. She took off her shoe and threw it at his back.

Demi was on her ass, turning, and pulling her from the helicopter as Bails barked like, "Don't forget about me too."

"Don't let your attitude get you fucked up," he threatened.

"You're being mean to me," she said. She was a pout away from splitting his heart wide open. He would have to walk light with this girl. He would fuck around and spoil her in ways he had never imagined spoiling anyone. Charlie would walk all over him whenever they disagreed if she poked her lip out like she was now. It was a secret weapon or something. Demi hated it.

"You fucking that nigga from the club?" he asked.

Oh, the ways men made up shit in their heads. Demi's jealousy could no longer take a back seat.

"If I was, I wouldn't be fucking you," Charlie said. "If I wanted him, I wouldn't be here with hurt feelings over you."

Demi blew out a sharp breath, nostrils flaring, face serious. He looked off to the side. Charlie turned his head back to her. "Stay here with me, babe," she said.

"Your hands, Bird. You been touching every fucking thing." He grimaced.

"Oh my God! Somebody get this weird nigga some sanitizer!" she exclaimed, letting him go and turning toward the helicopter to get Bails.

Charlie turned and Demi was there. In her space. Looming over her. He was so damn intimidating.

"You think I'm a ho or something," she said. "First the doctor's records and now thinking I'm sleeping with Justin. It's hella disrespectful how you keep coming at me."

Demi kneeled in front of her, grabbing her shoe and then placing it on her foot, before standing. He was so close to her that his cologne invaded her space. A magic potion, dizzying her. Demi smelled like he was made of crisp, clean water, bergamot, and money. It was intoxicating and she hated how her heart raced, especially in the middle of a fight because she couldn't stand her ground.

"I'm grown, Bird. I don't even believe in that childish shit, man. What you do with your pussy is your business. Just let me know if you giving the shit away cuz I won't make it my business," he said. It was a rude accusation, but Charlie felt butterflies. His jealousy did something to her, making her stomach flip. She just wanted him to close the space between them and kiss her, manhandle her, anything. A man who didn't trip over anything but tripped over her was the ultimate turn-on. She didn't even know what it was about this man that she liked, but she craved him. His presence was the highlight of her days lately. In the short time she had known him, he had become the best part.

"I'm not giving any part of me away unless it's to you," she assured. "I lowkey don't even want to give it to you. I'm in a stage of my life where I want to be a little selfish with me, but you came out of nowhere making me love you and I can't help it. It's you, Demi. I just..." she shrugged because it was hard to explain. "It's just something about you."

He stood there, staring sternly, facing off with her. Charlie was one of the only people who didn't shrink under his menacing eye. He had met his match. Charlie's young, free-spirited, unorganized soul had claimed his. He was mated. He could pretend to reign, but she was queen, his queen. He was just fighting it. It was so hard to contend.

"Say, man," he said, sighing.

"Say, man," she shrugged.

"Keep that nigga out of your house, Bird," Demi said, sounding defeated like he was tired of thinking about it.

"You can't make the rules in somebody else's house," Charlie said.

She shrugged and walked around him, heading to the table to eat.

Silence.

The rest of the night was filled with silence and Charlie was sick. Fighting with him felt like grief, like she had lost someone dear to her. Demi used silence as a weapon and she hated it, but she wasn't in the business of begging a nigga. If he didn't want to speak, she wouldn't force it, but when he was ready to drop it, she hoped he knew she wouldn't be. She was stubborn that way. Demi might have started this fight, but she would decide how, when and *if* it ended.

He spent the next three hours on his phone, texting, and stepping away for phone calls. They hit a mall, walking in and out of stores without acknowledging each other. Charlie didn't even tell him what she liked. She just threw whatever she wanted on the counter for him to pay for and he did, all the while, typing away in his phone and ignoring her. His calm was the fuel to her anger. They both knew it and she hated it. There was nothing worse than a passive-aggressive man. If they were going to fight, she would rather they scream it out. The ignoring and avoiding was torture. It was a prolonging of pain and manipulation of her feelings. It was cruel and Charlie wanted to take his head off.

By the time they were done with the day, she had already decided they were done.

He can lose my number.

She had never had a worse date. The sex was bomb but the treatment afterward was trash and Charlie wouldn't excuse that in search of an orgasm. As they headed back to Flint, she noticed he sped past her exit.

"Where are you going?" she asked.

He didn't answer.

"That was my exit, Demi," she said.

"I don't need a passenger seat driver, Bird," he replied, tone impatient and eyes straight ahead. It was the first thing he had said to her in hours.

She crossed her arms and pushed back in her seat in frustration. When they pulled up Downtown to the newly-built loft building, Charlie frowned.

"Who lives here?" she said.

"You do, get out," he replied.

There was a woman waiting in the lobby.

"Demi! A little more notice next time would be nice!" she said, smiling as she hugged him.

"My fault. Virginia this is Charlie. Charlie, my realtor, Virginia," he said.

"Well, Charlie, it's nice to meet you. I hope you enjoy the condo," she said. "I just need your signature in a few places."

"What? Demi, what is going on?" she asked, perplexed as Virginia held out a pen for her.

"Sign the papers, Bird. I'ma be upstairs," he said.

Virginia handed him a key. "One for you," she said. Demi walked away.

"Oh, and one for you," Virginia said, giving the second key to Charlie. "The furniture has all been delivered."

"Furniture? What am I even signing?" Charlie asked.

"He bought you a condo. Congratulations," Virginia said. Charlie signed what felt like a hundred pieces of paper before she made her way upstairs. She was stunned. She didn't know what to feel as she used the foreign key in the foreign lock. "Come on, Bails." She walked inside and bent to take Bails' leash off and he took off, to explore the new space. Three thousand square feet of luxury was in front of her. Brand new everything. It even smelled new. She heard the shower running and she headed in that direction.

"What the fuck, Demi?" she shouted as she walked in on him as he climbed out of the shower.

"Bring that nigga in here and they gon' have to zip him up and carry him out," Demi said. "House rules, Bird."

Charlie was floored. He bought an entire property just so he could be the man of her house.

"You ain't got no slick shit to say?" he asked. He was soaking wet, thick brows bent in challenge, dick relaxing against his thigh. Comfortable. How had they gotten this comfortable around one another?

"I've got nothing," she replied, smirking. The nigga wanted to kick up dust in her life, so she was going to let him. She knew when to shut the fuck up and listen. Certain men you just didn't back talk to.

"I got something for you, though," she said. She went into her bag and removed the envelope she had been holding onto. She handed it to him.

"What's this?" he asked as he opened it.

"Negative for every single STD known to man," she said. "I'm healthy, as you can see from my perfect PH balance," she said standing on her tiptoes to point out the number. "I'm sweet. So, what you gon' do about it?"

Demi scooped her up by her ass, growling in her ear, and scaring the shit out of her, causing her to scream and then laugh uncontrollably as he took her straight to the shower. Water on, ripping her clothes off, lust filled the room along with steam as Demi went down on one knee.

"She real pretty, babe," he said, playing with her clit piercing. "You stay wet, Bird."

"I been wet all day for you," she moaned.

He lifted both legs over his shoulders and she leaned against the wall as he pulled her flower in his mouth. Demi didn't play with pussy. He demolished it, those full lips making love to Charlie's clit, wrapping around it, kissing it, sucking, smearing his face in it, flicking it, as he moaned like crazy. The sounds he made. Like he had been starving and she was a meal. Charlie looked down at him, her mouth open in agony because he was torturing her clit, murdering it. He was eating it so good that she felt like she was having an out-of-body experience. Like she was watching a tape of some man doing something to a woman that she wished a nigga was skilled enough to know how to do to her. She was dreaming... fantasizing, in fact, she had to be. No way was this pleasure real. She gripped the top of his head as water poured down over them. His hunger came from wanting to taste her from the very first time he had laid eyes on her.

"Just like I thought it would be, Bird," he said, between kisses to her flesh.

"You fantasize about eating my pussy, Demi?" she asked, eyes fluttering in surprise. "You don't put your tongue in anything wet. That's what you said."

"All day, baby. Every day, since I met you. A nigga lied," he groaned, standing, coming face to face. His tongue entered her mouth. "That's you. That's how you taste, Bird."

The test results were all it took to remove every reservation he had about her. "Turn that ass around." Charlie listened. She would listen for the rest of her fucking life if he was buying condos and eating pussy like his name was the pussy monster. Fuck it. She would submit every day of the week for this man.

Demi entered her from behind and Charlie's hands went to the wall. She was flooded, dripping from the aggressive seduction. It was the stings from the slaps to her ass that took her over the top and she threw it back.

"Fuck, Bird, wait, wait, wait," he said, breathing hard as he pulled out and rubbed her clit. His dick was so damn thick and long that he reached her clit from the back, rubbing it, teasing her entrance as she closed her stance, squeezing his dick as he slid back and forth against her sex. "Fuck, baby, I'm trying not to nut. Damn, girl."

Charlie reached between her legs and forced him back inside.

"Me tooooo, but I can'ttttt," she cried, cumming. Charlie pushed out rapids as she grunted her approval. The sight of her cream all over him made Demi explode. He pulled her waist to his body and filled her with his seeds, grunting and stroking deep until he was empty.

"I'm not on birth control, Demi. Thank God I'm not ovulating, but I just thought you should know," Charlie said, turning to him.

"I'ma need you to get on something, Bird, cuz I can't pull out of that and I don't want nothing between me and you," he panted.

She nodded as he grabbed the brand new loofah that sat in the shower.

They showered, extra-long, talking, about least favorites this time. Food. Places they had been. Holidays. Every detail that was normally learned over time, they squeezed into this moment in their eagerness to know one another.

"How the fuck you hate Christmas?" he asked.

"I haven't had a good one in a long time," she answered, shrugging.

"I'ma have to change that then, Bird," he whispered, trapping her against the wall. He pressed his nose to hers and rubbed his forehead to hers. So much touching. In the shower, Demi was normal. When he was sure she was clean, she could see his relief. He had no limits under the stream of water, even though it was running cold.

"Can we be normal and get out now? Look at my fingers," Charlie laughed, holding up wrinkled skin. He bit one and a titter fell from her lips. Since when did she even laugh this much?

He turned off the water and they went to the bedroom.

He knew he wasn't going home tonight. Probably not for a couple nights. He couldn't. His new addiction wouldn't allow it.

"Demi, why did you buy me a condo?" Charlie asked as she sat on the opposite side of the bed, applying lotion to her legs. Charlie was surprised at the way he had moved her in effortlessly. He hadn't missed a single detail. It was completely stocked. From her favorite foods, to the fragrance she wore, to the lotion bottle in her hands. Her every need had been attended to. Demi stood and reached across the mattress, grabbing her ankles, snatching her across the short distance. Charlie yelped in surprise.

"Hand me the lotion," he said. She did and he took his time rubbing her down, starting at her feet and working his way up.

"I never understood why people put this shit on their skin after getting out the shower. You wash the day off you and then put some shit right back on you. It makes me feel like I'm covered in dirt," he said.

"Everything makes you feel like you're dirty," Charlie said. "I swear this shit better not be hereditary. I don't want a bunch of dry-skinned, weird-ass babies."

His hands stopped, mid-thigh. She felt the energy in the room change.

"That scares you? You don't want kids?" she asked.

Demi's son flashed through his mind and he lowered his head. He knew he should tell her. It was the perfect opportunity to be honest with her, but if he told her about DJ, he would have to tell her about Lauren. She would undoubtedly ask questions about the mother of his child and then everything they shared would change. Even if it didn't end, it would be different, and he just wanted more of what she had given him thus far.

I'ma tell her. Just not tonight.

"Kids ain't a problem, Charlie," he answered. "You moving real fast, though."

Charlie felt the speedbump they had hit, and confusion wore her.

"Moving too fast? Really? Coming from the man who bought me a condo. You just learned my last name today!"

He shook his head and put the lotion on the nightstand, wiping the residue off his hands. "I can sell a crib. I can't sell a kid."

Charlie laughed, her bold voice filling the space between the walls, making it come alive, making it feel like theirs. He would remember that laugh one day, remember the smile, the sex, the girl because he knew it was only a matter of time before she was a thing of the past.

"So, why did you do it?" she asked.

"Because I want you around, Bird. I want the responsibility of killing your spiders and taking out your fucking trash and filling up your gas tank. I fuck with you. I want access without asking and I want every other nigga on freeze. So, I got to take care of you. Make you mine," he replied as he climbed in bed beside her.

"Not because you're in love with me?" she asked. "Shouldn't that be a reason?"

"That's the main one," he replied, kissing her nose.

The bedroom door creaked open as Bails' big, blocky head peered in.

"Come here, Bails," Charlie said, climbing out the bed and picking up the dog as Demi's face screwed.

"You bet not put his big ass in this..."

Before he could even finish his sentence, Bails was on the bedspread.

"You want me, you get us both. Ain't that right, Bails?" she asked. She climbed under the covers, as Bails laid on top and Demi leaned against the headboard. Demi-0, Bails-2.

"Go to sleep, Demi," Charlie said as she turned out the lamp on her nightstand. "I'm in love with you."

He mumbled under his breath, talking shit, but he replied, "I'm in love with you."

CHAPTER 15

Complete peace. Charlie hadn't felt it in a long time, but as she rolled over, reaching for Demi, she felt nothing less than comfort in her soul.

His wrinkled, cold side of the sheets convinced her to open her eyes and when she registered the smell of food, she crawled out of bed. Charlie went to the master closet. It was filled with clothes in her size. Everything from new lingerie to expensive shoes had been meticulously organized for her. She chose a silk robe before following the smell to the kitchen.

The place really was beautiful. Decorated in blue hues, gold, and black. Their favorite colors combined, and she was sure it was intentional. To her surprise, Bails sat at Demi's feet, eating out of a monogrammed dog bowl. Demi had not missed a single detail and the fact that he had planned for Bails too warmed her because she knew he hated animals. He stood over the stove shirtless, wearing hoop shorts and socks with slides. Her eyes studied the tattoos before she walked up behind him, wrapping her arms around his strong waist, and tucking her hands in the front band of his shorts.

"I woke up different today," she said, feeling him tense. He didn't question it because he knew what she meant. The moment he opened his eyes he had felt the same. Different, blessed, endowed to a girl named Charlie. She made a man feel brand new. "Relax, Demi. My dirt is your dirt," she whispered, kissing his strong back and feeling his dick stiffen in her hands. "So, you cook?"

"Not really," he snickered. "I don' burnt these eggs twice."

Charlie eased between him and the stove. "Here, let me help," she said. This time, it was his arms around her waist. His dick pressed into her and she quivered a little as he reached around, grabbing her neck. Morning sex. Demi forced her head against his shoulder and then turned her to the island, lifting her silk robe and bending her over.

They burned another pan of eggs as they made love on the countertops. This was an overdose of pleasure. They were gluttons for one another. This was a sin, a bigger one than Charlie realized, but even in her ignorance, she could tell this was too euphoric to be good for you.

"I want to see where you come from, Demi. Who else is in your life? Meet your mama. I just want to know the person that has come into my world and made it about him. If my every waking moment is going to be about you, I want to know you," Charlie said as she sat on the kitchen counter with Demi standing between her thighs, picking grapes off the bunch he had laid out. One for her, one for him. That's the kind of man he was. He fed a woman's soul first, filling her up before catering to his own.

He fed her casually as he answered, "I don't talk to my parents. My daddy ain't really shit. Never been shit. My mom has some handicaps. She had a stroke while giving birth to me, kind of fucked her up. My dad blames me for that. Never really treated me the same as my other brothers and sisters. Used to beat my ass for the smallest shit but the rest of my brothers got away with murder. The last time he touched me, I fought back, broke his jaw, and then took off. I ain't really had a good relationship with him since."

Charlie saw pain in Demi. The kind that had taken years to build.

"And your mom?" she asked.

"I speak to her every Sunday. She calls. I haven't seen her since I left home, though. She won't leave my daddy. She loves him. She put me out for fighting him back. He ain't shit but she worships that nigga. I can't see her without seeing him, though, so I just ain't seen them," he said. "My brothers or sister either. I don't fuck with none of 'em."

"Have you always had OCD?" she asked.

"Not always," he said. "My ma, she ummm..." he paused, searching for words as he scratched his temple. "She can't really move around like that. She's dependent on my dad. He used to take off all day, drink, fuck around with other women or whatever and she would sit in the same spot. Sometimes, for days. Sometimes, she would be a mess. Soiled, you know? When I was little, I couldn't help her to the bathroom, couldn't bathe her, couldn't help her when she needed to relieve herself. I would have to clean her up with a rag and a bucket. My other brothers and sister were too young. I was the oldest, so it was on me. Cleaning up urine and feces just gave me a complex, I guess. I just don't like no dirty shit."

Demi's heart ached with every word. He had never told this to anyone. Not even Lauren or DJ knew about his past. He had never planned to revisit it, so what was the point in talking about it?

"She's disabled? I'm so sorry, Demi," Charlie said.

"She has Parkinson's," he revealed. He hadn't spoken about it in years. He sent money and paid for care but he never called and he never went home. "She lives in Cali. That's where I'm from. We don't really talk. The shit with my dad… I don't know, he was a mean drunk and she defended it. I haven't gone back in some time."

"You should check on your mom, Demi," she whispered. "I'll go back with you. Help you face it. I'm sure she misses you." He kissed her shoulder. His sweet Charlie. She was so much more than a casual fling.

"You're comfortable this morning," she said, smiling, changing the subject intentionally. He was grateful for the shift.

"Your dirt is my dirt. That shit makes so much sense in my head, Bird," he said, speaking into her neck because he was kissing her there now too.

"It doesn't burn?" she asked.

"It does," he whispered. "I don't care, Bird, I can't stop. Shit with you feels good than a motherfucka. So good it hurts a little. I know I'm not making sense."

"It makes sense," she replied. She leaned back to stare at him. "You should check on your mom. My mom's dead and I would give anything to get one more day with her. It's been years since you've seen her face."

"I can't, Bird. I would love to introduce you to her, but I can't go back," he said.

"You won't go back, Demi. I can't see my mom. You won't," she replied. "That's two different things, and one day when you really *can't* see her… When it's not even a choice anymore… When she is gone… You'll wish you had," she said.

She could tell her words landed hard. She could practically see the thoughts running through his mind.

"Yeah, I hear you," he said. "I've got to get to the studio. You want to meet me there later? Day would kill to lay down something for you. He's been talking about the girl who stole the showcase non-stop. I can make that dream a reality, Bird."

"I can't. I have my dad's anniversary dinner and then a set at the club," she said. "Like you, I have my own issues with my father. He's an asshole, but I kind of have to show up. Stassi will kill me if I don't. Would you want to come? I mean, I'm not big on introducing people to my family, but if I'm going to be here with you, they should meet you, right?"

Demi grimaced as the idea of meeting her folks turned him off.

"I mean, you don't have to; I just hate the way my dad's wife picks me apart. I never have an ally at that table," she said chuckling. "Stassi's too afraid to stand up to her mom and my dad is too far up her ass. Just thought you could keep me company, but it's cool. I get it."

"How about you do your family thing and I handle my business and we link after that?" he asked.

She nodded. "Yeah, that's cool." He heard the disappointment in her voice, but Demi couldn't be out here meeting parents. They were already crossing lines. What should have been low-key was becoming very blatant. He would have to remind himself that Charlie wasn't his home. He was playing pretend with her, investing in something he knew would eventually end.

"What about my old place, Demi? I'm in a lease. I can't just..."

"You telling me a lot about what you can't do, Bird," he answered. "Unlearn that shit. You can do whatever you want to do. Whatever is in the way can be removed. I'll pay out your lease on the other spot. Do you want to live here?" he asked.

"With you? Or by myself?" she asked. "Is this our place, Demi? Or mine?"

"It's whatever you want it to be. Your name is on it, Bird," he replied.

She paused, thinking. It was crazy to move in with Demi. Charlie liked her space. Her solace. Her old apartment was her piece of safety. She had designed it to be exactly that, a refuge from harm. This new place was luxury, but it was cold. It was too perfect. Too clean. Demi would want it to stay that way. Charlie needed to dirty it up a little, live in it, for it to be her new safe haven.

"Can it just be mine for a little while? I just don't want to rush into living together. I need my own space," Charlie answered. "Is that ungrateful? I don't want to seem ungrateful."

"Whatever you want," he said. He pulled back. "I got to get dressed and get out of here. Enjoy your dinner with your people. I'ma call you later."

Lauren felt her life slipping from beneath her. If Demi had never been anything else, he had been consistent. Lately, inconsistencies had been his routine. She had never had to wonder where he was. She had never stayed up late at night questioning his intentions, his fidelity, but as she watched Demi walk through the front door, she could feel the shift.

"DJ! Your dad is here to take you to school!" she shouted.

"Yes!" DJ shouted as hurried steps echoed through the house.

"Lo," Demi started.

Lauren shook her head and held up one hand in protest to stop him from speaking. "Just take him to school, Demi," she said. "I have a client that can't wait this morning, so whatever lie you're about to tell, I don't have time to hear it."

Her eyes were red. He knew she had been crying and it made him feel like shit. She didn't deserve this.

"DJ, wait for Daddy in the car," Demi said.

"Okay, Dad," his son replied. Demi and Lauren waited until they heard the garage door close before saying one word.

"This is not okay," Lauren said. "The disrespect. The coming and going when you want to. The bullshit explanations about where you have been. I am not okay with this. I don't know how we even got here. Things were fine and then they weren't, but you need to get your shit together. My son should not be asking me where you are. He has never had to question why you are gone all the time. Never had to fight for your time. Neither have I. You know he has a game tonight. Are you even going to show up for that? Or do I need to start looking for excuses to explain your absence? You know what I gave up to be with you, Demi. I don't have anyone but you and DJ. My entire family disowned me because I chased behind you when you were in the streets. Are you throwing me away now? I chose you and now I'm old news, so you just throwing 15 years away? Because that's what it feels like. It feels like you're abandoning me."

"I'ma be there, Lo. When have I ever not been at one of his games?" he asked. He thought of the promises he had made her over the years. She had always put him first. She had defied her entire family to run away with him. When he was worth nothing, had nothing, but a hustle and a dream, she had been patient, while he built an empire. "I'm not throwing you away." Guilt forced the lie out of his mouth. He had never liked to hurt her. Her tears crippled Demi, but he couldn't help but compare his connection to Lauren to what he shared with Charlie. He was present for Lauren but even she followed his rules. Limited touching, designing a life around his preferences. Their home barely looked lived in it had to be so spotless. Their life was sterile. Safe. Charlie was a beautiful mess. Still, Lauren didn't deserve to be abandoned. They were family, one that had withstood the test of time.

He had walked into his home with every intention of telling her he needed a break, but he couldn't do it. He couldn't pull out on her. "It's just work. Trying to help Day with the company and the street shit and breaking a new artist."

"Work?" Lauren repeated. "This doesn't feel like a work problem, Demi. It feels like there is someone else. Like another woman is breaking up my home."

"I want you to stop worrying. Ain't nobody breaking up shit. I wouldn't let that happen. I'm here, ain't I? I'm home, Lo. Look," he said, blowing out a breath of frustration as he swiped one hand down his head. "You got your meeting. I don't want to send you out in the world like this," he said. If it were Charlie, he would hug her; he didn't know why he had so many rules for Lauren. They lacked intimacy. He was hard with her. What he once thought was soft was ice cold and callous. He didn't know soft until he experienced it with Charlie.

"DJ's going to be late for school. Go ahead, I'm fine," Lauren said, wiping her tears away with the back of her hands and rolling her eyes to the ceiling to get them to stop. "If you say it's work, I'll believe you. It's work, right?"

"Just work."

Demi felt like he was suffocating inside the house and he was grateful when he stepped outside.

He got in his car and pulled off, rubbing the back of his son's head as he reversed out of the driveway.

"You want to play hooky with your ol' man today, D?"

He needed his son's energy. He needed to feel a love that didn't come with pressure. Charlie came with unspoken pressure because his soul called to her. Lauren came with the pressure of obligation. DJ gave the purest form of love, unconditional, and Demi wanted to soak that up.

"What about Mom? She'll get mad," DJ said.

"I'll handle your mama, boy. Roll with me for the day, bet?" he asked.

"Bet," DJ nodded

Demi looked down at the football in DJ's hands. "You remember we used to toss that around at Gundry park?"

DJ smiled wide and nodded his head as Demi rustled his son's head. "Yup, remember you taught me how to spiral? Now, I'm colder than you."

"You ain't got no heat on that arm, boy," Demi said, snickering.

"Dad, you crazy!"

Demi made his way to the same park he taught his son how to play catch.

"Come on," Demi said as he climbed out of his car. It was too early in the morning for anyone else to be out, so Demi and DJ had the park to themselves. "Leave ya backpack."

DJ shed the school bag and ran after Demi toward the open field.

"Go long, ain't no short passes," Demi said, tossing the ball up like he was still a 16-year-old football star. DJ went running and caught the ball effortlessly.

DJ ran it back toward Demi, who was guarding him, blocking his path.

"I'm finna juke you, Dad!" DJ said, faking left but going right, only for Demi to scoop DJ into the air and over his shoulder, yelling and growling. He didn't think twice about touching his son and normally he would have. Things were changing. Charlie was changing him.

"If you gon' fake out on a nigga, better quit calling your plays. Never let 'em see you coming. You hear me?" he said, flipping his son completely over his shoulder and slamming him to the ground. Demi was rough with everybody, but it only made DJ rougher. He climbed up instantly, hitting Demi with a punch to the gut before taking off because he knew Demi was out for get back.

Demi picked up the football and launched it, forcing DJ's legs to work overtime. He dove for it but missed the ball by a fingertip's length.

"Dang, Dad!" he shouted in frustration.

Demi chuckled and made his way to a bench, taking a seat, leaning over onto his knees.

DJ walked toward Demi, throwing the football in the air.

"You tired already, old man?!" DJ teased.

Demi laughed. "Yeah, man, I ain't young like you. You got your whole life ahead of you, baby boy, Daddy got to put it on cruise control," he admitted. His son was his spitting image. He was his greatest accomplishment. He didn't know love until he had laid eyes on his seed. It was a bond he cherished, one he prayed over because Demi just didn't want to fail his son. He wondered if by failing Lauren, he was inevitably failing DJ too. "Come over here, let me talk to you for a minute."

DJ sat next to Demi.

"You good? Everything going good for you at school, champ?" Demi asked.

"Yup," DJ replied.

"That kid still fucking with you? I had a talk with his old man, you shouldn't be having no more problems," Demi said.

"Mommy said you beat him up. I heard her talking on the phone with grandma about how you can't pick me up no more because you not allowed on school grounds," DJ said.

"Man, ya mama need to stop yapping on that phone in front of you and ain't nobody do nothing to that scary-ass nigga," Demi said, mouth pulling in a smirk of amusement. Demi had barely touched that little boy's father. He had just broke one of his fingers as a warning for what would happen if his boy touched DJ again. He hadn't even intended to do that, but the little boy's dad had dismissed Demi. Trying to be a tough guy in the barbershop had gotten him punished. Demi had hemmed the man up in the barber's chair in broad daylight.

"What if I got you and your ma a fly new spot?" he asked, tiptoeing because he didn't know how to have this conversation.

"Would you come to?" DJ asked.

"Sometimes," Demi said, honestly. "Not all the time, though. Daddy got a lot of business to handle. I can't be home all the time. You getting older. You can hold it down when I'm gone. You think you could handle that?"

"Not yet, Dad. That's what I got you for. You make sure me, and Ma are safe. So, you have to move to the new house with us," DJ said.

Demi's shoulders bricked. He had always wanted to be present for his son. It was one of the reasons he had made sure to make it work with Lauren because he couldn't see himself being away from his kid. He had been a super father over the years. He hadn't missed a beat with DJ. He had given his son every fatherly connection he wished his father had given him growing up. Their bond was solid, but in this moment, Demi felt like he was stuck. Leaving Lauren felt like the same thing as leaving his son and he couldn't do that. He wouldn't. Charlie wasn't worth that. No matter how much he loved her. He couldn't choose her over his child.

"What if I didn't DJ? If a day came when I didn't live with you and your mom? How would that make you feel?" Demi asked.

He was praying for clarity. Searching for strength in his son that would make him feel okay about deciding to move out, but when DJ's eyes prickled, Demi knew there was no way this would not hurt. Their little family, the three of them, was DJ's foundation, his sense of normalcy, his confidence, his security came from their unity. How could Demi divide that? Destroy that? For pussy? Only Charlie was more than pussy, but was she more than temporary?

"I don't want that, Dad," he said. "Everything would be all messed up. You said you and Ma weren't getting a divorce! That's what divorced people do! They live in different houses! Are you going to live somewhere else?"

His son was trying to be tough. His chest was poked out, but the tremor in his voice gave away his weakness. Demi pulled his son close. "Nah, DJ, Daddy ain't going nowhere, man. We just talking. I'ma stay with you and your mom."

He spent the rest of the morning with his son. He felt like he had something to apologize for. The notion of leaving his family was crazy. His mind told him it was, but his heart, his heart wasn't even with him. It was back at the condo with Charlie, waiting for him to double back and retrieve it like it was some item he had forgotten to take with him on his way out the door. He dropped his son off at school after lunch, and as he walked him into the building, Demi paused, turning to DJ.

"No matter what, I love you, man. Remember that. You're me without all the bad. You're made of everything good, DJ. I love you and no matter what, I'ma always be here for you. No matter where I am, you hear me?"

DJ nodded and Demi gave him a light push to his head. "A'ight, boy, get to class."

"See you at my game!"

"Yup, top of the stands, baby boy. You know where to find me," Demi said. DJ ran back over to him and they did their handshake. Two slaps, pinkies locked, then drop it. DJ took off running down the hall as Demi watched until he disappeared around a corner.

"Fuck, man," Demi muttered. He didn't know what he should do. He knew what he wanted to do. He knew what he needed to do, but he couldn't. He just couldn't. For now, he would have to do both.

CHAPTER 16

"No, noooo, come on, don't do this right now!" Charlie cried as she turned her key over in her ignition. The engine sputtered and her entire car shook but it wouldn't start. "I'm already late." Charlie sat in the parking lot of Target, stranded. "I knew I should have left it running." She had turned off her car to run in and grab a gift card for the occasion, only to come out to chaos.

She picked up her phone and dialed Stassi, only to be sent to voicemail.

"Come on, Stassi!" she said, sucking her teeth. Demi was her next call. She knew he was busy. She hoped she wasn't crossing lines, but he had told her to call him first when she needed something. She prayed he meant it.

"Talk nice to me, Bird," he answered.

She smiled. Only Demi could make her smile when she was completely overwhelmed.

"Hey, babe," she greeted. "Are you busy?"

"A little but what up?" he replied.

"I'm stranded. My car died and I'm late to this family thing. I wasn't gonna call you, but Stassi didn't answer and..."

"Where you at?" he interrupted.

"Target, on Miller Road," she said.

"I'm on my way," he answered. That was all he needed to say for Charlie to feel saved. If he said it, he did it and he didn't do it halfway, so she knew the problem would be solved. A man. Her man. She couldn't believe it. After everything she had been through, it was hard to trust in it because niggas had always led her astray. It was the pace that made Charlie give into it. It was happening too fast to be manipulative. What they were doing was impulsive, it was passionate. She loved it. She loved him. She didn't care that it was what most would call "too soon." She knew what she felt in her heart and that was enough.

When she saw Demi's Cadillac pull into the parking lot a half hour later, she felt instant relief.

"I'm so sorry," she said as she climbed from the car to greet him. Demi commanded her chin between his fingertips, pulling her lips to his. A quick peck, probably because he couldn't give more without his soul dying a little, and then his face in the groove of her neck as he hugged her, picking her up. He walked her to the passenger seat of the car, seeing her safely inside before going to the driver's side.

"I missed you," she said when he climbed inside. How? It had only been hours since being in his presence, but that didn't make it any less true.

"Show, don't tell, Bird," he said. Charlie smiled mischievously as she reached for the seat of his denim.

"Slow down. You press go on that and you ain't going to ya daddy's little dinner," Demi said.

Charlie pouted and faced forward in her seat.

"I'd never hear the end of it," she said. "I really appreciate you dropping everything to come get me."

"Don't worry about it," he said. "I'ma have my little niggas take care of the car for you. Come ride with me."

"I'm so late," she complained.

"I'll take you where you got to be," he said.

Charlie showed up to her father's house an hour late and she was practically shaking as she opened her door to get out.

"He's going to be so mad," she said. "I had one job. I'm always fucking shit up."

Demi frowned. Seeing her rattled bothered him. She was frantic and he took a finger to her chin, causing her to take pause as he commanded her eyes.

"Relax," he said. "This your family, Bird. You a little late. It's not the end of the world. They better be lucky they getting a piece of you at all, cuz a nigga want to be real selfish with your time."

She smiled, but there was something in her eyes that called to him. Something that said she needed him there.

"If you gon' need a ride back, I might as well stay," he said.

"Would you mind?" she asked.

"Come on. Guess I got to try to impress ya daddy and all that, huh? Young-ass." He shook his head and scoffed because he couldn't believe he was in a position where he was attempting to win over anybody. Demi was an IDGAF kind of nigga, but for Charlie, he had too many fucks to give.

His fingertip was still under her chin. She shook her head. "No, babe. He got to try to impress you," she replied.

"You got my head fucked up, Bird," Demi admitted. "I been thinking about how not to be crazy when it comes to you all day, but then I see you and a nigga just get crazier."

"You're not crazy, babe," she whispered. He pulled her across the seat, stealing her lips and forcing her into his lap. They were so squished they honked the horn. The front door to the house opened and a man stepped out onto the porch. His face bent in irritation.

"Fuck you looking at?" Demi asked. "You ain't never seen a nigga kiss his girl?"

Charlie laughed as she put her hands over his mouth.

"Shhh!" she snickered. "Demi! That's my daddy."

"He ain't exempt. Interrupting my time with my baby. I got smoke for anybody getting between us, Bird," he said, smiling lazily and moving his head because her hands over his lips made him want to rinse his whole face in bleach.

She couldn't help but laugh harder. "Yeah?" she asked. "That's how you feel?"

He laughed too. "Knock yo' fucking daddy on his ass, Bird, no lie," Demi said.

Charlie looked back to the porch and saw her father coming down the steps.

"Uh-oh, Bird, you in trouble," he teased.

Her father knocked on the driver's window and Charlie buried her face in Demi's neck, laughing as Demi rolled down the window.

"Can I help you with something?"

It was the way he said it. The baritone of his voice. The challenge in his tone. Charlie had never been so turned on.

"I'm going to fuck you so good," she whispered in his ear. He tapped one finger on her ass and Charlie lifted her head, sheepishly smiling as she greeted her father with a flushed face. She was still straddling Demi and his recklessness didn't even allow for him to take his hand off her ass. He was gripping it. Yeah, it was a new daddy in town.

"Hi, Daddy," Charlie greeted. "This is my boyfriend, Demi."

"I ain't been a boy in a long time," Demi said, biting her ear. Charlie was on cloud nine and couldn't even compose herself in front of her father.

Unenthused, her father let uncomfortable silence linger for a few seconds.

"The photographer has been waiting long enough, Charlize," her father said. He turned and walked back in the house.

"Guess he don't like a nigga," Demi said.

Charlie hollered. Charlie absolutely hated to visit her father. Stassi's mom had never been the friendliest. Since her mother's death, her father acted like she was a burden. The only person in her family who had treated her well was Stassi. The "step" had never meant much in stepsisters. They were closer than blood could have made them. Demi exited the car, wearing Charlie like she was a second skin. Ass in his hands, her arms around his neck. He carried Charlie like her feet didn't work. Spoiled. Charlize Woods was spoiled by a man named Demi Sky and she loved it.

When they got to the front door, he placed her on her feet.

"Thank you for staying, Demi," she said. She pushed open the door.

"Finally! We can begin! Leave it to Charlie to make a day that's not about her, about her," Yvonne, her wicked stepmother, said.

"Nice to see you too," Charlie replied. "Yvonne, this is Demi."

"And this is a family event," Yvonne responded.

"If he leaves, I'm right behind him," Charlie said.

"You've shown up with worse, I suppose," Yvonne focused on Demi. "Welcome. Might as well make yourself at home."

Demi simply nodded. If he used words, shit would get ugly so he didn't speak.

Yvonne held out her hand for them to walk ahead of her. When she placed a hand on Demi's shoulder to guide him, his entire soul left his body.

"Don't touch him," Charlie said. She offered no explanation afterward and Yvonne jerked her neck back, offended. Charlie grabbed Demi's hand and led him through the house.

When they entered the kitchen, Stassi frowned. "Charlie! Hey! What is... I'm surprised you brought a date. You know how Mommy and Daddy are," Stassi paused. "Hi, Demi." It was a dry greeting.

Another nod. Demi didn't seem to be speaking at all today. Demi stared at Stassi for a beat, and in the time it took her to blink, an unspoken threat had been made. She didn't know what it was, but the look in Demi's eyes told her she didn't want to find out.

"And they're going to be that way regardless of who I show up with so..." Charlie shrugged.

"Well, let's get you together so we can get these pictures over with," Stassi said. "There is a makeup artist upstairs."

Charlie nodded and turned to Demi.

"You don't have to stay," Charlie said.

"Go handle your business, Bird, I'm right here," he said.

"It'll give me a chance to see who you brought into my house." Her father interjected, entering the kitchen from the hallway.

"Daddy..." Charlie's tone was pleading, desperate almost, and Demi didn't like it.

"Bird..." Demi said, eyes boring into hers. He hated that she looked like she wanted to cry. She feared what her father might say. What he might reveal. How he might offend. Her name on his lips seemed to freeze her. "We're good."

His confirmation told her that nothing could happen in this kitchen that would make him leave. She nodded and retreated, leaving Demi to fight the war downstairs.

Stassi led the way to the guestroom that was being used for hair and makeup for family pictures. It was always an event. The annual celebration of her father's marriage. Yvonne made such a production about it. Charlie had missed six years. It was a joyous occasion for everyone else. For her, it represented the day she had lost her dad. He hadn't been the same since and it was the date that should have been engraved on her mother's headstone because the day her father got married was the day her mom's heart broke.

"Hi, everyone, this is Charlie. We'll be all set after she's done," Stassi said to the team waiting in the room.

"Hi, sorry I'm late," Charlie said as she sat in the chair.

Stassi sat on the bed behind her as Charlie closed her eyes so the team could start on her face.

"You and Demi. That's serious?" Stassi asked.

"Yeah, I guess you can say it's kind of serious," Charlie said. "I honestly have no idea how it got here, but I've never been more serious about something."

"What do you really know about him, Charlie?" Stassi pushed. "I mean, you've known him all of what? A month?"

"I know enough," Charlie replied.

Conflict tortured Stassi. She wanted to come right out and tell her. Demi wasn't what he appeared to be. He had an entire family that Charlie knew nothing about. Stassi had seen the photos of Lauren's son plastered all over her office and the little boy was Demi's twin. Stassi could see Charlie's happiness. It was all over her. Whatever Demi was doing, was working. Charlie was glowing. She looked like a woman in love and Stassi wanted to be happy for Charlie, but how true could it be if Demi was lying?

"I heard he's a dog, Charlie. You need to be careful with him," Stassi said.

Charlie wasn't even phased by the warning. She was too caught up in what Demi made her feel to heed Stassi's words.

"Better stop listening to miserable bitches saying miserable shit," Charlie defended.

"Charlie, he's..."

"Not your business, sis." Charlie finished the sentence. "I

don't care what he's known as to anybody else. It actually makes hella sense that other people would misunderstand him, call him mean, call him a dog, think he ain't shit. All those things might be true to somebody else. To me. For me. He's different. They don't get the part of him that I get. Nobody gets that part. I don't really expect you to get us. We get us and that's all that matters; so, yeah, we not speaking about him because I get real defensive about that nigga."

Stassi hated that Charlie was stepping so hard over a man who had a whole family in the shadows. If she told Charlie what she knew and she decided to fuck with Demi anyway, Stassi would be the bad guy. She would be the gossip. She would prove she can't separate personal and professional and the business she was building... the connections she had made would all be in vain.

"I'm happy that you're happy. I just want you to be careful and get to know him. I've watched you piece yourself back together before. I just don't want to see you hurt like that again," Stassi said.

"Demi wouldn't do that," Charlie said.

"What is it that you do, Demi?"

Demi rubbed a hand down his goatee as his brows hiked. He had never done this dance before. Been interrogated. Had a girl's father question him. Not even with Lauren. So, this interaction with Charlie's father, a father he had a feeling hadn't treated Charlie the best, was a challenge for him.

"I'm in music. I own a record label," Demi answered, deciding to walk light. Whatever this tension was that thickened the air in this house was awkward enough. He didn't want to add another layer to that. If Charlie's father kept it respectful, so would he.

"And let me guess, you're filling Charlize's head with promises of fame to get her into your bed. Playing on her desperation. Charlie's always been easily manipulated. She's like her mother. She uses the wrong things to get what she wants. Whoring herself out. I swear it's in her blood. I always have to save her from a bad situation because she doesn't use her head."

If looks could fucking kill.

"What you say your name was, again, man?" Demi asked. His impatience was not to be missed.

"Major," her father replied.

"Major, Charlie been in my bed since the day I met her," Demi answered. "No promises were made to get her there. No manipulation needed to keep her there. I don't know how well you know your daughter, but what she's using to get her way with me ain't got nothing to do with sex. I don't really know what type of niggas she's brought home in the past, but this thing you're doing, this degrading her to me, won't end well for you."

"Is that a threat?" Major asked, his temper flaring as he pushed back out of his chair. Demi stood too because he had never let another man take a dominant position over him.

There would be no towering, no hierarchy. Demi was the head nigga in charge in every room he occupied. It didn't matter that he was a guest in this house.

"Take it how you want it as long as you take it," Demi stated calmly, hiking up his pants.

"You need to leave my house!" Major shouted.

"Major!" Yvonne hissed as she entered the kitchen. The sound of footsteps descending the stairs quickly announced Charlie and Stassi. "What is going on in here?"

"This thug! Another one of Charlie's bad decisions just threatened me in my house!" Major said. "Call the police."

"Daddy!" Charlie exclaimed.

"It's cool, Bird. You stay with your family. I'ma slide, though," Demi said. Charlie shook her head and crossed the room.

"If you leave, I'm leaving," Charlie said.

"I'm not doing this again with you, Charlize. If you leave this house with another man. If you choose another no-good-ass negro off the streets over me, over this family, you can stay out. Stay in the streets," Major shouted. His voice was filled with so much judgement that it filled Charlie with shame.

"That's where she belongs anyway," Yvonne said.

"Mommy!" Stassi protested.

Charlie's eyes prickled. "You know what? Fuck this fake-ass family," Charlie said, voice trembling as she stormed out.

Demi lingered.

"Follow your whore..."

Before Major could finish his sentence, Demi had his hands wrapped around Major's neck, lifting him clear off the ground as he choked him. What kind of father spoke that over his daughter? Demi didn't even have a daughter, but if he did, he knew he would never. He could never. If Major spoke this way about Charlie in front of other people, Demi couldn't imagine the damage he had done over the years in private. The thought made him more aggressive.

"I'll kill you about her," he said through gritted teeth.

He couldn't even hear Stassi and Yvonne shouting around him. All he saw was Major as his eyes bulged and his hands clawed, trying to get Demi's grip to loosen.

Charlie heard the commotion and came running back into the kitchen. She rushed to him.

"Demi, babe, no," she said, placing her hand on his forearm. Demi released Major with a shove, sending him to the ground as Charlie positioned herself between Demi and her father. She pressed her forehead to Demi's. She could feel his pulse, racing, through the vein in his forehead that was protruding. "Stay here with me, Demi. It's okay. Let's just go, okay? I'm fine. I'm used to this. Let's go. Fuck this shit. I don't need them. All I need is you."

"You're defending him?! This man just assaulted your father, and you take up for him? Get out! Get out and don't come back when he's done abusing you and using you!" Yvonne shouted.

Charlie looked to Stassi, down at her father, and then to Yvonne.

"Let's go, Bird," Demi ordered. She followed, walking out without hesitation.

The car ride was silent. Charlie couldn't look at him. She lent her eyes to the window, watching the city pass her by as she fought tears. She had known it would go bad. Her relationship with her father was the reason why she had run away from home right after high school. It had been the worst decision of her life, but she had needed a place to escape to. Her escape just so happened to be hell. Coming home with her tail tucked hadn't been easy. Her father and Yvonne had never taken it easy on her. There was always judgement. They took it so easy on Stassi but handled Charlie in the harshest of ways.

Demi didn't know what to say.

"Maybe I overreacted, Bird. I'm sorry for fucking up your day," he said.

Charlie didn't respond, but he heard a small sob and Demi reached for her hand, lacing his fingers between hers, ignoring his pain to absorb hers. He even lifted her hand and brought her fingers to his lips, biting one softly before kissing her knuckles. Charlie didn't even care that he was driving, she climbed across the console and straddled him, burying her face in his neck. He felt her wet tears on his skin.

"You trying to kill us both?" he asked.

She laughed through her tears as Demi drove in the most uncomfortable position.

"I got you, Bird," he whispered. Kissing her shoulder and lifting his neck so he could see better while steering with one hand.

They rode just like that for ten miles until they arrived at the club.

He parked in the back of the lot and opened his door to give them more room.

"You want to talk about it?" Demi asked.

Charlie shook her head as she pulled back, still in his lap, but now eye to eye. "Will you come back later? To watch the set?"

"Yeah, I'ma fall through. Let me go handle this business first, a'ight?" he asked.

Nodding, she closed the space between their lips and rolled her ass into his dick.

"You gon' make me want to fuck, Bird. You keep going and you ain't singing shit tonight," he said, hands on her ass, squeezing, pressing her into his body.

"Stassi thinks I'm being stupid for you. That I don't know enough about you," she said, pulling back. "She just doesn't understand."

She right, he thought. How he wished this thing with Charlie could be built on truth. He would be able to enjoy it so much more if he could do so with a clear conscience, but he couldn't. If he told her about Lauren and DJ, Charlie would leave him alone and he just wanted her to bother him. To call him. To crave him. To touch him. To dirty up his life like only she could.

"It ain't her business to understand. You understand? Cuz I understand this shit clearly, Bird."

Charlie nodded. "Me too."

"Then that's all that matters," he responded. "I'ma see you in a little bit, though, a'ight?"

"Okay," she replied.

"Bitch-ass club owner should be handing you another bag today," he said. "You still got the rest put up?"

"Yeah, it's at my old townhouse."

"Good girl," he said. Another kiss. His mind was gone. He didn't even recognize his need for her. He had never put himself in a position to rely on anyone, but he relied on this. Charlie climbed out and Demi looked down at his phone. Day had called him ten times in the last hour.

Demi picked up the phone and dialed him back.

"Niggas got problems," Day answered.

"We got answers," Demi responded.

"Half oowee," Day informed. Day and Demi had known one another long enough to know it was the code they said to one another when they needed to meet in private. The rendezvous when discussing dirt was always their old recording studio. The little run-down brick building on the corner of Stewart Avenue and Detroit Street. They had recorded out of the rinky-dink studio for three years before Day had laid his first hit. It had been up from there. The only time they humbled themselves and revisited the past was when they needed to tap into some street. Apparently, it was needed tonight.

When Demi arrived, Day was already parked in front of the building. Demi reached beneath his driver's seat, retrieving his pistol. Demi didn't mind coming to the hood. He was a rich nigga who didn't mind being in the trap if he was strapped. His burner gave him a pass in every hood because Demi was known to use it. He got busy and word had reached the streets that he was ruthless. Niggas had learned that it was easier to show Demi love than to receive his hate.

"Wassup, boy?" Day greeted.

Demi nodded.

"What's the word?" Demi asked.

"That shit behind the club owner? Apparently, he's connected," Day said.

"How connected?" Demi asked. His mind instantly went to Charlie.

"He's 5th Ward. His Uncle is Tracy Hart," Day informed.

Demi stilled. Tracy Hart was an old-school gangster. Where New York had John Gotti, Flint had Tracy Hart. It was rumored that the older gentleman had started Benny Atkin's organization. Both men were Flint legends. The game had swallowed Benny whole but Tracy still had respect in the city and his reach was long.

"How the fuck we miss that, Day? Huh? You the one put the product on this nigga! You brought him into the fold! You ain't know who his family was beforehand?!" Demi barked.

"He ain't mention it! We don't be in Flint like that! I ain't know 'til I knew, but now that I know, nigga, it's a problem," Day explained. "He already sent shooters to one of the studio sessions. Followed Lil' Reo to the crib, wet him up, now I'm picking caskets out with his mama."

"He did what now?" Demi asked.

"I already got our people outside your crib," Day said. "Word is, when you beef with this nigga, it's bloody. Ain't no rules. Women and kids apply."

Demi pulled out his phone. His mind went directly to his wife and son. He didn't know if it were habit, love, or loyalty, but saving Lauren echoed in his mind.

"Hello?" Lauren answered.

"Aye, Lo, you good?" he asked, finding relief in the normalcy of her tone. She was pissed at him, which meant things were okay, she was safe. She was just waiting for him to walk through the door.

"No, Demi, I'm not good. Where are you?" she asked.

"Shit thick out here. I need you to drop the attitude and listen. Grab DJ and go to your mom's. I got some shit to handle but I'ma come for y'all as soon as I can. Just stay out the way for a few days. Keep DJ home from school and you take a couple days off. I need you out the way. You understand?"

The line was silent. It had been a long time since Demi had handed down those types of orders. She knew what the makings of war looked like. "Demi, come home," Lauren said. She was afraid. He heard it in her voice.

"I will when it's safe. I got to handle some shit first, though," he said. "Take care of my son."

"I love you," Lauren said.

"Love," Demi replied.

Demi looked at Day. "A lot of niggas not gonna make it 'til morning. You got the alibi lined up?" he asked. They would need an alibi. A good one. When murder was on the menu, they had to prepare the table the right way to avoid being caught.

"Hotel rooms in Detroit already checked into under both our credit cards. Camera system is down, the desk clerk been paid to say we been there all night. We're covered," Day informed.

A workable Alibi. Demi never committed murder without one.

His next call was Charlie. His stomach tightened as it rang longer than usual. She was at the club, with the enemy.

If anything happens to her...

Before he could manifest the thought, she answered. "Hey, babe."

"Bird, I need you to go home. Go home right now and text me when you get there. Don't open the door for nobody," he said.

"Why? I'm singing tonight and I still have to..."

"Bird, do what I said, baby. No questions. Go home. That bitch-ass nigga, Frankie, there?" Demi asked.

"Yeah, he's here, but he's in his office with the door locked. I haven't gotten your money yet," Charlie said.

"No, don't worry about the bread. Get your friend, Justin, to take you to the condo and wait for me," Demi said.

There was silence on the other end of the phone, like Charlie was trying to decide what to say next. If Demi was telling her to ask Justin for something, she knew something wasn't right.

"What's going on, Demi?" she asked.

"I'll explain later, just get out of the club," he responded. "Listen to your man, a'ight?"

More silence. He could practically hear the thoughts in her mind. She wasn't trained like Lauren. Demi hadn't been with her long enough. She was taking too long to follow instructions and Demi could feel himself losing patience.

"Demi?" Her voice was small.

"Yeah, baby?" he responded, turning away from Day.

"You know I just got you, so I'm not really trying to lose you, right?" Charlie asked.

"I know, Bird," he replied.

"Whatever is about to happen… Be careful," she said. "Because I need you to be okay. I'm in love with you."

"I'm in love with you, Bird. You don't even know how much I'm in love with you, girl," Demi answered. He ended the call after that because Charlie was a distraction. What he felt for Charlie would get him killed. Tonight, was not the night to have her on his mind.

Demi hung up the phone, turned it off and looked over at Day. "Got to get the cells to the hotel so they ping off the nearest tower. Then, it's time to put in work."

CHAPTER 17

Lauren's hands shook as she packed an overnight bag. "DJ! Make sure you pack up your game and the charger!"

"Why do we have to go to Granny's, Ma?" her son asked, popping his head into her bedroom.

"It's just for a few days, baby. Keep her some company. Hurry," Lauren said.

It took her thirty minutes to pack. She hated that she was so hardheaded. Demi had told her to park in the garage repeatedly, but she never listened. She parked in the driveway and she felt exposed as she ushered her son to the car. Whatever was going on, she knew it was serious if Demi had asked her to leave their home.

She ushered DJ to the car. Her nerves were tattered.

"Put your seatbelt on, baby," she said. She was halfway down the driveway when she remembered she had forgotten her cell phone inside. "I'll be right back."

She hopped out and went back into the house, locating her phone quickly before running back out. Her worst fears were realized when she saw the man in a black hoodie and full ski mask pulling DJ from the back seat.

"Mamaaa!" DJ's cries broke through the air as he fought, kicking, and screaming as he was dragged toward an awaiting vehicle.

"No!" Lauren shouted. She sprinted across the yard, fighting, and clawing for the man to release her son. "Let go of my fucking son!" She was pulling at DJ's feet as the man flung him like a rag doll.

"Ma! Help me! Mama!"

Lauren wasn't a fighter but the one thing that would always bring the lioness out of a woman was a threat to her cub. She swung on the man repeatedly, her hand connecting to the back of his head and the side of his face. She was screaming at the top of her lungs, praying one of her neighbors intervened.

"He's trying to take my son! Help! Somebody help me!"

The man backhanded her so hard Lauren's vision went white, but she didn't let go of her son. When her neighbor across the street came out, the man released DJ. She saw the spark from the gun and heard the blast in her ear, but she didn't feel anything. Shock absorbed all her pain as she scrambled for her child.

"Ma! Ma! Help me!"

"Pleaseeeeee nooooo!"

DJ was stuffed into the back seat of the tinted car as Lauren used all her might to pull at the man. She reached inside the car and the man wrestled with her, flinging her, but she didn't stop... couldn't stop. If they got away with her baby, she knew she would never see him again. Her neighbor came outside with a shotgun, running across the street and firing into the air. Lauren grabbed her son's shirt, ripping the collar as she snatched him from the car and throwing her body over DJ, shielding him, bleeding all over him. She felt another gunshot to her back and then choked as blood came from her mouth. The last thing she heard was the screeching of the tires as they burned rubber against the pavement and the sound of DJ screaming for her before her eyes closed.

Charlie sat in the condo alone. Her heart hadn't beaten right since she had gotten his phone call. She had tried to call him repeatedly for hours, but the phone just rang. Charlie had never been so unsettled. It was 2 o'clock in the morning. She couldn't sleep. She wouldn't sleep until she heard from him because something just felt wrong. Off.

Please be okay, Demi, baby, please just come home, she thought. She was desperate. If he would just call her so she could hear his voice. The silence was maddening. The silence made her make stories up in her head. The ringing of her doorbell made her scramble to her feet. She pulled it open, hope filling her, only for her entire body to deflate when she saw Stassi standing before her.

"What are you doing here?" Charlie asked. "It's late and Demi isn't home and..."

"Something's happening, Charlie. I have to tell you something about Demi," Stassi said.

Charlie frowned but stepped to the side, letting her sister in.

"He's not even here. Don't come over here with this bullshit about..."

"Demi's married, Charlie. His wife and son were attacked tonight. There is some kind of street war going on right now. He told Day to have me come get you. You can't stay here," Stassi said. "It's not safe."

The words hit Charlie so hard she stumbled backward. "He's what?" she asked. "He's not married. You don't know what the fuck you're talking about."

Her eyes filled with tears as Stassi nodded, her eyes matching Charlie's sorrow.

"He is, boo," Stassi said. "His wife's name is Lauren."

All of Charlie's air left her lungs as her fingers bawled on the fabric of her shirt, gripping her stomach to stop the grief from ripping through her.

"How do you know... what you mean.... how do you know this? Bitches talk all the time. I would know if he was married," Charlie said, reasoning with herself, running every single day since she'd met him back in her mind.

"My new job is with his wife. Her name's Lauren Sky I saw Demi come into her office a few days ago," Stassi admitted. Hiroshima. The bomb that went off inside her body was worse than Hiroshima. It leveled everything.

"You knew he was married and you..." Charlie shook her head in disbelief as she stared at Stassi like she was a stranger.

"I'm sorry, Charlie, I didn't know how to tell you!" Stassi defended.

"And you work with her! You smile in my face and you're out here kiki'ing with his wife?!" Charlie shouted. "You're my sister!"

"I wanted to tell you!" Stassi screamed.

"Where is he?" Charlie shouted.

"I don't think it's a good idea for you to..."

"Where the fuck is he, Stassi?!" Charlie shouted. Stassi struggled. Charlie saw her, weighing her options in her mind until finally fessing up.

"They're at the hospital. Beaumont in Troy," Stassi said in a low tone. Charlie grabbed her purse. This was a mistake. It had to be. No way was Demi married. No way. It wasn't possible. Not after the things he did to her...the things he said.

"Take me," Charlie said as she pushed out of the condo.

The entire ride, Charlie felt like she would throw up. The feelings they shared were real. There was no way to manufacture energy like that. Or was there? Was Demi so skilled a liar that the deceit felt like truth? He was out here masquerading ill intent for love and she felt like a fool.

"He's not married," Charlie whispered. Stassi's silence told her that he was. She was being polite, not wanting to pour salt in her wounds.

She called his phone, repeatedly. Each time he didn't answer, another tear fell. The 40-minute drive drove her crazy. Charlie didn't even wait for Stassi to park before hopping out the car and rushing inside. She heard him before she saw him. His voice. His angst boomed through the entire first floor.

"What the fuck you want to know?! My fucking wife in surgery and my kid almost got snatched but you pussy-ass cops in my face asking questions that ain't gon' matter cuz these niggas is dead anyway!"

There it was. The words from the horse's mouth. His wife. His son. He had said it. Stassi had not lied.

She stood in the doorway to the waiting room, frozen. It felt like he had cut her open, sternum to pelvic bone and all her insides were falling out. This was a hospital. This was the emergency room. Why wasn't anyone helping her? Why couldn't anyone see her bleeding out?

"Yo, Demi," Day said, nodding toward Charlie.

Demi followed Day's eyes and when he saw her, Charlie's lip quivered.

She put both hands over her mouth and nose, shaking her head as she closed her eyes.

He stared at her, eyes red, chest heaving, a look of distress and defeat wearing him.

He saw it. He was the only person in the room who saw her insides were on the floor, in a bloody pile at her feet. Her guts, her liver, her spine… yeah, definitely, her spine because she had lost her nerve, her kidneys, her heart. All outside of her body. That's how bad it hurt, and Demi could see it because he was the one holding the knife. A fool. Charlie had played the fool. Again. Another man had made a fool of her. She had never been so disappointed in herself. His eyes said what his lips couldn't. She looked around the room. A grieving woman sat among a room full of soldiers, Demi's soldiers. People she had never met. His family. Parts of his life that he had not shared because he couldn't because he shared a life with a woman and a child. Charlie was screaming on the inside. Dying. Pleading. A riot of conflict lived in her, but she refused to give him anything else. She had given him her heart. She had done it effortlessly without asking him for anything in return. She hadn't questioned anything. Damn it, why hadn't she questioned anything? How stupid could she be? She wouldn't give him anything else. Especially not her dignity.

She turned and prayed to God that her shaky legs would carry her out of the hospital.

"Bird!" he said, calling her in a low but desperate tone as she walked frantically down the hallway.

When he caught her elbow and turned her toward him, Charlie couldn't talk herself out of laying hands on him. She slapped Demi so hard he tasted blood as the inside of his lip hit his teeth.

"How dare you," she said. The calm of her tone caused his eyes to widen in confusion and alarm. It would have been better for him if she were loud, if she were making a scene. If she was fussing and fighting. Charlie was certain. Certain that this was not for her, that he was not for her. She shook her head. If only she could stop her eyes from watering. "All that love you gave me belongs to somebody else. You're married."

"Bird, baby, now ain't the time..."

"Are you married, Demi?" she asked, but it was rhetorical because she knew the answer. She had seen the evidence for herself.

He rubbed the back of his neck and then ran both hands over his head, blowing out a breath so deep it felt like it would blow her away.

"I can't even think right now. Go home. I'ma come home to you, baby. I'll explain, but right now..." he paused and bawled his fists, bringing them to his forehead and blowing out another limited breath. He couldn't breathe. Her man. Her love. He couldn't breathe. She could see the invisible ants crawling on his skin. The hospital was overwhelming him. The germs. The doctors. The smell. Then, there was his wife and son. "I need you, Bird. Niggas tried to snatch my son."

Charlie didn't know what to say. He was hurting over a son she hadn't even known existed.

"Demi, the doctor has an update."

Charlie looked at the woman who had come out of the waiting room and then scoffed, giving Demi her misty eyes one final time. "I'm drowning, Demi."

"Me too, Bird," he replied.

She sobbed, once, one sob slipped out before she could chase it down. "How could you?"

"I can't gather a thought right now, Bird. You got to give me a minute here. I'm seeing fucking red, Bird. I can't think. Take my mind, baby. I'm losing it."

He didn't even care that his mother-in-law was behind him watching. He trapped Charlie against the wall, pressing his forehead to hers. She didn't know how the roles had reversed but his touch now burned her. It hurt so damn bad. Toxic. All of this fucking love was bad for her health.

"Oh, Demi," she whispered, touching his face as tears escaped her. One by one they slid down her face. "I gave you me. Why would you do this to us, babe? How could you do this to me? You fucked up so bad." She covered her mouth, stopping herself from falling apart. She shook her head, drawing in deep breaths. She was hyperventilating she was so damn angry. She was trying her hardest to make up an excuse that made him loving her make sense, but it didn't. None of it mattered if he belonged to another. Giving men the chance to explain after they fucked up was stupid. Women know what it is when they discover the betrayal. Allowing the explanation is merely a chance to allow yourself to find an excuse to believe the lies. Charlie knew better. She had learned that lesson before —the hard way— and she wouldn't willingly play the fool again. "We're done."

"Nah," Demi said shaking his head.

"I'm done," she repeated, shrugging before clearing her tears. She said it stronger the second time, with more certainty, and with no hesitation. It scared the fuck out of Demi.

She turned to find Stassi at the end of the hall, looking on in angst, and as she walked by her sister, she said, "I'm done with your ass too."

CHAPTER 18

"She's going to die, isn't she?"

Demi looked at DJ. He was growing every day, trying to be hard, pretending to be a man. Day by day, his innocence was leaving him. He was going from a baby to a young boy, tapping on adolescence, but as Demi stared into his son's eyes, he saw him shrink. He was a baby clinging to his mother, terrified that he would lose her.

"Your mom is the strongest woman in the world, baby boy. She's going to be okay. She's just resting for a minute, that's all," he said. He sounded more certain than he was. She was hooked up to so many machines. Two bullets had ripped through her and as Demi listened to the machine breathe for her, he knew that he was going to murder niggas. Demi was going to murder everybody. The streets hadn't been that bad in a long time. A little uprising had occurred not too long ago when a nigga named Isa from Flint had torn up the Northside of the city. Word was it was over his girl, but that was nothing. That was a flash in the pan compared to the tyranny Demi was about to bring. He had been holding himself together by legitimacy, being responsible, getting money on the low and investing in his record label so that his family had security. The streets had still touched him. Had it been a bullet to his back he would have been okay with that. He would have accepted that as fate because he had chosen that life, but Lauren didn't deserve it. His son was above it. If she died, he was taking mothers and sons. Right now, only the men responsible would pay. The men who attacked her. The man who put down the order and the fucking pussy-ass nigga who had caused it all. As long as Lauren breathed, he would keep it street, but if she died...if his son was forced to watch his mother take her last breath, Demi was going to keep it gutter and wipe out entire bloodlines.

"What if she doesn't wake up?" DJ asked.

"She will," Demi said. His jaw ached he was gritting his teeth so hard.

"But what if she doesn't?" DJ pushed.

Demi bent over and closed his eyes, rubbing the back of his neck.

"She will," Demi repeated.

"But what if..."

"She will!" Demi barked.

His son's clipped silence told Demi he was scaring him.

"She will," he said in a softer tone. Demi was inflated with despair. Life was attacking him from left and right. With Lauren on his mind and Charlie on his heart, he felt like he was losing it a little bit.

"I'm going to send your mee maw in here, a'ight?" Demi stood and hugged his son. "Be strong for her, man. When she's weak, that's our job, to be strong."

DJ nodded and Demi released him before walking out of the room.

Lauren's mother sat in the waiting room. Lillian was a woman of a particular age, but she was beautiful. Black didn't crack and Lillian looked more like Lauren's older sister than her mother. Her swollen eyes were red with worry as Demi approached.

"Can you stay with them? I need to step out," Demi said. "Call me if anything changes."

"This is disrespectful, Demitrius. I know you're not this stupid."

Lillian's words caught him off guard. She didn't talk to him like this. No one talked to him like this. They knew better but the challenge he saw in her eyes was real.

"My daughter is on her death bed behind something involving you and you're running to the next woman? Who was the girl who showed up here today?" Lillian questioned. "I come from the day when men would keep their affairs in order. Her showing up here while my daughter is fighting for her life is out of line."

Demi put her under his tense stare as he chose his words carefully.

"Focus on Lo. That's where I need your head, cuz I got to go handle the niggas that's responsible for this. I can't be there and here. Nothing else is your concern," he said.

Charlie laid in her bed, in their bed, the one they had made love in for hours just the night before. She didn't know why she kept checking her phone every few minutes. He hadn't called, and even if he did, she wouldn't answer. She wanted to see his name on her screen just so she would know he was thinking about her, but he wasn't. She had never felt so distant from him. He wasn't thinking about her because he was with his family. Tears rolled out of the corners of her eyes, soaking her pillow. Wrapping her mind around Demi's betrayal was tearing her up inside. It was hard to believe that he hadn't been in her life a month ago. It felt like she was letting go of someone she had loved for years. She was weak. Her legs didn't work the same and her stomach was non-existent. She could still smell him in the sheets. Bails whimpered from the doorway because even he could feel that Charlie was heartbroken. Her distress filled the entire condo.

The knock at the door felt invasive, like it was interrupting her mourning. She forced herself from the bed and looked through the peephole to find a man she didn't recognize on the other side.

"I'll call the police!" she shouted through the door. Stassi had said she wasn't safe. She had said that Demi had sent her to get her because there was a street war.

"Demi sent me," the voice called back. "I just wanted to let you know I'm out here. Looking out for you. Demi's orders."

Charlie pulled open the door.

"Tell Demi I don't need protecting," she said.

The man held up a car key for her.

"What's this?" she asked.

"He said your old car was beyond fixing. That's the key to the new one. It's on the first level to the parking garage. Spot 6A," the man said.

Charlie snatched the key from his hand and stormed out of the apartment.

"Show me where the car is," she demanded, as she headed toward the elevator.

When they made it to the garage, a beautiful brand new Audi SUV sat in her parking space. Charlie climbed inside and started it. Putting the car in reverse she hit the gas, ramming into the pole behind her.

"Yo! What the fuck you doing? That's a seventy-thousand-dollar car!"

Charlie put the car in drive and rammed the front fender into the barricade wall ahead. She hit the wall with so much speed that it ruined the entire front of the car.

"Tell Demi I don't want this shit and to bring my old car back," she said before storming back upstairs. "And stay off my doorstep before I call the police."

Her phone was ringing by the time she made it back to her apartment and Demi's name on the screen made her silence it instantly. Seconds later, the text came through.

DEMI
Answer the MF phone, Bird.

There was nothing to say, however. No conversation to be had. He was married. There was nothing he could do to take that fact away.

Charlie powered off her phone and then climbed back into bed. She just wanted everything and everyone to go away. She was exhausted. She hadn't slept the night before and now she just wanted to close her eyes. In her dreams, it couldn't hurt this bad. She wasn't sure how long she had been out before he began infiltrating her unconscious thoughts. The scent of his cologne interrupted her peace and when she heard Bails barking, she knew he was there. Her eyes fluttered open and he sat there, beside the bed, leaned over onto his elbows, staring at her in the dark.

"I got the nigga blood all over me," Demi whispered. "I took three showers and it's still all over me."

Charlie didn't even sit up. She didn't have the strength. She just laid there, with her head flat on the mattress, looking at him. He evoked instant emotion from her.

"Say something, baby," he said.

Charlie turned over in the bed and faced the wall so that she could let her tears fall without him seeing them. She felt Demi's weight in the bed as he spooned her.

"I'm sorry, Bird," he whispered in her ear as he wrapped one arm around her body.

"I don't want the car. I do not want anything from you. I need my car back," she said, sniffing, holding back as best as she could. She didn't move, though. She laid there, in his arms, staring at the wall. She could hear her heartbeat in her ears.

"The car was scrapped, Bird. Wasn't no point in fixing that old shit. I junked it and bought you a new one."

Charlie sat up and turned to him. "You did what?"

"The shit was 25 years old, Bird," he reasoned. "You needed a new..."

"I needed a man who wouldn't lie to me! Someone who was available to me and only me! That's what I needed!" she shouted. She jabbed his ass with every word.

"Say, man, you pushing it with the fucking hands, Bird," he said.

"You pushing it with the fucking wife!" she shouted. Her resentment was so loud that Bails began barking.

Demi couldn't say shit. She was right. The shit had hit the fan, so he had to let her get her shit off.

"How long have you been married?" she asked.

"Does it matter?" he asked. "Married is married."

Charlie's nostrils flared as she stared at him in contempt. "Just like a nigga, man." She shook her head in disgust.

"Stop asking for details to make this worse," Demi said.

"How long?" She was vehement about it. She wouldn't let up. They both knew it. Demi blew out a sharp breath.

"15 years, Bird," he admitted. There was so much solemn in one room.

She almost choked on the notion. She didn't even have a response to that. She scoffed. There wasn't even room for her in his life. There wasn't room for her to compete if she wanted to. His wife had paid for that dick in full. Charlie was just test-driving it.

"Just give me my car and go on your way," she said. The defeat in her voice was crippling. It haunted him.

"Can we talk about..."

"Where is my car, Demi? Just give me my fucking car and go! Where is my car? I need my car!" she screamed, hitting him, again, this time slapping him, her hand connecting with so much force that he exploded.

He pinned her to the mattress, holding her hands above her head. "Calm the fuck down!" He barked. He was so close to her face that she felt his spit as he yelled. "The fuck is wrong with you?"

"I lived in that car with my mom for a year before she died! It's the last home I shared with her. That's the only place that feels like home! I don't want your stupid-ass car! Where is MY car?" Charlie's tears were rolling out of her eyes, one after another, and Demi lifted off her.

"I didn't know about the thing with your mom, Bird. They took it apart at the junkyard," Demi said.

It was that revelation that destroyed her. Charlie fell apart, crying inconsolably as Demi pulled her into his lap.

"Life been on me heavy. Keep me here with you. Burn me, Bird," Demi said, voice low, pleading almost as he pulled at her hand, forcing her into his lap. She straddled him and his nose touched hers. Her entire face was wet, and Charlie quivered as he took his tongue to her tears. "I'm in love with you Bird," he whispered. "I tried to fight the shit. Tried to stay away from you. I felt it when I met you that you were going to dismantle my life. That's why I didn't call. After the first time, I went ghost because I knew I had no business being with you. I tried, Bird, but your voice. Your burns. You. I just need you, baby."

"You turned me into somebody I would never choose to be. You are somebody's husband. I do not sleep with unavailable men. I don't cash in on another woman's pain. I would have never done this with you. Ever. It is not who I am. I watched my mother fade away and die after my daddy left her for another woman. I would never, knowingly, be a part of that," she whispered.

"I understand that, and I know I put you in a position that's fucked up, but ain't no backtracking, Bird. The way I am with you," he paused. "The way I feel about you. The way you touch me without permission. The way we fuck. The way that pussy feel sliding down on a nigga dick."

"Demi, stop," she interrupted.

"I want to take your soul out your body while you call to God," Demi said, as he placed his lips on her neck, then his tongue, then his teeth. OCD where? He was accustomed to Charlie now. Whatever covered her was a delicacy. Her germs. Her sweat. Her dirt. Demi was infected with her and he wasn't seeking the anecdote. He could die just like this and he would die a happy man.

Charlie hated that she wanted that too. God, how she wanted that.

"I can't do shit with somebody else's husband," Charlie said. "You need to get out."

"I'll leave her, Charlie," Demi answered.

Charlie looked around the room to make sure the second hand was still ticking on her clock because it felt like time stood still.

"It's that easy for you? To leave your wife? She's your wife, nigga. She has your son! If you'll do that to her, what the fuck will you do to me?" Charlie asked, confused, disgusted.

"Just give me some time to figure shit out, Bird, damn. I ain't got all the answers, and I ain't trying to do nobody dirty. I want you, though. If that's wrong, shit, that's what it's going to have to be. I'll leave her. Yeah." It was like he was convincing himself, psyching himself up for the challenge.

"If you were going to leave her, you would have done it already. You should have done it before you ever touched me, before you ever promised me one thing. You should not have to be caught up to move accordingly. I am not interested. I meant what I said. I'm done."

"You don't mean that shit, man," he said, forcing her out of his lap as he stood.

Charlie turned to walk away but he snatched her back. Charlie swung on him, going crazy, her anger building as she pushed him, smacked him, scratched him. Bails jumped and barked, getting between them as their toxic energy put him on edge.

Demi hemmed her up, breathing hard as she screamed, "Get Out!" at the top of her lungs. "I hate you! I don't want to see you! Just leave me the fuck alone!" She was a mess and Demi released her, realizing that he was only making things worse.

"Don't do this to me, Bird. I cannot be out here fighting a war with niggas and thinking about losing you. I can't handle both at the same time," he said, honestly. From the moment she had discovered his secret, he had been in turmoil. Hurting her, hurt him. He couldn't think straight knowing she was in pain. "We not done, baby. You the one. I don't know how, or why the shit happened, but you belong to me. Tell me how I can make us right."

"Go home to your wife and your son," Charlie said.

Charlie climbed to her feet and retreated into the bathroom, shutting the door, and locking it. Bails was going crazy, barking, and scratching at the door, trying to get to Charlie.

"Bails!" Demi said, clapping his hands. Bails came to his feet and Demi picked him up, carrying him to the front door. He opened it and handed the dog to his young gunner, Malachi.

"Take the dog out to piss and when you in her face, you make sure your eyes are in the right place. Keep it respectful with my lady, my nigga, and keep her safe. Ain't nobody coming or going without permission from me. If you don't hear it from me, they don't enter this door. Have the dealership pick up the car and fix it, then park it back in her spot. Understand?"

"Got it, big bro," Malachi replied.

Demi went back inside, washed his hands, and then turned to leave. The pen and notepad on the counter halted his tracks.

He picked it up and wrote a message before leaving. He wanted to stay but Charlie needed some time and he had somewhere to be.

"I'ma kill this nigga, man," Demi said as he sat in the darkened car, pulling on the blunt, words choking out with the smoke.

"You want to wait until he comes out or we running in the joint?" Day asked.

Ski masks were rolled up on the tops of their heads and pistols sat in their laps. They were prepared for anything.

"I'm too old for this shit," Demi stated. "Every time a nigga try to be normal, motherfuckers bring me back to the dark. I want him alive. I need him to take me to his uncle."

"Understood," Day replied.

Demi mashed out the blunt and popped open the door and then rolled the mask down over his head as he stepped out. They wore black coveralls, gloves, and black boots. There was nothing distinguishing about them except for their height and build. It was four o'clock in the morning. The club had let out at two. If the parking lot indicated anything at all, it meant that only Frankie was inside.

Day and Demi ran up to the door. Two shots to the lock and they were inside the club. Rushing onto the main floor, Frankie let off shots instantly, missing because he was shooting out of fear. Demi put him down instantly. A bullet to the leg took him down to one knee.

"Where can I find your uncle, nigga?" Demi asked.

"Fuck you, man," Frankie said, writhing in pain as he grabbed at his bleeding thigh.

"Oh, he a tough guy?" Day asked.

"Let's see how tough," Demi added.

Day pulled the trigger again, blowing a hole through Frankie's right hand. The scream reverberated through his brain like a pinball, but it wasn't Frankie's. He turned to find Charlie standing at the bar, shaking, trembling.

"Demi, please..." she said, choking on air as she gasped through the hands that cupped her mouth in disbelief.

"What the fuck are you doing here?" he asked, walking over to her. "What are you doing? I told you to stay out of this club!" He barked. "You're hardheaded, Bird."

"What are you doing, Demi? Please, you don't have to do this," she pleaded.

"We got an issue?" Day asked.

"No issue," Demi replied. "Go get the security tapes, Bird. You just said my name all over them shits. Hurry, baby, go now."

"Are you going to kill him?" she asked.

"No questions, Bird, just do it," he instructed.

Demi watched her rush to the back office and then stalked back over to Frankie.

"Tell me where to find him? You got five seconds," Demi said. He put the gun between Frankie's eyes. "5...4...3...

"Okay! Okay! At Rube's bar. He plays an all-night poker game on Friday nights," Frankie said.

BOOM!

Demi laid him down without remorse and then looked into Bird's eyes as she came back into the room.

"It's a new system. I deleted it," she stammered. She looked at the blood on the floor and then up at Demi.

"Go home. I'ma be by there," he instructed. "Straight home, Bird."

She was unable to find her words and he knew it was her first time seeing a murder. He remembered that feeling but he had been responsible for so many men meeting their maker that it no longer affected him.

"You sure about letting her leave?" Day asked.

"Yeah, she's solid," Demi replied. "Let's get this over with so I can get back to her."

"How you know, bro?" Day pressed the issue. They had never left a witness alive. Ever.

"Because a nigga gon' have to kill me to get to her. We not doing that. She's off fucking limits, Day," Demi said. "You hear me?"

Day gritted his teeth. "Yeah, man. I hear you."

Six hours had passed, and Charlie couldn't get the sound of the gunshot out of her mind. She had called him every 30 minutes since then. When she heard him put the key in the lock, she stood. She didn't know why. She just needed to be on her feet. Her anxiety was rotting inside of her.

"Are you okay?" she asked.

Demi paused at the door, looking at her. She was scared.

"I'm good, Bird," he answered. "I can't stay, though, baby."

She nodded. "So why come at all, Demi?" she asked.

"You saw something tonight that you were never supposed to see," he answered.

"I was at the club, writing. I stay late sometimes to soak up the vibe while I write my songs. I write songs when something hurts. Everything hurts right now, Demi," she explained, wiping away effortless tears as they fell silently.

"I need you to forget what you saw. You were never there. You went home. When you left, Frankie was still there alone. That's your story," Demi said. "If anybody asks."

"And that's it. Tell me my lines and now you go back to your wife? And your son?" she asked. She was trying so hard not to care. Demi approached her, caressing her face as he pressed his forehead against hers.

"My Bird," he whispered. He was soft for a millisecond before he turned it off. "I need you to focus on getting this right. Nothing else matters. I know you're hurting. I know. I'ma fix everything. That's my word, but tonight, I need you to get your story straight."

He kissed the tip of her nose and then walked out, leaving her with more questions than answers.

CHAPTER 19

Charlie barely felt like herself. She was tired all the time. Sleeping all the time. Crying all the time. She just wanted to make the pain go away. She was walking around with this pit in her stomach and it made her weak. It was like losing Demi made her feel all her past hurts too. It all came at her at once. She carried her guitar case into the club. He had said to go. To show up. To not go would seem suspicious, so despite her fleeting nerves, she walked into the building.

She expected to see the blood still staining the floor, but it was clean. It was like the night before hadn't even happened.

"Hey, Charles," Justin said.

"Hey," she greeted, her eyes never leaving the spot on the floor. She wondered if Demi had killed Frankie. Every time he called, she couldn't bring herself to answer. The way he had beaten Frankie the night before had terrified Charlie. Deep inside, she knew he was dangerous but seeing it... Charlie just couldn't shake her fear of him.

"You heard from Frankie? His car's here and the door was unlocked when I got here but he's nowhere in sight," Justin said.

She shook her head but couldn't quite find the lie she was searching for.

Her face was pale, and she was sure she would throw up. The room was hot.

"Charles, you okay? You look kind of..."

Before Justin could finish his sentence, she was falling.

"Whoa, Charles." He caught her and Charlie clung to him as he scooped her off her feet.

"Can we just get out of here?" she asked. "This place makes me sick." It reminded her of Demi, of the way his fist had crashed into Frankie's face, of the way his eyes had gone completely blank, of the sound Frankie's hand had made when Demi broke it. If she stayed, she may reveal something she shouldn't. She was grateful when she heard the clang of the heavy club door open and felt the sun on her face as Justin carried her to her car.

"You good to make it home?" he asked as he put her in the driver's seat.

She nodded. "Yeah, it's been a long night. I don't feel that great and I just don't feel like being here."

Justin looked back at the club and then toward the car pulling into the parking lot. The rest of the band was arriving for rehearsal.

"Get home, Charles. Get some rest. I'll check on you later after I get these niggas together in rehearsal, if that's okay with you," he said.

Charlie nodded. "Yeah. I could use a friend right now. I'll text you the address," she agreed.

She felt everything as she drove home. Fear, regret, anger, disappointment. Her life felt like it was spiraling out of control. In hours, heaven had become hell and the man she loved had become the man she hated to love. She just wanted to go back to not knowing him, to not needing him. It was hard to believe there was a time when Demi hadn't been hers. The craving was too strong to be new. She walked into her shiny new condo that her shiny new man had purchased her but the perfection of it all made her sad. Without Demi, it felt like she was visiting. It didn't feel like home. She wished she had somewhere else to go. Anywhere. Her old place, even her father's home, but she couldn't. She had given it all up. For love. For Demitrius Sky. She had never felt so lonely, even in her darkest times she had always been able to find a light. All she saw was darkness.

Charlie dropped her purse at the door and didn't bother taking off her shoes, a spite to Demi, as she made her way to the kitchen. Liquor. Charlie needed liquor. The brown shit because it would get her fucked up faster and she just wanted something to take the ache in her tummy away.

She helped herself to Demi's fifteen-hundred-dollar bottle of cognac and downed a shot. He would have gone crazy had he seen her because he sipped the expensive liquor slowly. Charlie poured another and took it to the head.

The knock at the door startled her and Bails barked at the intrusion.

"Good boy," she said as she went to answer. His loyalty was unmatched because Bails was right on her heels. She pulled open the door and the sight of Justin standing there made her eyes pool with tears.

"I canceled rehearsal," he informed. "I had somewhere better to be."

Charlie stared at him for an awkward beat. She didn't realize a tear had escaped until he wiped it away.

"You know every man I've ever loved has chosen someone else. Am I that bad?" she asked. She was so sick of this shit. This hurting. This curse of the side chick that Demi had put on her. Women in her position never won. She knew it. The problem was she hadn't known she was in second place. She hadn't even known it was a competition. She just wanted to be first. Only. Charlie wanted to be someone's only. Even if it was temporary. Even if it was just one night.

"The nigga's stupid, Charles," Justin said.

"Is he? Or am I just expendable?"

Justin stepped across the threshold and Charlie's breath hitched as he caressed her cheek.

"You're gorgeous," he whispered. Charlie's eyes closed as he came closer. Peppermint. She could smell peppermint on his breath. He had popped one before knocking on her door. It flattered her. The simplest act of wanting to smell good before she let him in. Demi had done the most and been a disappointment. She wondered if Justin doing the least would make him the exception. Would he be like all the others or would he prove different? Charlie surprised herself when she leaned into Justin for a kiss. Cognac and mint were the flavors they made and as soon as their lips touched, Charlie felt their chemistry ignite. He liked her more than she liked him, and tonight, that was okay. He picked

her up, kissing her as they made a trail made of mistake and resentment all the way to the kitchen island.
Her shirt. On the floor. How did it get there?
He had to be a magician because before her very eyes her jeans had disappeared. Her heart screamed.
Bitch, you don't want this!

Oh, but her head...her head was filled with pride, with ego, with resentment, with pain and it screamed,
"FUCK THIS NIGGA GOOD!"
Justin slid her thong down her leg like he was a professional panty-taker-offer and then he went down like he was a professional pussy-licker-upper. Charlie bucked so hard as he ate up her clit. He was exactly like she thought he would be. Amazing. Justin was a pretty-ass, hippy-ass nigga who had been on national tours playing guitar for artists for years. He wasn't new to pussy and Charlie could tell. The way he pulled back her hood, exposing all of her before diving in like he had been thinking about it for months, told her he was sexually fluent. Musicians always were. It wouldn't be her first time with one, but the way Justin was ravishing her, he made her want to make him her last. She came. Hard and loud as she pressed his face into her wet, drowning him. *Die down there, nigga.* Somebody had to pay for her pain. Why not him? He swam, though, all through her waters, pushing his tongue so far into her that he pushed her legs backward so he could go deeper and deeper. Goddamn, orgasm number two she didn't even see coming.

When he stood, the way his dick bulged through his denim made Charlie blush.

"You sure about this, Charles?" he asked as he placed a hand on his dick and biting into his bottom lip. "I ain't plan on none of this, so if you want to hit pause, I'm with that."

She shook her head and Justin picked her up, kissing her, sharing the taste of her as he took wide-legged steps through the condo.

"Mmm... the bedroom is in the back," she whispered. She hopped down. "Wait... give me a second."

She rushed back to the kitchen and took the bottle to the head. It burned a path straight to her heart, making it ache, making her remember that this drink was a numbing agent... if she was honest with herself, so was Justin. He was attractive. He was attentive. If she had to guess, he was good in bed, but as she stood there with the bottle in her hand, her chest hollowed.

He's not Demi, though.

It took two more shots to make her feet move toward him and another one to get her to lead him to the bedroom.

By the time she was on her back in her bed, staring up at him, the room was spinning. The smell of latex filled her nose as Justin ripped open a condom with his teeth and then he was inside her. Sex with Justin had Charlie coming for hours. He pleased every inch of her body, and by the time he was done, she could barely lift her head off the bed. She felt the kiss to the nape of her neck, and she was grateful for it. He had handled her with care, and it was needed. She didn't know if he was staying or leaving and she didn't have the strength to ask. Sleep captured her, and before she could overanalyze anything, her eyes closed.

Charlie groaned as Demi infiltrated her dreams. She smelled him. His signature scent filled her mind, and it was so potent that it felt real. Her eyes fluttered open and the room instantly felt like it was on an axis. The hangover hit her full force as she groaned. She reached over, rubbing her hands over the wrinkled sheets, before grabbing the empty condom wrapper that laid under the pillow.

"Fuck," she whispered, remembering the mistake she had made repeatedly the night before. The condom had broken by the time they were done.

I've got to get to CVS.

Her head felt like someone was taking a hammer to it, and as she rolled over, her eyes fell on him. She screamed, caught off guard as she pulled the sheet over her naked body from instinct alone. It was pointless. He knew every inch of her body by heart, but still, she clung to the sheet. Demi sat in the accent chair in the corner of the room, staring at her. He was so still that his presence sent chills down her spine.

"What the fuck is wrong with you?!" she shouted in exasperation. Just like a woman to lash out when someone scared her. Fear turned to instant anger when a motherfucker snuck up on her.

He didn't respond. He just sat there staring while rubbing his chin and nodding, his eyes blank, but on her.

It wasn't until Demi's goon walked into the room with moving boxes did she realize they weren't alone. She was both enraged and relieved. Embarrassment filled her as she covered her body better with the sheet, although she knew that Demi's goons knew better than to look.

"You got ten minutes to grab what you need and go," he said.

Charlie's eyes welled with tears and her heart sank. She was caught. Caught cheating. But it couldn't count if he had been caught first, right? He was married. So, he was the foul one at play, right? She honestly didn't even know anymore. It all just felt so wrong. She was staring at the man she loved with the scent of another man on her skin. She wondered if he could smell it, her night of passion...from the look of contempt on his face she was sure he could.

"Go where, Demi? Huh? Where am I supposed to go? You made me give up my apartment. I'm not even talking to my dad or sister. So, where exactly do you suggest I go?" she asked.

"I don't really give a fuck where you go. Better have that other nigga save you," Demi said.

It was a punch to the gut. It hurt, eventhough she saw it coming a mile away.

"You know, when my lil' nigga hit me and told me you had a nigga over here, I ain't rush to get here. I was handling business. I knew he had to be mistaken," Demi said, scoffing. "Guess God knew what I would have done had I pulled up while that nigga was still here. When he sent me a pic of the nigga leaving out the crib I bought you, I snapped. I don't even know how I got here. You lucky I don't hurt you in this bitch, Bird. I sat here, thinking about it all night. So, you might want to get your shit and get out."

"You have a lot of fucking nerve," she said, coming up on her knees. "I found out you were married days ago. Do you know what I've been through?" It was rhetorical because she knew he couldn't possibly know. She hadn't told him. He was adding pain to years of expired hurt that had been sitting on her emotional shelf. "You looked me in my face and told me you loved me, knowing you had a wife at home, but I'm the bad guy?"

The cave in Demi's chest was dark. Deep and wet with pathways so intricate that even the most experienced lover would get lost in them. She had no idea how much he loved her, how much it damaged him to see her lying there all night with the remnants of another man all over her. Was it hypocritical? Yes, but he couldn't help it.

"It's not a conversation," he said. Charlie recoiled. Dismissive was something he had never been and his coldness stunned her. Conversation meant there was room to fix things. A conversation left her with a voice. This wasn't that and as Demi stood to walk out of the room, hopelessness settled over Charlie.

"Demi, please just listen to me. Last night was a mistake. I'm just confused, and I'm hurt," she cried out. Clinging to the sheet that covered her indiscretion, bunching it at her heart as her eyes followed him out the room first and then her feet followed when he didn't stop. He was fleeing. Leaving. She was chasing. How the hell had they gotten here?

"Yo, get all her shit out of here. I want it to feel like she ain't never been in this bitch," he said. When she discovered two more men in her living room, Charlie lost it. The lump in her throat spilled out of her as she cried.

"I'm not leaving," she said. "I'm in love with you."

Demi laughed and her blood ran cold.

"Say, man," he snickered as she shook his head. "You hear this shit, man?" he asked, pointing at Malachi, his young gunner. "Bitches be on that bullshit."

He was embarrassing her, reducing her to someone unimportant in his life. Demoting her, or perhaps she had never occupied a place of significance at all. His wife had to be his priority, right? So, what did that make her? Number two? Damn. Charlie was a pencil ass bitch — #2 might as well have been etched on her forehead. She was sick.

"Get over here," he said. His tone didn't leave room for anything other than compliance.

She stood before him at his mercy. He was wrong. He was married. Yet, she was the one on trial.

"You led us here," she said, her words breaking under emotion as she lowered her eyes to the floor, taking a break from his scrutiny. "I was in it until I found out you weren't, Demi. You at least owe me a conversation."

"I don't owe you shit," he said. "You fucked a nigga in my bed, in my crib. Ain't no love after that."

"So you being married is okay? You're going to pretend like I'm the bad guy? You're destroying me!" She sobbed, tears of resentment ruined her pretty face, causing her cheeks to stain in red as a migraine built from the pressure. "What am I supposed to do? Be faithful to a married man? You got me out here looking stupid."

"I was gonna tell you," he said.

"When?" she shouted. "Huh? After you made me fall for you? Fuck you! Fuck your wife! And fuck your son!"

Demi grabbed her throat so abruptly that Charlie gasped.

"Nah, fuck you," Demi said with a nonchalance that cut deep. He wasn't even bothered by the fact that this was ending. It had run its course. Charlie had proven disloyal, and for Demi, there was no coming back from that. He had cut people off for less.

Charlie wasn't prepared for her own damn reaction. She slapped him so hard it felt like she broke her hand. It was like a match that lit a firework.

"You got to go," he said, grabbing her by her upper arm, squeezing so tightly that she was sure bruises of his fingertips would linger on her skin.

"Go where, hmm? I have nowhere to go!" she shouted, resisting, as he pulled her toward the door. The rest of the room was still, spectators to her heartbreak as she fought him, swinging and twisting and grabbing onto whatever she could get her hands on to stop him from getting her to the door. She fought so hard her nails broke with every blow, but Demi was unmoved at her effort.

The scuffle was out of control. The more she fought to stay, the more he tried to get her out. Demi lost his grip as Charlie fell to the floor. He was livid. Disgusted. Done. Demi was done as he snatched her ankle, dragging her into the hallway, naked. The sheet was gone. Her body and soul were on display.

Her skin was burning and red from being dragged across the carpet and she tasted blood on her lip, somehow, through the chaos it had busted.

"All yo' shit is out here already," he said. There was no sympathy, no love in his stare, just nothingness. It was like he was passing a bum on the street. Even then, he would have felt more than he felt in this moment. Charlie had turned Demi off. Once that occurred, he lost interest quickly.

"Where's my dog, Demi? What about Bails?" she asked.

"Bails is on me. He's good," Demi said, crushing her heart because Demi had no idea how much Charlie needed that dog. He was her emotional stability when she had none.

"He's mine! Demi! You can't take my dog!" Charlie said. "Please, I need him!"

The *him* she was talking about wasn't the dog. It was Demi. She loved him so damn much and he was leaving her. Permanently. She felt it. Even when she had discovered he was married she felt in the back of her soul that one day they would find one another again. One day. She hoped. She was sure she had touched his soul in a way that he would hunger for her so badly that she would be worth leaving his unhappy home. But now, she knew that her *him* was never coming back.

Demi ignored her tantrum and changed the subject. This wasn't a debate. It was a dictatorship. This was going his way and his way only. He was too enraged to give a damn about her feelings, even when he could see them being crushed under the weight of every word he spoke.

"Anything that's left out here after an hour, toss that shit," Demi said. He walked away and Charlie felt the abandonment issues creeping to the surface.

"Fuck you, nigga! I hope you die!" She didn't even know she had that much rage in her and apparently neither did he. He turned, staring at her one, long, final time, a flicker of pain flashed in his eyes and disappeared in a milli-second, leaving her wondering if he felt anything at all.

"I really never knew you, huh, Charlie?" He searched her eyes. "I'm finally meeting the real you and you fucked up just like the rest of us." The elevator arrived and he stepped on. It took everything in Charlie not to go after him. She marched back to her door, distraught.

She grabbed jeans and a top from the mess that laid in the middle of the hallway as one of Demi's men guarded the door. It was clear she wouldn't be getting back inside.

"I.. I... need my bag and my keys," Charlie said, voice shaking. She was so hurt. Her pride was incinerated. This was a stage of shame and she was the star of the show. "They're on the floor right next to the door."

Demi's goon looked at her sympathetically. She knew she looked pathetic. Still, she held her head high, despite feeling like Demi had walked all over her.

The man disappeared inside and by the time he came back out, Charlie had managed to pack a survival kit. She stuffed as much as she could inside one box that she could manage to carry alone and then she took the purse and her keys before walking out.

Heartbroken.

CHAPTER 20

"I went hard on her," Demi said as Bails sat beside him, his big head resting in Demi's lap. He was alone in Lauren's hospital room. The glow of the machines and the bathroom light cast a shadow over her. Bails whined, undoubtedly because Demi had stolen him from his comfort, his master. Bails missed her.

"I know, man," he said to the dog. Demi missed her too. Bails whimpered as he lifted his head and blinked big, watery eyes as Demi feathered his coat. Before Charlie, he would have never taken a liking to a dog. After her, he just wanted to feel something, even if it was hard for him, even if it felt unordinary, even when it hurt. Charlize Woods made him feel. In this moment, he was just a lonely man with his dog. The door opened and a nurse walked in.

"Sorry to interrupt your rest," she said.

"I'm good. Do your thing," Demi said, his eyes remaining on Lauren.

"She's doing better," the woman said as she pulled down the IV bag. She replaced it with another and then lifted the blanket from Lauren's body. A quick change of Lauren's dressings and she was popping off the latex gloves. "All of her vitals are stabilizing. We're just waiting for her to wake up."

Demi watched like a guard dog. Bails was his. He was Lauren's. He just wanted the doctors and nurses to treat her right.

"I'm not supposed to tell you this, but the doctor plans to release her. She could be home by the end of the week as long as she continues breathing unassisted," the nurse informed. "She can heal at home."

Relief. It flooded him. He would never forgive himself for her falling victim to a game he started, but he thanked God that she was being spared. He would never allow himself or his family to be caught slipping again.

He had locked his entire team down, to salvage lives. He didn't want anybody else under his watch to feel what he was feeling. Inadequacy. Like a king who had lost one too many soldiers in war. Demi had murdered those responsible, but still, it didn't erase what had occurred. While he had been distracted with Charlie, his family had been left uncovered. It was a stain on his soul like none he had ever felt before. If a man couldn't protect his family, what was he good for?

"Surprise!"

Lauren smiled at her son and her parents as Demi pushed her through the doorway.

"Be easy, D." Demi's warning didn't stop DJ from pummeling her with hugs.

Her pain was still immeasurable, but she was grateful to be home.

"My baby," she said, hugging him tightly, relief flooding her as she pulled him into her lap. She had never been so grateful. Her entire life had flashed before her eyes. She hadn't taken time to think. When she saw her child being snatched, she reacted. It could have cost her life, but if that was the toll to pay to keep him safe, then she was willing. Pain had never felt so good.

"Guess what, Ma? Dad got us a dog!" DJ shouted. "His name is Bails and he's..."

"A dog?" Lauren asked, peering over her shoulder in confusion. "You hate dogs."

"It's temporary," Demi said, without giving further explanation.

"Aww, Dad! Why? I swear I'll be responsible if you let me keep him! Ma, tell him!" DJ pleaded. Lauren didn't know what to say. She had just gotten home and already she was overwhelmed. She looked to her mother for answers.

"Okay, Granny's boy, let's take it slow on your mama, okay? We'll talk about the dog later. She needs to rest. She still has a lot of healing to do." Lauren kissed the top of his head as he pulled back.

She could feel his relief and the gratefulness on the faces of her parents warmed her. It was Demi's energy she couldn't quite read. He had been silent the entire ride home from the hospital. He was brooding. Moody. Mean even, but the feather strokes he soothed her shoulder with as he stood behind her wheelchair told her that he was happy she was alive. He was appreciative but she knew him well enough to know that this entire situation had sent him into a deadly headspace.

"This is nice and all, but she needs to rest. I'ma get her set up in the bed. The nurse should be here any minute," Demi said.

"You hired a nurse?" she asked.

"Just until you're up and moving around without pain. You'll need the help," Demi said.

"I don't need help, I have you," she said.

"It's done," Demi said.

Lauren left it alone as Demi wheeled her through the house and into their bedroom.

"You know this isn't your fault, right?" she asked.

He didn't respond as he lifted her from the chair and placed her gently on the bed. He removed her clothes, eyes flashing in the darkness, as his brow wrinkled. He was displeased. She touched his face and Demi maneuvered away from her fingertips.

Her heart ached. After all these years... she wondered if it were possible to spend a lifetime with someone and never get used to their touch.

Slipping a loose silk gown over her body and then turning her feet up onto the bed, he tucked her in without one word.

"Stop blaming yourself," she whispered. "I'm fine. We're fine."

"If I ain't to blame, who is?" he asked.

She couldn't answer that one. She only watched him walk to the en suite, wash his hands, and then walk out. Before he disappeared, he said, "Get some rest."

Her mother's presence in the doorway didn't surprise her. She was overbearing in that way. If Demi was the caregiver, her mom was going to come behind him every time to make sure it was done correctly. She didn't mean harm. They all were shaken up over the shooting. Lauren smiled and patted the bedspread.

"Come on in, Mommy."

The hesitation in her mother's stance made Lauren frown, and when her mother stepped inside and closed the door behind her, Lauren knew... she just knew whatever was about to come out of her mother's mouth was bad.

"There was a woman at the hospital for Demi."

Lauren's stomach sank.

"It was probably just one of his artists, Mommy," she replied, covering, lying. She was shielding herself from the embarrassment that admitting that her husband was a lying-ass nigga would bring. Anger and shame filled her. She didn't even know the full story yet but somehow, she didn't need to. She had felt the presence of another woman in her marriage long before she had been revealed. Lauren knew it was true. Still, she covered for his ass.

"It didn't look like it was business to me. The way he held her. She was crying and I don't think she knew about you because she was angry. She showed up to the hospital and..."

"That's enough, Mommy. I promise you. It wasn't what it looked like. We're fine. Everything is fine," she assured. Only it wasn't. "You and Daddy should go home. Get some rest. I know Daddy's missing his own bed. He always complains about my guest room." She forced a lighthearted chuckle. Her heart was slowing, stopping even, and she couldn't even ask for help because what ailed her was disloyalty by someone who had sworn to love her.

Her mother knew when to back off.

"Okay. You call me if you need anything."

Lauren nodded. "Love you, Mommy. Thank you for keeping DJ occupied and taking care of things here," she said.

"I will hurt anybody for hurting my baby."

Lauren smiled. "I know." The kiss to her forehead healed something inside her, even if only a small piece, and Lauren let her head rest against her pillow as the pain medication dulled her heartbreak. She closed her eyes, running from the truth. Sleep was a better option than facing Demi right now. She was afraid for him to leave but wondered what it would mean if he stayed.

Charlie winced as the cold towel touched her bruised skin.

"Did he do this to you, Charles?" Justin asked as he nursed the evidence of her run-in with Demi. Charlie looked exactly how she felt. She had cried so many tears that her eyes were swollen and red. Fighting with Demi had left her body with scratches all over her legs and her nails were broken from hitting him so hard. She had been swinging with all her might, and she knew that she was taking something out on him that had been building in her for a while. The pain she felt was unbearable. The abandonment was choking her.

"I don't want to talk about it," Charlie said. "Thank you for letting me stay here for a couple days. I don't know what I was thinking. I gave up my place to be with a man I barely know."

"You can stay here as long as you want," Justin said. "I'll go get the rest of your stuff."

Charlie nodded as her chin quivered uncontrollably and she lowered her head. "He threw me out," she whispered. "Like I was trash."

"He put hands on you. A nigga that will put his hands on a woman is a bitch, Charlie..."

"He didn't. I mean. He didn't mean to," Charlie said. "He asked me to leave. I should have left. He didn't hit me, but Demi is just a rough man. He doesn't know gentle. He doesn't do gentle." She couldn't believe she was defending him. Justifying. She knew why he had handled her with so much disrespect.

I deserved it.

"He just needed me to get out. I refused. I fought him. I put my hands on him. He drug me out because I wouldn't leave. I was touching him everywhere. He just needed me out. He couldn't even look at me," she cried.

"I hate that you make excuses for him, Charles," Justin said. "He doesn't deserve you."

Justin leaned into her. A kiss to her lips lowered her head in despair. She sobbed. "I can't right now, Justin."

Justin nodded. "I get it."

Charlie didn't want to say that she could never. Repeating the thing that had caused Demi to turn his back on her would be like digging into a fresh wound.

"I can't believe he put all my shit out. He threw me away," Charlie said. "My whole life is probably in dumpsters by now."

"Look, I'm going to get your shit. You get some rest," Justin said. "I'll take care of it."

Demi stood in the middle of the condo. The site of Charlie's boxes cut away at his gut. She hadn't even taken the time to take her things. He felt like shit but the disrespect that had occurred between these walls was too great to go without punishment. His pride was stopping him from forgiving her, but he knew in his heart that what Charlie had done was fair play. He had given her pain and she had flipped that shit. Women were always the ones with the most power, whether men liked to admit it or not. He hated the power she had over him. Even her lingering scent between these walls put emotion behind his rib cage.

A knock on the door and then a voice that followed pulled his attention.

"Brody, what up?" Day asked as he entered the space. He looked around in admiration. "Nice. When you pick this up?"

"A little while back. Bought it as an investment," Demi said. It wasn't a full lie. He had been investing in Charlie.

"And now you getting rid of it?" Day asked.

He eyed the pile of Charlie's belongings. "Let me guess. Little light skin with locs and that pretty, little ass?" he asked.

Demi didn't answer but it only signified confirmation. "You done with that?" Day asked.

"My nigga. Not the one," Demi warned.

Day smirked and shook his head. "Lil' baby bad, no lie," Day said.

"Shit just got out of control," Demi said. "She did wrong, but I did worse, man. I need you to give her a deal, a big one, make sure she straight. I would just hit her with some bread, but she wouldn't accept it. Just put her on the label, give her the push her voice deserves and some paper."

"Every nigga got that one," Day snickered. "I'll have the lawyers draw up the agreements and connect with her through her people."

Demi nodded. He didn't know if it was residual love or his conscience wailing, but he felt obligated to set her up right.

"Say less. I got you," Day assured. "And about this place? What's the ticket on it? You crazy to let it go. It's the best investment in the city."

Before Demi could answer, another knock interrupted them.

"You expecting somebody?" Day asked.

"It's probably just the realtor," Demi responded. He swaggered to the door, pulling it open and his blood stilled in his veins.

"I'm here for Charles' stuff, man," Justin said, standing toe to toe with Demi.

Demi couldn't even stop himself from reacting. He beat the audacity out of Justin, wrapping one tattooed hand around his neck, and drawing on him with the other. Demi didn't even want to pull the trigger. He wanted to kill Justin slowly. He pistol-whipped him mercilessly as everything around him went dark.

"Demi! Bro!" Day shouted as he pulled Demi away from Justin.

"Pull up to my door again and I'ma send you back to her in a bag," Demi said, too calmly for the moment. Certain. Still. Like he could deliver a bullet to Justin's skull without thinking twice.

"My nigga, we don't need this heat," Day said in a low tone over Demi's shoulder. Demi pulled the condo door shut and stepped over Justin's writhing body as he called for the elevator.

When the doors slid open, two cops emerged, guns drawn.

Day pulled Demi's burner out of his back waistline and slyly tucked it in his own as the cops put Demi in cuffs immediately.

Security had called the police as soon as Demi had entered the building. His last run-in with Charlie had caused enough problems. This new stunt was the last straw. Demi held his head high, arrogance dripping off his sneer, as he looked down at Justin.

"Call my lawyer, brody," Demi said. "I'll be out by morning. Better stay away from my bitch before that pussy be the death of you, boy."

Demi didn't have a care in the world as they forced him onto the elevator. It was a charge he would gladly take. His lawyer ate shit like that up in court anyway.

CHAPTER 21

"Oh my God, Justin," Charlie whispered as he entered his home. Charlie sat in his living room, hugging her knees to her chest, on his plush couch. She had been there for hours, calling him repeatedly, wondering what had gone down. His face was every indication of how things had gone horribly awry.

She rushed to his side and he shrugged her off.

"It's alright. I'm good," Justin said.

His pride. He was saving his pride. That's all it could have been because Demi had left him bloody.

"Let me see," she said, fighting for a view of his face as he pulled away.

"I'm good, Charles, I'm good..."

"Justin, let me see your face," she said, persistent, as she cupped it tenderly. "I'm so sorry." She should have known better than to let this happen. She knew there wasn't a nigga alive that could handle Demi's gangster. Only she had been able to tame him, and even then, it had backfired.

I'm so sorry," she said. "I should have never let you go there."

"I'm a big boy, Charlie. I'm good," Justin said. He snatched away from her and pulled open the freezer, retrieving a bag of frozen vegetables.

"Let me help," she said, taking them and placing them to the eye that Demi had blacked.

"He broke my fucking nose," Justin said, wincing. He was pissed, triggered, aggressive as he thumbed his bloody and swollen nose. "He's a madman, Charlie. You need to stay away from him," Justin said. "Next time I see him, know I'll be strapped."

"I don't want it to come to that. Not over me."

"Don't defend him," Justin said.

"What? I'm not!" Charlie pulled back.

"I went there for you and you acting like I'm just supposed to let this shit ride." Justin was deflecting, taking his anger out on Charlie.

"I didn't ask you to check Demi about shit. I didn't ask you to save me. It's not my fault that you confronted him, and bit off more than you could chew!" Charlie knew she had said too much when she saw his ego flare.

"Fuck you, Charlie," Justin said. She was speechless as he pushed by her. "I'ma take the couch. You can take the bedroom, if you're still staying."

"Do you want me to stay?" Charlie asked.

Justin turned to her. "Do what you want, Charlie."

"What happened?" Lauren's voice came over his shoulder as Demi sat in the darkened living room. "You were arrested in Flint. What were you doing in Flint? Who is this man you assaulted?"

Demi didn't turn. Instead, he sipped his cognac and flexed his swollen hand. His hand looked bad. Justin's face looked worse. Bails laid at his feet. A man and his dog. What a lonely existence.

"You shouldn't be out of bed," Demi said.

"I've been with you forever and the only time I've ever seen you lose your shit like that was when I cheated on you in college."

"Don't bring that shit up, Lo," he said, voice revealing his disdain at the mere mention of that indiscretion in their relationship. Demi had hustled back then, hard, on the block, moving major weight across the Pennsylvania turnpike. He had taken care of her every need, including her six-figure tuition, and in return, she had cheated on him. While he was consumed with proving that he could take care of the young college girl who had her heart set on taking over the world, she was investing in someone else... a ball player that was slated to go pro, his roommate at that. Demi had never felt a betrayal so cold. Demi would have never found out if one of his runs hadn't been rescheduled. Demi had doubled back to her apartment the same night he was set to leave for Philly. Finding her in bed with another man had sent him into a rage he couldn't control. He ended an NBA career that night. He ended a life that night. It had taken them a long time to come back from that. It was one of the reasons why he had never grown accustomed to her touch. She was covered in disloyalty. He had never quite let it go, no matter how much he claimed it to be "old shit."

"I'm just saying, Demi. You don't fly off the handle. I know you have your business to attend to. You're disciplined with that... calculating. You've only ever popped off over me. When you caught me cheating, so I can't help but ask what caused all this tonight?"

"What I'm hiring the nurses and chefs and shit for if you up on your feet, Lo? It's not the time to have this conversation. I just want to make sure you're straight," he said.

"There was a woman at the hospital. Who was she, Demi?"

The sigh that left his soul unlocked the door to the truth. He stood and faced Lauren. It wasn't the time to have this discussion, but if he knew her, she wouldn't let it go. There would be no getting her back in bed.

"This yo' payback?" she asked in confusion. He would be a cruel nigga to go tit for tat with her after all these years... to get her comfortable in their bliss only to purposely do her harm. This wasn't that. This was a case of the universe handing Demi something he couldn't keep and him being too selfish to release it.

"I ain't on no bullshit like that. What I did had nothing to do with getting back at you for some old shit," Demi said.

"So, you did cheat?" she pressed. "Oh my God..."

"There was a girl, Lo. It's over now. I don't know what that mean for us, but I'm tired of covering shit up. I was fucking with somebody."

It was like someone deflated her. He saw her reach for the back of the couch to give her some stability, but it wasn't enough. She came to her knees, wailing. It was the sound someone made when they found out someone they loved had died. That someone, was their existence as they had known It. Their normal was now abnormal and it ached so bad.

"How does a man who hates to be touched, cheat with another woman?" she asked.

"I fucked up, Lo," he admitted.

"What was I not doing?" Lauren asked.

"It was never about you. Women like to make it about them. Internalize the shit. I was selfish. It was about me, not you, and it's over," Demi said.

"When did it start? How many times?" Lauren asked. "Do you love her? Has she been in this house?"

Demi groaned and shook his head as he swiped both hands down his face. "We not doing that. The torture shit. None of that shit matters, man," Demi said. Her self-deprecating ways would only make a bad situation worse.

"It doesn't matter because she's been here? Because you love her?" Lauren asked.

"It don't matter cuz it don't change shit. I ain't trying to punish you with the details. I'm wrong, Lo. That's all you need to know. I did some fuck shit and you ain't to blame. A nigga just get shit wrong sometimes."

Demi's chest tightened because he wasn't sure if he believed that. Charlie had felt too right to devalue her in this way. Nothing about her felt wrong but the way that they had concluded. The fight. The lies. The cheating. All of that was wrong. It was the opposite of what they stood for. Still, Lauren didn't deserve that part. The intimacy. The exceptions Demi had made for Charlie. It was those things that would hurt Lauren most. So, he omitted those parts. For the sanity of his wife, he reduced Charlie to a fling.

"I can't do this, Demi," Lauren said. "I can't become the woman worrying about my husband's dick every time he steps foot outside. "I will divorce you and I'm not talking about a nice, neat divorce. I will leave this marriage with what I'm owed and take my son so far away from your existence that you won't even be able to find us. I'll be bitter. So, you decide right now what happens next. Is it over? Because if it's over, we can move on from this. You forgave me once; I could do the same."

"I never forgave you, Lo." His words silenced her. She stood, painfully slow before facing Demi with wet eyes.

"You don't forgive shit like this. You just learn to live with it," he said. He turned his back on her and recaptured his cognac, pouring another glass... neat. "I ain't never letting a soul keep me from my son. You know that. We don't play that game with one another. You either leave or stay, but using DJ as a pawn, it's not your best move. He's a king. He's my young. I'm asking you not to do that because I know how it'll end."

The eerie void that lived in the room after that made the silk hair stand up on the back of his neck. He could practically hear her breathing it was so tense. He hated that it felt this way in his home. It wasn't what he wanted.

"I can't heal if you're still hurting me, Demi." Her voice was almost non-existent. Had he beaten her down that low? Demi tipped the drink to his lips and then lowered his head as he nodded

"I know. It's over."

The words echoed in his mind, reverberating in his gut, ripping through his soul. Charlize Woods. His time with her. He recalled her entire face with every blink of his eyes. Her deep and doe-shaped eyes. Her dewy skin. Her pretty, little Chiclet teeth and those full lips that he had learned to love to kiss. It was over. Damn if he wasn't losing all his gangster from just the thought of that. Charlie had served him a single dose of his own medicine and it was so bitter he couldn't swallow it.

"Damn," he said.

He downed the last of his drink and kicked one foot up on the coffee table in front of the couch.

"I'ma sleep out here tonight. Go to bed."

CHAPTER 22

Humility was a motherfucker. Charlie stood on her father's doorstep, too nervous to ring the doorbell as she replayed her last encounter with him over again in her mind.

"Your key still works, Charlize."

Her father's voice oozed through the Ring camera and she looked up at it.

"Can we talk, Daddy?" she asked.

"Yeah, come on in," he replied.

At least I'm welcome, she thought as she pulled out her keys and unlocked the door.

She never thought she would be here. Begging for forgiveness. Her pride was too big, but her desperation was greater. She had nowhere to go. Her old place had been leased to someone else, she had no money, no job, and no plan.

"You okay?" he asked.

She nodded, but her nods quickly transformed to her head moving left to right. She wasn't okay. She didn't know if she would ever be "okay" again. Charlie ran into her father's arms. She bawled as he hugged her. She couldn't remember the last time he had done this, been her haven, and held her close.

"I miss Mommy," she wailed. She didn't know where it had come from. That wasn't the reason for her tears. Or was it? Was everything she had been through with men a reflection of the love she had lost when her mother had died? Charlie had never been lonelier than she was in this moment.

"I know you do, Charlize."

"I need a place to stay," she said. "I won't make it long. I just need a little help while I figure out what I want to do with my life."

Charlie felt him pull back and he walked to the sofa and took a seat.

"You're at a point in your life, Charlize, where you have to figure things out on your own," he said.

"If I could do that, do you think I'd be here, Daddy? I'm asking you for help because I need it, not because I want to. I need my father. I don't have any other options."

Charlie knew it sounded a lot like begging and she hated herself for it.

"I have a family. You can't just run in and out when I have a wife to look after. It's disruptive to my marriage. It makes things hard."

The audacity. The motherfucking audacity. Charlie might as well have been breathing flames.

"And what am I, Daddy?" she asked.

The fact that he disassociated her from his notion of family hurt so badly that Charlie couldn't stomach it. She felt sick. Word vomit was coming up and it burned the back of her throat as her eyes prickled. Rejection from men was one thing, but rejection from the man responsible for her existence made her feel worthless. No wonder she put up with bullshit from niggas. How could she hold men up to a standard of care when her father never cared for her at all? She had no one to measure love up to. No example had been set.

"You're a grown woman, Charlie," he answered.

"But what about the little girl? Huh? What about the little girl that came to live with you when her mother died? You've treated me like a stepchild ever since!" Charlie screamed.

"My wife..."

"Stole you from my mother!" Charlie interrupted his praise of his precious wife. "She stole my childhood, and you idolize that bitch! If it wasn't for Stassi, this house would have been miserable! Come on, Daddy! For once! I'm asking you! Choose your child!"

Major cleared the discomfort from his throat. "If it was as bad as you say here, I wouldn't expect you to ever want to come back," he said.

At that exact moment, Charlie knew they weren't alone. Her stepmother's Elizabeth Diamond perfume had sickened her for many years and today was no different. The sound of Stassi and her mom filled the home as they came waltzing through the front door. Their mother and daughter Sunday ritual. Shopping. Lunch. Just the two of them. It was a trip that Charlie was always excluded from, even when Stassi begged her mom to include her when they were kids.

Charlie scoffed. She shook her head. "I don't know why I even came here," she whispered. Disappointment was oozing from her soul. Nobody would ever have the power to hurt her like this man. "Bye, Daddy."

She stormed out and Stassi followed her.

"Charlie, wait!" she shouted.

Charlie couldn't wait. If she stayed there another moment longer, she would lose it.

"What did I ever do to them?!" she shouted. "And you!" Charlie shook her head. "Nobody in this fucking house ever loved me. I've always been an outsider."

"That's not true, Charlie," Stassi replied. "What would you have done? Huh? If it were me? How would you have looked me in my eyes and broken my heart?"

Charlie recoiled, stunned like she hadn't thought of how hard it might be for Lauren to be the one to break it to her.

"You should have told me," Charlie said, adamantly. "How could you work with her?"

"She's not a bad person, Charlie," Stassi said. "I know you probably want to believe she is, but she isn't. It was selfish to not tell you, but I just didn't know what to do or how to handle it or even if you and Demi would last. If I could go back..." Stassi stopped talking. "You need somewhere to stay?"

Charlie hated to need her, but she was in no position to be stubborn. She nodded. "I gave up everything for him."

"Come on. Let's go to my place. You can stay in my spare bedroom," Stassi said.

Charlie nodded. "I'll pay you back. I'll get a job and pay my way. I swear."

"From where I'm standing, I kind of owe you," Stassi said.

Charlie scoffed. "Yeah, bitch, you do. Your ass should be paying me rent. Emotional fucking rent."

"Forgive me?" Stassi asked.

Charlie nodded as Stassi pulled her apartment key off her key ring and handed it over. "I'll be there later. I have to be somewhere but make yourself at home."

Charlie sat in front of the camera on the floor of Stassi's guest bedroom. The solitude was loud. The pain was screaming, and Charlie needed an outlet. Her YouTube channel was private so it wouldn't matter if she uploaded her emotions tonight. She only had a few followers. People she knew. No way would *he* see it.

She just needed to let this feeling out. She was suffocating and music was oxygen.

She streamed live for two hours, playing, and singing until she felt like she was drained until she had nothing else to feel. She didn't even say a word, she just clicked off the camera, ending the video for the one viewer who had sat there, listening until the end.

The knock at the door terrified her. She jumped at the unexpected interruption and crawled to her feet as she made her way through the darkened apartment. She flipped on every light in Stassi's house as she made her way to the door.

She pulled it open and when she saw Demi an invisible hand wrapped around her throat. She took a step back.

Terror replaced shock as she put a little more distance between them. It felt like miles to Demi. The gap. How desperately he wanted to close the space.

"Don't be scared of me, Bird," Demi said. He took a step toward her and she took a step back. She was bracing herself. Hands subtly lifting to defend herself.

Like I'ma hit her, Demi thought. He was crushed, destroyed under her presumptions that he would bring her harm.

"Demi, please leave," Charlie said, her voice unstable, barely making it across the threshold of her lips.

Her reaction to his presence injured him. His eyes took in her trembling hands and her wide eyes and his stomach knotted. He saw the evidence of what he had done. Because he loved her, it was all over her. Subtle scratches. Bruises where he had grabbed her. Manhandled her.

I took this shit too far, he thought.

He had hurt her, and now witnessing the damage, he was remorseful in her debt. He just wanted to pay the debt. All her debts. In whatever ways she made him settle up, he was willing to.

"Leaveeee!" Charlie yelled.

EXCEPT THAT WAY. He didn't want to leave. He wasn't going to leave. He had watched her sing online for hours. He had practically bribed Stassi's address out of Day. Leaving was the last thing he would oblige.

She picked up the Aloe plant that sat on the kitchen island and threw it at him.

"Bird," Demi said. He took a step toward her and she took a step back.

"Demi, please leave," Charlie said, her voice unstable, barely making it across the threshold of her lips.

Her wounds had physically healed. The bruises were visibly gone. The scratches had disappeared, but he saw evidence of her pain all over her.

"Leaveeee!" Charlie yelled as she reached for the aloe plant that sat on the kitchen island and threw it at him. Demi narrowly dodged the vase, leaving the wall to receive the blow.

"Fuck, Bird!!" Demi's bark was loud enough to shrink her. She had seen a side of him that was volatile, a side that was menacing, and he could see her anticipating abuse. Would he hit her again? Would he lose control? He had come to her to deliver an apology, but it was going terribly wrong.

"Just get out! I didn't say anything to the police. I didn't press charges; Justin isn't going to press charges! Just leave!" Charlie shouted. She was hyperventilating, she was so shaken, and Demi wanted to soothe her. He wanted to undo everything he had done but hearing Justin's name on her tongue reignited a blaze in him.

"Fuck you talking bout? You speaking for that nigga now? You still fucking that nigga, Bird?" He didn't give a fuck about space. Didn't give a fuck that she was like a deer in headlights. He cornered her, digging his finger into her forehead. "You fucking that nigga? He dropping charges for you now?" He was irrational. Jealous. His hand was around her throat and she was withering beneath his hold. He wanted to get control of himself but he couldn't. The thought of her with another man drove him mad.

"No! Demi, no!" Charlie shouted, crying as he stood in her face, fuming, breathing so hard he felt like his heart would explode. He couldn't even see her sincerity he was so livid. Knowing Justin had been inside her, remembering the chemistry he had witnessed between them, thinking about Charlie letting somebody else in the place where he sought refuge... Demi was going to murder somebody. The nigga Justin. He could go. He could catch every single bullet in Demi's chamber. Demi had done a good job of keeping his temper in check over the years. He didn't bring this side of him home when he was with Lauren. Hadn't cared enough, or perhaps, she didn't provoke him the way Charlie did. Charlie giving her love away was motivation for murder. Charlie was gasoline to an uncontrollable fire. "Demi, please. Please, Demi. I just want to feel safe. You're hurting me so bad."

He took her face in his hands, pressing her into the wall and meeting his forehead to hers.

"I know," he said. "I know, Bird. I fucked up. I fucked up. I fucked up. Burn me, baby. Sing me a song, Bird."

Demi was riding a line between sane and insanity and Charlie could feel the clock of her life ticking down. Demi was dangerous. A fucking lunatic. He killed people. He had told her in so many words. He had warned her, and she hadn't heeded his words. Staring in his eyes where she saw nothing but rage, she feared that he could very well kill her.

"Demi, no," she whispered, turning her head away from his persistent lips.

"I'm sorry, baby. I fucked up. My head is fucking spinning. I can't think of you with that nigga, Bird. I'm on another level with this shit. I'ma kill niggas out here over you. I need to go there, Bird. To Charliezonia. Take me with you, baby. Sing to me, Bird."

Charlie was sobbing. He was scaring her. He knew it, but if she sent him into the streets tonight, Justin was dying.

This is insane. This is NOT right, she thought. *This isn't love.* Only it was. It was love, unlike any love Charlie had ever felt. It was the kind of love that didn't make sense. The kind that hurt just as much as it healed. The kind you needed space from but craved when it was gone. Charlie loved and hated this man. Felt calm and fear around him. Demi was everything. He was her everything. Every possibility of emotion, he made her feel. Charlie trembled she was so terrified.

Her face was a mess. The prettiest fucking mess and he swiped her tears and her snot, craving her dirt. He kissed her, forcing his lips on hers as she moved her head from side to side. "Demi, stop, Demi, stop," she protested. She reached for the knife block on the counter. She didn't even realize what she was doing until he released her.

He took a step back and looked down at the blood as Charlie dropped the knife.

"You stabbed me," he said in disbelief. It was the calm in his voice that made him crazy, like he was okay with dying if she was the one doing the killing.

Weird-ass fucking psychopath.

"Oh my God, Demi," she whispered. "Demi! Demi, what do I do?"

Demi stumbled to the wooden chair and sat, his legs weakening by the second because Charlie hadn't only stabbed him, she had pulled the knife out and blood was gushing everywhere.

"I'm so sorry, Demi; don't die, don't die," she cried.

She scrambled for a towel and came to her knees in front of him, pressing the towel to his wound. Huge tear drops clung to her lashes and Demi took her hand, pulling her into his lap. "You gon' have to get me to a hospital, baby. Shit kinda deep."

He dug in his pocket and pulled out his key, handing it to her.

He didn't know if she was nodding in agreement or just completely in shock, but she helped him from the chair. With his arm around her shoulder, he left a blood trail through the house as they made their way to the car.

"Fuck!" he hollered as she helped him into the passenger seat.

Charlie hurried to the driver's seat and threw the car in reverse, clipping the curb as she pulled out.

"You don' fucked enough shit up tonight, Bird. Try to keep my whip in one piece," Demi grunted. The towel in his lap was soaked.

"I didn't mean to. I just grabbed it. I thought you were going to hurt me. Demi, I'm so sorry," she stammered.

"Bird," he moaned. "Sing, baby."

"I can't, Demi," she was panicking.

"A nigga in hella pain, Bird. Just sing me a song," he insisted.

What have you become? What have you becomeeee?
Matter fact, nah that's what you've been
I was blind. I was in it. I was blind. Ohhhhh

Charlie glanced over at Demi and her stomach sank at the sight of his closed eyes.

"Demi, wake up, wake upppp," she cried. She punched him and then shook him. He groaned in pain.

"Fuck, Bird!" he shouted.

"I'm sorryyyyy, I thought you were dead!" she shouted, completely overwhelmed. Terrified as her adrenaline terrorized her.

Demi sat up, struggling, blood-soaked towel in his hand as he leaned across the armrest. He arrested her face between pinched fingers, denting her cheeks, and pulling her toward him. He kissed her. He kissed her like he was okay... like she hadn't just put a hole in him.

"I ain't gon' never die on you, Bird." He whispered the words like they were true.

"You're not invincible, Demi," she sniffled.

"Sing to me, baby. That shit make a nigga feel invincible. Sing to me and a nigga gone be A-1," he replied, leaning back into the seat.

"Let it go, let it go-ooo."

"Fuck Summer Walker, sing something else," Demi interrupted.

Charlie laughed as relief flooded her. Even in this moment, he was trying to make sure she was okay. Even though he wasn't. Even when he was hurt, he didn't want her to feel the weight of it.

"Ma'am. The longer you continue to lie to us, the longer this will take. We can tell from the wound that he was assaulted. Telling the truth will make this easier for everyone."

Charlie's eyes were wide with fear as she shook her head. "I...I..."

"Ayo, my man, she said what she said. It was an accident," Demi said as the doctor stitched his side. "As a matter of fact, y'all can get the fuck out. Ain't nobody going to jail today. I was walking with a knife and tripped. There's nothing more to the story, so quit asking her the same shit over and over again."

Charlie couldn't believe he was lying for her, but she was grateful.

"Yes, well, this is a pretty deep cut. You're lucky it wasn't worse," the doctor said.

The police officer closed his notepad and gave Charlie a skeptical glance before exiting the room.

The doctor wrapped Demi's stitches, taking it around his entire mid-section.

"Keep these clean. I'm going to prescribe you something for the pain and you should be all set. It'll heal completely in a few weeks' time. Until it scabs, don't submerge in water. I'll go have the nurse discharge you."

"That's a plan, Doc," Demi answered. Charlie looked on; guilt-ridden. The doctor walked by her.

"Demi, I'm sorry," she whispered.

"Come here."

Charlie walked to him, standing over him as he sat on the examination bed. His stare held no disdain, but it was brooding as he inspected her.

"I'm not fucking him," Charlie said. "I haven't even spoken to him."

Demi nodded and then lowered his eyes to his hands.

"I got a problem, Bird. When it come to you. I just lose it. A nigga ain't right in the head over you," he admitted.

"You scare me," she whispered. "You kicked me out of your condo, Demi. You dragged me out, kicking and screaming. You said you loved me and then you treated me like I wasn't shit."

"I'm wrong, Bird," he said.

Tears built up in her eyes, but she held them.

"I been going crazy, baby. I been living in hell, Bird. Going through the motions, sleeping in a bed where I don't belong. Living in a house that don't feel like mine no more."

"You're married, Demi," she whispered.

"I told you where I'm at with that," he revealed. "That can be over."

"If I tell you to leave," Charlie said, scoffing and shaking her head. "If you wanted to leave you would be gone already, Demi."

Charlie closed her eyes.

"I'm not a homewrecker," she said.

"Nah, you a Demi wrecker, Bird. You just knocking my shit down. Every rule. Every wall. You just come in a nigga life and do what you want. Let me come home. It'll never happen again, Bird, but you got to come back to me."

Charlie shook her head. "No, Demi. I'm not coming back."

Demi hit his chest with a balled fist, like he was trying to get an old vending machine to work, like his heart had clunked out and a knock in the right place would get it to work again. Charlie had broken his shit. He had tried to stay away, tried to let it go. He was fine until he heard her voice, until he heard her pain in a song. He had come running.

"Bird..."

"It's not just you, Demi. It's me too. You lied, I lied. We're both wrong. We argue and we fuck and then we argue some more. We don't belong together. The shit is toxic," she argued.

"So be toxic with me! Who the fuck we comparing our shit to? I want this toxic shit. Whatever it is. I want all of it. I want to fuck and fight. It's the best fucking and fighting a nigga ever did, Bird. I'ma do better by you. The lies and the hiding shit and losing my temper. I ain't gon' be about none of that no more with you. You can't let this shit go. I'm up like a fucking teenager, sick and shit. You can't tell me you been good?" he asked.

"I've been dying," she gasped.

"Then why you running, Bird?" Demi asked. "Huh?"

"Because I have to do better than this. I'm on a journey, Demi, and you are disrupting that. I am trying to get my shit together. Trying not to keep making the same mistakes..."

"We ain't no mistake, man," he said, hanging his head and rubbing the back of his neck.

"We are. All of this. I should have never given in to this. I was fucked up before you came along, and now, I'm even more fucked up," Charlie said hopelessly. "I can't do this with you, Demi. I can't be with someone who chokes me and manhandles me. I don't feel safe."

"I'm in love with you, Bird," Demi said, shame and desperation transforming a gangster to a man.

"Stop saying that," she whispered.

He reached for her balled fists and brought her hands to his face.

"Say, man," Demi said, holding her in place with a strong hand to the small of her back.

"Say, man," she repeated, shaking her head as her eyes betrayed her, exposing just how much this hurt.

She caressed his face. He didn't even flinch. The man who resented human touch embraced hers. It was an honor. To be the recipient of his comfort was incredible, but he wasn't hers. She couldn't keep him. He had given her something she couldn't claim. "Oh, babe," she soothed. "Love doesn't hurt. I don't know what this is that we've built but it hurts me, Demi. This feeling I give you, hurts you. Like a burn. You said it burns. That's not love. I stabbed you tonight. How much worse does it have to get before we let it go? You have to let me go."

He nodded. He knew he had to. He didn't want to, but he knew it was necessary to let birds fly. If he tried to hold onto her, she would die, and he just wanted to admire her heights.

"There's a deal with the label. Day will be in touch. If you want me to let it go, you got to take the deal, Charlie. I can't walk away without leaving you with something, and I can't live a life without hearing you sing to me, baby," he said. "Can you do that for me? To ease my mind, Bird. Leave me with a piece of you at least."

"I can't, Demi," she said. "I can't take a deal. My face can't be out here like that," she whispered. "Just let go. I don't want anything from you except that."

Her words scraped away at his manhood. He nodded, biting into his bottom lip, restraining his anger, his hurt.

He reached for his bloody shirt, slipping it over his head. He pushed by her and Charlie felt herself choking as she reached for his arm to pull him back. Why couldn't love be simple? Free? The price of love was too expensive. They had done too much to one another. They had mixed in too much hurt to the pot and ruined their recipe.

"I'm never going to love a woman the way I love you," he said. He caressed her face and Charlie closed her eyes, holding her breath. His goodbye was her defeat.

She watched him walk out of the room and her legs gave out. She sat on the edge of the bed, chin to her chest, as she finally let her anguish flow.

"I'm in love with you too," she whispered. It took everything in her not to go after him. The way she loved him was terrifying. The way she forgave anything, sweeping all his missteps under the rug like they hadn't happened at all. She would love him to her detriment. She would forgive him over and over. Charlie felt it in her soul that she would love him so much that she wouldn't have any love left for herself. That scared her. That stopped her from telling him how she really felt. He would have to learn to let go because Charlie was certain that they were over. The overwhelming urge to work things out were thwarted with the idea that this pain was self-inflicted. It was her karma for sleeping with someone else's man to begin with. Demi had never been hers, and even though he was willing to leave everything behind to change that, she would always feel like a second choice. Their relationship was stained with lies. No matter how much love was present, no matter how good they could have been, karma never would forget how they began.

CHAPTER 23

Demi entered his home. It had never felt this foreign. He was a guest between these walls. In a place he had built, a place where he paid bills, a place where the sound of his son's laughter filled the air...he was uncomfortable.

"Oh my God, what happened to you?"

He didn't even mean to mug her. His face just went tense, his entire body... rigid... resentful... but she wasn't to blame. Lauren hadn't changed. It was he who was switching up and her presence in place of Charlie's was like alcohol on a wound.

"I'm fine," he said.

"But you're bleeding," Lauren protested.

"We got to talk, Lo," Demi said.

Lauren seemed to know what was next before he even said another word. She braced herself, reaching for the arm of the couch and then lowering to sit.

"I love you, but this ain't gonna work." There. He had made it plain. No dancing around it. He wanted out.

"You saw her, didn't you?" Lauren asked. "I felt it when you left here earlier. That you were going to her."

"I won't ever not be here for you, Lo. I'ma stay here until you're better and then I'll sit down with DJ and explain this shit to him. Let him know it's on me. Let him know that just because you and me aren't together doesn't mean his life will change. I'ma still be here," he said. He wasn't sure if he was trying to convince her or himself.

"Of course, his life will change. Everything will change, Demi. You're ruining our lives for a fling!"

"It's not about her. It ain't about nobody but us," Demi said. If he was honest, he had been walking around half living, half loving way before meeting Charlie. He just didn't realize it until she had put her hands on him. Now, he needed that feeling. Charlie's hands were like jumper cables to his heart.

"I'd beg if I thought it would change something, but I know you. You decided this a long time ago," Lauren said. "Don't do me any favors. You can get your shit and get out tonight."

"If that's what you want," he said.

"Why can't you just try, Demi?" she shouted in frustration.

"I been trying, Lo." His calm was her stimulant. It was the "been" for her.

How long had this been going on? How long had he been cheating? She hated that he was so certain, so unaffected. She couldn't see his indecision, couldn't feel the pull of his conscience. It was present but her hurt outweighed it all.

She laughed, a sarcastic, fed up snicker as she shook her head, but she didn't say another word. She turned and left him standing there in the middle of the living room.

Lauren had never been the type to do what she was doing now. Snooping. Hacking. Torturing herself with access to a man's private files. Yet, here she was, letting her insecurities take her down a rabbit hole of searching for validation. She sat at her computer, staring at proof of Demi's infidelity. His predictable iCloud password on her MacBook had pulled up the evidence of his affair.

Videos of the two of them in bed together. Pictures of the woman who had ruined her family. The fucking dog he had given to their son.

This dirty-ass nigga, Lauren thought. The discovery of this was worse than his admission of guilt. *She's touching him. She's all over him.*

Tears blurred her vision as she watched the homemade sex tape. The fact that he was comfortable enough to film himself with another woman. The things he did to her. The things he said. She didn't know which part was worse. Lauren was gutted. Fifteen years and Demi had never touched her the way he was touching this girl. It was four o'clock in the morning and Lauren had been in this same seat for hours. She remembered seeing the girl on Day's story after the talent showcase. She had stolen the show.

Demi's sleeping with his artist, she thought.

Lauren would be damned if she would let a bitch come up off her pain without repercussions. She logged into Demi's company Instagram account, and without thinking twice, she uploaded the video. Then, she changed the password so that Demi wouldn't be able to take it down.

"Bitch," she whispered, slamming the laptop closed.

"Charlie! Wake up!"

Stassi's voice and the banging at her room door forced Charlie from her restless sleep. She had just gone to sleep. Hours of crying into her pillow had kept her awake.

Stass! I'm sleep!" she shouted, groaning.

"Wake up and check Shaderoom," Stassi said. "It's important, Charlie. He's going to find you."

Charlie popped out of bed and staggered to the door, unlocking it. Stassi shoved her phone in Charlie's face. Charlie read the post.

Charlie Woods, the new songstress at Dynasty Music Group, is sleeping with the BOSS. Bad boy and street legend, Demi Sky, has new arm candy under his label and in his bed... and apparently, he's not the only one. She has tapes with Shad Brooks too!

"Shad's the first comment Charlie," Stassi said. "I clicked on his page and he has pictures of you all over it."

Charlie's soul left her body. She and Demi were all over the internet, and while she was mortified, that wasn't the worst part. Her ex, Shad Brooks, a man who had ruined her life, a man she was running from. Demi's tape was fuel to a fire she had been trying to put out for months.

"Oh my God, oh my God, Stassi. Why would he do this?" Charlie asked. "He's going to find me, Stass."

She couldn't stop herself from clicking on his profile. She had left home with Shad Brooks at 16 years old with the promise of fame as bait. He was in the industry. A music legend as far as the streets were concerned, and he had "signed" her to a deal when she was still in high school. When her father had refused to let her explore music, he convinced Charlie to follow him to New York to network and make connections that would help her "career." She had been too young to see it for what it was. He had wanted a traveling groupie, someone who was too young to understand that she was on the road pussy. He had sold her big dreams and Charlie had bought them in bulk. It had been the worst decision she had ever made. Once he had gotten her away from home, she never saw the inside of a studio. Instead, he made her earn it. She didn't eat unless she earned it. She didn't sleep unless she earned it and the act of "earning" it was some of the most disgusting things she had ever done. What had started out as being pressured to prove she was grown had transformed into suggestions that she give his friends a try. The day Charlie refused was when the beatings began. He would fight her so mercilessly that Charlie felt like she would die. His manipulation knew no limits and Charlie cowered as she remembered the ways he had cut on her body to make sure no other man would want her. He filled her with Ecstasy and kept her so doped up that Charlie stopped fighting. It had taken Charlie seven years to find her way out. She set a house fire while he was gone, hoping that the police and firefighters would get there in time to save her because every time he left, he kept her locked inside.

She had come back home to her family after years of no communication. Now, he had found her. She had been reckless to fall for someone like Demi, to trust that his influence in the streets and with his label wouldn't leave a bread crumb trail back to her. She was exposed and the terror that came along with that was paralyzing. She had been careful, until Demi. She had been rebuilding her life quietly, hoping Shad never found her, and now that he had, she knew it was only a matter of time before he came to take her back.

Demi's phone rang non-stop. He reached for the nightstand, snatching it up to silence the ringing, but when he saw there were 19 missed calls, he sat up. Six calls from Day, numerous texts, and a bunch of random numbers.

He opened Day's message.

DAY
My nigga, somebody hacked your page. It's all over social. Let me know how you want to spin it.

He didn't need to press the play button to know what it was. His heart stopped; not because he was out there but because Charlie was. Demi went to his Instagram account and when he saw the damage his temper skyrocketed. Every Black-owned blog had run the video, but when he saw that the story was taking on a life of its own, he saw red. He clicked on a post.

**SHAD BROOKS LEAKS TAPE OF CHARLIE WOODS.
"SHE FOR THE STREETZ!"**

Demi was out of bed, throwing on yesterday's clothes before he could stop himself.

"What's wrong with you?" Lauren asked. It was her tone. The tone she used when she asked a question she already knew the answer to. She was baiting him, testing to see how affected he would be by what she had done. She prayed for indifference. If he didn't care about the girl on the tape being put out there for the world to see, then Lauren would know that it was just a jump-off. She could recover from unattached sex, but the look in his eyes, the worry, the pure rage, and the hurt not for himself but for the other affected party... for his side bitch...that shit peeled away at all the reserve Lauren had left.

"You went through my shit?" he asked.

"Don't check me about finding some shit that wasn't supposed to be in your phone anyway," Lauren said. "And for damn sure don't check me about your filty side bitch. Dirty-ass bitch. I bet you won't wife your little whore now, will you?" Lauren asked as she sat sipping coffee at their dinner table.

Demi was on her ass, rounding the table, and yoking her up before he could talk himself into self-control. Lauren pushed him and then slapped him so hard that she instantly regretted it, bringing her hands to her mouth in shock. She didn't touch him like that. She knew better. She could see the steam shooting out of his ears.

"We're done, Lo," he said, temple throbbing, hands wrapped around her neck as Bails activated at the commotion, barking. Demi released her and clapped his hands. "Let's go, Bails."

"Fuck you, Demi! You mad I exposed your slut for what she is?! She was fucking a married man! You thought she was worth it? Huh? You see niggas came running. Guess you ain't the only one she on the mic for. You gave up your entire family for a bitch that's for everybody."

Lauren was so out of character she didn't recognize herself as she followed Demi as he stormed out. She was glad her son was at school because this was the makings of World War III.

"You're done with me? You cheat on me, now you playing victim? Got this bitch dog in my house, acting like it's a gift to MY SON! You dirty! That fucking whore got you turning your back on the people that been in your corner and now you salty because I exposed her! Should watch the company you keep! I been here! That don't count for nothing?" She was barely out of the hospital. She hurt everywhere. Her body nor her mind was in any condition to handle this battle, but she couldn't stop herself. The pain was overwhelming and she didn't know if it was coming from the betrayal or the bullet.

Demi grabbed his keys and was out the door, but Lauren was on his heels.

"Where you think you going? Huh? Now you running to save this ho?" Lauren shouted. He brushed her off and put Bails in the back seat.

"Move, man," he said, pushing her away roughly.

"No!" she said. "You want to go check on your whore?! Take your wife! Take your wife to meet your whore, Demi!"

Lauren was irrational. She was a woman scorned, and the way Demi felt he would knock her fucking head off if she didn't let him leave.

"Get the fuck on!" Demi barked. "You out here making a fucking scene in front of my house! You want to take my shit? What I built? Take it, Lo! Take all this shit! The money! The house! The cars! I don't give a fuck about none of this shit no more! You can do all that and it's still not gon' keep me here. You just ruined a girl's life, Lo. She's twenty-four-fucking years old!"

The intensity of his words caused her to stop fighting as her anger turned to grief. Shock wore her. She remembered what she was doing at 24. How young she had been. How naïve. "You love her," she whispered. "How could you love her?"

"I ain't mean to, Lo," he said, defeated. "Go in the house before you hurt yourself, man. You just got out of the hospital."

"Demi, please don't go to that girl. Please don't. Please just stay home with your wife."

"I can't stay, Lo."

Demi cleared her from near his door and then slammed it shut before pulling recklessly out of the driveway.

Demi told himself the entire drive that he would be calm, but the closer he got to her the more rage filled him. He pulled up banging on Stassi's door.

"Open this fucking door, Bird!" he shouted.

Stassi pulled it open.

"Where is she?" he asked, pushing her aside, disregarding that it was even her house.

"You fucking bastard! You leaked a sex tape of my sister and you got the nerve to come here making demands?" Stassi asked.

"Do it look like I would do some shit like that?" Demi barked, he asked, marching straight to the closed door, barging into Charlie's room. He found her curled in bed, the lights out, and the shades drawn.

"You fucking Shad Brooks, Bird? Huh? Who else you fucking? Huh, Bird?" The bass in his voice shook the entire apartment, but when he saw that she didn't react, he looked on in confusion.

Charlie was trembling.

He looked back at Stassi who had tears in her eyes as well.

"He's her ex, Demi. She's been hiding from him," Stassi revealed.

For some reason, the scars on Charlie's body flashed in his mind and he put the story together in his head.

"He's going to kill me, Demi," she cried.

Demi picked her up and sat down on the edge of the bed with her in his arms. She bawled. "He's going to kill me!"

"Shhh," Demi said. "Why you ain't tell me, Bird? Hmm?" he asked, kissing the top of her head. "Tell me everything, Bird. Who is this nigga? Cuz I'ma kill him, but I got to know everything first."

By the time Charlie was done telling Demi about her past, he was in the mood for murder.

"Listen to me, Bird, and hear me clear. You don't got to fear a nigga walking this earth as long as I'm breathing. You hear me?" he asked.

Charlie nodded.

"Are you keeping anything else from me? What else don't I know?" Demi asked.

Her eyes widened slightly, and he knew there was something else. Something more.

"I'm pregnant," she whispered.

"And you weren't going to tell me? Why wouldn't you tell me that, Bird?" he asked.

"Because I'm not keeping it," she answered.

He eased her out of his lap and stood. This just might be the worst day of his life.

"Just like that?" he asked. "You'll get rid of my seed without even thinking about it?"

"I just can't, Demi," she whispered. "We said goodbye. We were done. We're supposed to be done."

Demi nodded. He was gritting his teeth so hard he thought they would chip.

"Yeah, I guess we are," he said. He walked out of the apartment and didn't look back because there was nothing left to say or do.

FINAL CHAPTER

One Year Later

Must not have beeeenn, paying attentionnnnnn
Stepped right on in itttt, didn't even noticeeeeee how deee—ee-ee-eep I wasssss

Charlie's face stretched in emotion as she sang the song with conviction. She felt that shit. She felt it like Demi felt her dirt all over him. It had been a year of no contact. A year of space. He had done what he promised and erased her fears. Shad Brooks had been found dead in his apartment from an apparent overdose three months after the infamous sex tape, but Charlie knew Demi had been responsible. Her life had been a whirlwind since. An abortion, a record deal, and instant fame. The sex tape had caught everyone's attention but her voice had kept it. She hadn't even dropped an album yet. She was recording a mixtape of cover songs called *Idols*, from artists who had inspired her to sing. It was the most anticipated project of the year.

Day was producing, and as she sang, she saw him falling into his infamous head nod. Whenever she was knocking it out the park, he became so engrossed he got lost.

I went from the ground to the top of the clouddddd
And nowww as I look down I see where I felll into your armssss
now
I've got looooveeeeee
All over meeeeeee

The song was so appropriate. For him. To Demitrius Sky. The man who had freed a bird from her cage and allowed her to fly. She missed him. She thought of him every day, hoping that he would pop in to one of her studio sessions, but he never did. He was more of a silent partner these days. After accompanying her to the doctor and holding her hand through the abortion procedure, he hadn't communicated with her since. Charlie sang the song to its end and then smiled at the thumbs up Stassi gave her through the window from Day's lap. They were off and on, hot then cold, but it worked for them. Her sister was happy and that's all that mattered to Charlie.

"Charlie, you've got to get out of here. You've got to meet that realtor so you can sign the papers for the condo," Stassi said, as she pressed the button to speak into the recording booth.

Charlie nodded, pulling out her phone to check the time.

"Damn, you're right. Am I good to go, Day?" she asked.

"Yeah, we can do adlibs tomorrow, superstar," Day said.

Charlie snickered. It was their inside joke. Her presence

had grown online ever since her sex tape had leaked. She hated it, but as soon as the tape had gotten steam, Day had dropped the video of her singing at the showcase, putting money behind it to get it on the same timelines of people who had liked the tape. Once they heard her sing, they became instant fans and the conversation changed. She had been the "superstar" of the label ever since. She grabbed her bag and her keys and rushed out.

"The realtor wants you to meet her at a property she's showing! I'll text you the address!" Stassi called after her.

Charlie followed the GPS for a half-hour before pulling up to a gated property.

"So sorry I'm late!" she said as she hopped out of her car and greeted the woman. "I'm so glad the condo finally sold. You're cutting the check back to Demi, right?" Charlie asked.

"Yes, arrangements have been made," the woman said. "The paperwork is right inside."

Charlie nodded. "Lead the way."

They stepped inside the massive mansion and the entrance took her breath away.

"Wow, this is a beautiful home. Oh my God." Charlie gasped as she admired the opulence of it all.

Her high-heeled boots clicked against the marble floors as she followed her to the kitchen. When she stepped inside her heart ached.

Demi sat coolly on one of the bar stools and Bails laid at his feet.

"Bails!" she yelled, dropping to her knees as her dog ran to her, barking in excitement as she rubbed all over him.

Charlie glanced up at Demi and then stood. The smile he wore was so relaxed. He was relaxed in denim and a white V-neck shirt. Demi wouldn't be Demi if he didn't have diamonds around his neck. Maybe he was trying to freeze her, because suddenly, she couldn't move. Her heart raced as she looked at him, stunned.

She felt like the room was imploding. She didn't know how to feel. It had been so long since she had laid eyes on him. So many things had gone wrong between them. So much hurt had been passed around. Still, her heart fluttered in his presence.

"Say, man," he said, giving her a slight nod, like he wanted to speak but was too taken by her to say one word.

She didn't know why but she loved when he said that. She could tell he was trying to gather his thoughts. Speechless. Charlie made Demi speechless.

"Say, man," she replied.

"It's been a year, Bird. I got the paperwork you need right here," he said. He handed it to the realtor who handed it to Charlie. Charlie's heart sank a little. Selling the condo he had purchased for her was like closing the book on their chapter in her life. This was their closure. Charlie had been okay for a few months. She hadn't felt this active pit in her stomach for quite some time, but just one look at Demi brought all her hurt back. To love someone but not be able to have them was torture. She took the paper and she sucked in a deep breath.

A divorce decree. Two signatures. Sealed by the State of Michigan. Demi was a single man. Charlie felt sick. He may as well had killed her. She had wanted him almost from the first time he had spoken to her. It had felt like love from the very beginning but she had spent the past 390 days telling herself that she had been wrong. So many nights she had convinced herself not to call him, that he couldn't be the one. She had forced herself to hate him and now here he was in front of her, available.

"You got a divorce?" she asked.
He nodded. "It was time," he replied.
She blinked disbelieving eyes up to him.
"I need you to burn me, baby," he said. "I want to go to Charliezonia, Bird," he said. "I missed you. Fucking missed my baby."
"You haven't spoken to me since..."
He thumbed her lips, stopping her words. He didn't need to be reminded of what they had lost. He thought of the baby they could have had often. He didn't want today to be about that. He turned to his realtor. "Can you give us a minute?" he asked. She nodded and clicked away in her five-inch heels, leaving them on the first floor of the home alone.
"It's been a year, Demi. You left me out in the world to deal for a year," she whispered. She scoffed and shook her head.
"I had some affairs to get in order, Bird. A lot of loose ends to tie. I had a family that I had to secure. I couldn't just leave. I had to get closure over there first, make sure my son was straight, get him comfortable with a new normal. It took some time. I'm sorry for that," he said.
"Shad Brooks? Did you-"

Demi didn't even let her finish the sentence. He simply put a finger to his lips, signaling for her to cease that line of questioning. Her instincts had been right. He had committed murder for her. A man who went to such lengths to protect you had to love you, right? It had to be more than lust. She didn't even know why she was questioning it. The way her heart beat for this man she knew they were so much more than the scandal of an affair.

"I've moved on," she said. It was only half a lie. Her life had moved forward. She had fallen in love with herself, with her artistry. The pain he had left behind was shaping up to be motivation for a damned fine album.

She turned and walked out the house. It was too much. This interaction. This love she felt resuscitating, it was all just too much.

As soon as she pulled open the door, her feet stopped working. She turned back to the house and Demi lifted out of the stool, taking steps in her direction. Her head whipped back to the car in front of her. Her mother's car. The one he had scrapped. It was pieced back together but better than it had been before and it sat with a red bow on the hood. It was restored. It was exactly how she had remembered it being as a child. This car had been her home. It had been her safety. She had spent moments with her mom in this car. He could give her a mansion worth millions of dollars and it would never outweigh the value of this car. He had given her the one place she considered home.

"How did you do this? You scrapped it for parts," she whispered, eyes flooded in disbelief. She couldn't even see him because tears blinded him. "This isn't her car. Is this her car?"

"Same car, Bird," he said. He spoke over her shoulder, nudging her head to the side and then sliding keys in her palm.

Charlie took steps toward the car and then unlocked it, sliding into the driver's seat. Her initials were still carved in the door frame and as she turned to stare out the windshield she noticed the box sitting near the gear shift.

Her heart stalled.

Demi pulled open the passenger side door and lowered into the seat.

"What is this?" she asked.

Demi finessed his newly-grown beard, a new look for him, one that she loved.

"A new life, Bird," Demi said. "A new car, a new house," he said, nodding to the massive home, and "a new ring." He picked up the box and flipped it open.

Charlie blew out a deep breath.

"I need you to burn me, baby," he said. "I want to go to Charliezonia, Bird," he said.

"What are you doing, Demitrius?" she asked. "I don't know what's happening right now. I just know I'm afraid of the way you make me feel. Please, Demi. Just let the past be the past."

"I can't do that, baby. It fucked me up, Bird. You getting rid of my baby," he answered. "But I took some time to look at the board from every angle and I understand why you wouldn't keep it. You deserved more than lies and a baby. I was being selfish. I wanted you to have my baby to keep you trapped with me, Bird. So, you couldn't leave, and I wouldn't have to change my ways because I would automatically have you. I was wrong, but I do love you and I want to do this right with you. You deserve a nigga that will do everything he can to do right by you. I'm sorry for every way I've ever hurt you."

She felt dizzy, like she wasn't breathing, like the room was spinning. She didn't know how she had let 390 days pass without this energy.

Demi took the brilliant ring out of the box.

"Nobody has ever touched me like you touch me, Bird. Burn me, baby," he said. "Burn a nigga for his whole life. Marry me, Charlie."

She searched his face for clarity, for an indication that this was a joke.

"Damn, Bird, a nigga trying to get his shit together for you and you just gon' act like it don't mean shit," he said.

She smiled, slowly, reluctantly, irresistably and then she shrugged. "Why not?" she answered. He snickered.

"That's all you got for me?" he asked. A hand to her cheek singed his fingertips. His burn. The burn he felt for her was back. It was the sweetest pain he had ever felt. "A nigga missed you, baby."

She blushed as the hue of love conquered her skin. "I have some conditions," she answered. He slipped the diamond on her finger. It was flawless. A single stone and a white band because the quality was so official that it needed nothing else to accentuate it.

Demi grabbed her chin roughly, forcing her to look into his eyes and then he pressed his forehead to hers.

"What's your terms, Bird? Put 'em on the floor. What does a conditional engagement look like?" he asked.

"I want to go slow. Everything went so fast last time and we crashed and burned. I want to get to know each other and date and meet your son and your parents."

He tensed.

"See, you don't like that, and I need to know the history behind that," she said, feeling his angst. "I just want to go slow. A long engagement."

"How long?" he questioned.

"As long as it takes. If you're good with that, then my answer is yes," she whispered.

"I can live with that," he replied.

"Then, I guess I'm a fiancée," she said softly, playfully, smiling wider than he had ever seen her smile. She was heaven. His heaven. He worshipped this woman. He had no idea that even if he disagreed she would have still said yes.

Charlie kissed him, long and deep, soul-stirring, and slow, and Demi felt it in his soul. A year's worth of I love you's tangled between their lips as he felt the heat from her soul. Her burns. Her touches. They were no longer foreign because she was his.

"I'ma be good to you, Bird. You can trust that," Demi said.

She didn't know how or why she had so much faith in him, but she believed him. He climbed out of the car and walked around to her door, pulling her to her feet, and lacing his hand in hers. Connection. Charlie had touched him. Stained him in a way that he couldn't scrub her out. Demi was dirty with her love. Charlie was the single bird in his sky, the one you would see flying alone on a bright, blue day as the sun blinded you as you tried to admire it. Sometimes, it would rain. Sometimes, it would storm. It wouldn't always be sunny, but they would endure. They would choose to love anyway because they knew what it felt like to be apart and neither Charlie nor Demi could bear the thought of living another day without the dysfunction of their love. What a beautiful sky indeed.

"My soul stuck on you, Bird," he said, holding her hand up and forcing her to spin so he could admire what he had almost lost. She fell back into his chest. Only Demi could make her feel this beautiful. He pulled her into his body and his large hand cloacked her neck, if he squeezed, he would choke her, but he didn't; he caressed there then used the other hand to undo the top three buttons of her silk shirt. Her scar greeted him, and he lowered his lips to it, kissing the place where she had been hurt. "I collected this debt for you, Bird. I'ma hold your life in my hands and you gon' hold a nigga heart in yours. How that sound? You can handle that?"

Like the money he gave her when they first met, he needed to give her collateral to make sure she would always welcome him in her world. He knew she was good for it. She would keep it safe, and in return, he would love her forever. He had made that promise to himself before she even walked into the house. It was his honor to love her, to have her, and he was forever grateful. She looked him in the eyes.

"I'm in love with you. Always, Demi. Always."

The End

DISCUSSION QUESTIONS

1. Are Demi and Charlie meant to be?

2. Was Demi wrong for leaving his wife?

3. How did you feel about Demi's OCD?

4. Is bird more than a side chick?

5. Do they have a chance at a real future together?

6. Is Demi abusive?

7. What was your favorite scene?

8. Who is your favorite character?

BE ON THE LOOKOUT FOR THE BOOK LOVERS APP!

COMING SOON!

BUTTERFLY 4 IS UP NEXT!

Thank you for the support and love Ash Army!